AcaPolitics

A NOVEL ABOUT COLLEGE A CAPPELLA

STEPHEN HARRISON

AFTERMATH PRESS
First Printing, November 2011

ISBN-10: 0-61551-305-0
ISBN-13: 978-0-615-51305-8

LIBRARY OF CONGRESS CATALOGING-IN-PUBLICATION DATA
Harrison, Stephen
AcaPolitics, A Novel About College A Cappella / Stephen Harrison

LCCN: 2011938648

First Edition

AcaPolitics

Chapter 1

Move-In

Taylor Stuart loved his college a cappella group. He wanted desperately for the Chorderoys to be successful.

For this reason, Taylor woke up at 4:45 A.M. on a muggy August Tuesday: Freshmen Move-In Day. He dressed quickly and arrived on campus by 6:15—a full half-hour before participating groups were technically allowed to show up—and was devastated to discover that the Harmoniums had already arrived and claimed the best spot for the Activities Fair. The Harmoniums' group president, Dani Behlman, was still flirting with the Director of Orientation, explaining just how awful she was at remembering times, and thanking him for letting her set down her things. She acknowledged Taylor's arrival with a smirk.

Taylor moved quickly to the second-best spot. Although his table was only a few feet from Dani's, her position was vastly superior because of its location beneath the hospitality tent, right next to a cooler of sodas and ice cream sandwiches. With horror, Taylor imagined the flood of students seeking shade and sugar who would be met by Dani's perfect sales pitch for the Harmoniums, masked by her ever-so-polite offer to provide directions. "Sheffield dormitory? Let me point that out to you," she'd say sweetly. The freshmen would be too naïve to know that it was all a façade, mere clever propaganda to paint the Harmoniums as the friendliest group of singers on campus. And once Dani charmed one prospective singer, she'd charm another, again and again, all day long.

1

With great effort, Taylor forced the dreadful image from his mind and proceeded to set up shop. He opened his gym bag and began pulling out flyers and arranging his group's a cappella albums at a furious pace. He set his iPod to "Chorderoys' Greatest Hits" and cranked the volume.

He'd been so careful, so prepared to ensure his group's success today. He'd ironed his group shirt the night before, laid out all of his clothes. He'd purchased bags of candy for them to use as bait, brewed and iced a giant batch of "singer's tea." How, he wondered, had he let *her* beat him on this most important day?

Olivia arrived shortly after Taylor finished setting up. She sported the Chorderoys' white and royal blue tee-shirt, a blue mini-skirt, and blue high heels. The Chorderoys' recruitment coordinator frowned at the second-rate table positioning. "We'll have to be more aggressive," said the alto resolutely.

As Dani and her cohort of fellow Harmoniums waited for the wave of college freshmen to arrive, they quietly discussed this year's strategy: Song selection. Promo gigs. Message-shaping. Group dress. Voice type-targeting. Inter-group alliances.

An hour passed. And then the flood began in earnest. Hoards of parents and students lumbered past carrying boxes, suitcases, flat-screen TVs, and ungodly amounts of toilet paper. The parental mood hovered between agitated and downright cranky, wary of the impending "goodbye" which would follow this ordeal.

Oddly enough, the moms and dads seemed to be relieved by the mere sight of older students at the Activities Fair, as if they'd only just realized that grown-up kids *live on* away from home. When not burdened by boxes, parents would meander up and down the lanes of tables, collecting fliers from random extracurricular groups in which their children likely had no interest, and quizzing upperclassmen about the *authentic* Brighton University experience, often with really embarrassing questions like "How much do kids party around here?" and "What do you mean by 'super-senior'?"

A cappella fliers were especially popular with parents. (Student-run "choir" seemed more wholesome than activities which had filled the average Boomer's college years.) But while charming a singer's parents helped occasionally, Taylor, Olivia, and Dani all knew students were more valuable targets for their a cappella sales pitches. Only students could be drafted.

By noon, the August air had heated considerably, and even more people were trekking through the activities field on their way to the freshmen dormitories. Even beneath her shady tent, Dani was severely regretting that black was the background color for her group's tee-shirts, which seemed to be absorbing all of the day's sunlight. More importantly, though, she felt the contrast between the tee and her skin made her look unfairly pale. Red was by far the shirt's superior color, their name penned in curving red italics: *Harmoniums*. She loved how it accented her strawberry blonde hair.

Dani beamed when an astute freshman complimented her "cute" ruby flip-flops. The a cappella president made a point of remembering her name—Nicole—and encouraged her to try out. "Here, take a few extra for your friends," said Dani, handing her a generous stack of fliers.

Yes, thought Dani, red was her color. As a junior, she still had two more years with her beloved Harmoniums. She decided right then that next season's group tees should be primarily red with only small black accents. Successful a cappella recruitment meant establishing a public persona, and outfit color was critical. Black was serious, formal. Red was tart but sweet, like red Skittles and cherry limeades—and upbeat, energetic a cappella. The Harmoniums should emphasize the latter attributes. They should wear more red.

Dani spotted a boy walking in her direction. She was not sure what it was about him that cried out "singer," much less "freshman." Was it the cargo shorts and Birkenstock leather sandals? The stylishly shaggy blonde hair? The black framed eyeglasses? The polite smile he wore while declining a flier from the Equestrian Society?

Whatever it was, she went with her instincts. She moved in.

"Have you heard about collegiate a cappella?"

Ben Jensen was beginning to wonder what about his exterior was making him the target of so many different student organizations. Already, he'd been singled out for the rock-climbing club, the debate team, and the pre-dental fraternity. He made a mental note to walk more quickly.

Ben smiled at his newest assailant and shook his head.

"Do you sing?" asked Dani, in her sweetest voice. Something about Ben—the sunburnt cheeks, the geeky glasses, the dimples—made him seem younger than his eighteen years. He was innocent-looking in just the way Dani found endearing.

Ben nodded and mumbled a few words about choir in high school.

"That's great! Let me tell you about the Harmoniums." Dani proceeded with her elaborate sales pitch, and thought she was doing an excellent job. In fact, Ben was too distracted to catch most of it. All around him, extra-curricular reps were yelling things like "Free soda if you join our e-mail list!" and "There'll be *pizza* at our group info session!" Consequently, he heard only snippets of Dani's life-changing monologue: "so much fun for people who love music" and "currently producing our fourth album" and "the clear highlight of my college experience."

"There you are!" Ben's mother was a petite woman, with small oval spectacles, little brown eyes, and a somewhat mousey disposition. Addressing Ben and his new friend, she relayed her saga of finding a decent parking spot. As she spoke, she placed an affectionate hand on her son's shoulder, as if to emphasize that he was still hers, if only till tomorrow morning.

Dani knew when to push for a cappella and when to let maternal instinct have its way. "You should come to the All A Cappella Recruitment Concert next Wednesday," she said, handing Ben a flier. "Then you'll see what it's all about."

"Okay. And what was your name again?"

"Dani Behlman," she said, smiling once more. During auditions season, Dani always gave her full name. This helped prospective auditionees look her up on Facebook, and she was rather proud of her internet persona. "My group is the Harmoniums. We'll be wearing *red* at the Recruitment Concert. Don't forget." Dani beamed. "And good luck with move-in!"

Ben's mother nodded and grasped Ben's arm, leading him gently but firmly towards the car and his belongings.

Just a few feet behind the Harmoniums' table, Taylor was shaking his head. He hated when Dani made the first impression with potential auditionees. It was hard enough for the co-ed Chorderoys to compete with the two all-male groups, the all-female group, and the Jewish music group, but the rivalry with Dani was by far the worst.

Taylor straightened, suddenly determined to be more aggressive in his salesmanship. The Harmoniums might be winning so far, but the battle for group promotion was far from over. He grabbed a few quarter-sheet fliers and moved towards the path with most foot traffic—

"Let me do it," said Olivia, pulling Taylor back. Olivia knotted her royal blue group tee into a single knot at the bottom, revealing a slice of her tanned tummy. She slipped her feet back into her high-heeled mary janes, and held out her hand.

Taylor nodded his approval and relinquished the handouts.

The Chorderoys' recruitment coordinator planted herself at the edge of the sidewalk. Unlike other student group reps, Olivia did not shout her message. She didn't have to. Males and females alike changed their entire trajectory to grab her fliers, drawn to the real sex appeal of Olivia's confidence. Taylor suspected he'd soon be running more copies.

"Should we be doing that?" asked Melanie, with a nod towards Olivia. Dani's fellow Harmonium had just arrived for her afternoon shift. "I wouldn't mind," she said, arching her back and tightening her stomach.

Dani sighed. Although the group president liked having another person with her, she wished Melanie wouldn't *talk* so much. The sophomore would be much more useful if she just smiled and nodded, silently observing an expert at work.

"No," said Dani. If anyone went, it should be the group president herself, but the idea of imitating Olivia was wholly unappealing. Since auditioning for the same a cappella groups freshman year, Dani had tried to avoid her rival alto as much as possible.

"It's not necessary," explained Dani. "She's distributing information on the *all* a cappella Recruitment Concert. If they come, they'll see us perform, too. We should save our energy for targeting specific singers. Let the 'Roys do our mass publicity for us."

Melanie consented and changed the subject. "Taylor's looking good this year."

Dani rolled her eyes.

"What?" cried Melanie. "Just because he's in the Chorderoys doesn't mean I can't *look*. Objectively, he's a fine looking man."

Dani inspected her adversary. His jet black hair was gelled up in its usual careful spiking. Dani loved mocking the Chorderoys' president for spending so much prep time in front of the mirror, but the hair style did fit well with the sharp angles of his jaw and cheekbones. And there was something appealing about his summer tan, the surfer look of his corduroy (he *would* choose corduroy) shorts and sandals . . . the bright gleam of his toothy smile . . . the way his pecs filled out his group tee . . .

"He's attractive, right?"

"He's . . . he's clean," Dani muttered.

"Clean?"

"Yes, he's clean-looking," Dani recovered quickly. "He obviously puts a great deal of effort into his personal appearance. But no, I'm definitely not attracted to him. How could anyone normal ever be interested in someone so . . . compulsive?"

Taylor had just begun arranging and re-arranging the albums on the Chorderoys' table. He stretched the tablecloth out so that it was perfectly pressed down and wrinkle-free.

"He is a little high-strung," admitted Melanie, although she thought the same criticism could apply to someone else in close proximity.

Dani believed in making her goals explicit, and Taylor's compulsive episode had just inspired her. She straightened her spine, stared straight at the rival group president, and calmly informed her subordinate, "The Harmoniums *will* be the best group this year."

Melanie followed the direction of Dani's sightline to see Taylor pour more candy into the candy bowl. "But what does it mean to be best?" asked the sophomore, genuinely curious. "Winning WAC? Scoring the highest audition rankings? Recruiting top soloists? Having the best sound? The group's social harmony?" Like most acatypes, Melanie was perhaps too fond of the easy musical reference.

The president's green eyes brightened. "All of the above," she said matter-of-factly. Dani beamed. "It takes everything."

Meanwhile, Taylor noticed Dani's teeth glinting in the sunlight, which only heightened his anxiety. The two Harmoniums stared at him, speaking in low voices. What were they conspiring about?

Taylor began pulling at his eyebrow hair. His nervous tic was back in full force. After tugging and ruminating for some time, he reached for his cell phone to send a mass text message to all Chorderoys. They were adding an extra hour to practice tonight. He'd determined they needed more time to prepare for the crucial Recruitment Concert.

When he finished typing the message, he looked up. Dani was still smiling. Taylor turned and cranked the volume of his group's album, hoping to drown the siren of those brilliant teeth. He proceeded to organize the

CDs on his table into even more perfectly symmetrical stacks.

Taylor could tell the Harmoniums were up to something. Dani was scheming, as always, but this time, he was determined to uncover her plans before she could put them into action. In the meantime, the Chorderoys would just have to be flawless. During recruitment season, they could afford nothing less.

♫ |

Chapter 2

Introductions

It was his first college class and Ben Jensen was already distracted. The student behind him had to *psst* and tap his shoulder before he remembered to "take and pass" from the professor's stack of syllabi.

Ben had been gazing across the lecture hall at the girl sitting in the fourth row. He had met her before, and while he had not yet caught her name, he remembered the circumstances of their meeting perfectly.

Last week was Freshmen Orientation, that glorious and uncharacteristic time at the beginning of a Brighton University college career when academic and extra-curricular stresses have yet to materialize and socializing itself is the goal. Incoming students were trying to form as many friendships as possible, as quickly as possible. The poor Residential Advisers delivered their nightly meetings on the "do's and don'ts" of college to an increasingly disinterested audience.

Floor meetings were usually scheduled late in the evening in order to curtail heavy drinking and partying. The concern was legitimate, but in practice, the precaution merely delayed, rather than reduced, such recreation. As soon as the RA's let them go, a whole crop of freshmen made a beeline to the door, already dressed for the night in the required polo with boat shoes, or tube skirt and high heels.

That particular evening, Ben decided to stay behind; he'd already learned that fraternity row was just exhausting. Instead, he joined a small gathering of his fellow freshmen who were sitting at the end of the dorm hallway, chatting.

The conversation bounced around—one minute they were discussing television, the next books, before finally settling on politics. Ben noticed how people perked up for this last subject, and thought how stereotypically "Brighton" (in other words, dorky) this would seem to his high school friends. Quentin from down the hall was wide-eyed and emphatic as he shared his profound political insights, all direct from Slate.com.

Eventually Ben's roommate, Wilson, and some other floormates returned from the frats. Each of them was still in that stage—far too prevalent, sadly—where one exaggerates one's tipsiness. Together, they were singing a rowdy and terrible rendition of "The Circle of Life" from *The Lion King*. Uninvited, they plopped down next to the comparatively subdued conversationalists. Mandy, one of the returning revelers, suggested Ben "bust out" his guitar. Ben was initially reluctant, but Wilson was eager to determine whether—by the doctrine of coolness by association—a guitar-playing roomie might prove handy with potential lady friends. He retrieved the instrument from their room and thrust it in Ben's face.

Ben tuned quickly and was soon strumming along as he played songs which had defined their childhoods, continuing the Disney magic with "A Whole New World" and the theme from *Duck Tales*. For the most part, they were simple tunes, and he figured out the chords easily as everyone sang.

"Do 'Can You Feel the Love Tonight,'" said Wilson, with a sidelong glance at his new female friend from the frats.

Ben smiled and complied. Although he was enjoying his first sing-a-long with his drunken floormates, it was by no means a magical experience. The overwhelming new-ness of his first week of college meant nothing seemed outside of his routine, not even spontaneous music.

But just when he'd finished the schmaltzy ballad, a raven-haired girl from down the hall walked up with her Spanish guitar.

"Ooh! Hers is special!" cooed Wilson, trying to be cute.

"It's classical," said Ben. Hers was lighter, with a thin rosewood neck. His was standard, a steel-string acoustic. It suddenly felt clunky in his hands.

Caroline smiled a little and sat Indian-style on the floor. Her long hair draped across her shoulders. The group had transitioned to nineties boy bands now, indulging in such masterpieces as "Quit Playing Games with My Heart" and "It's Gonna Be Me." Caroline joined in at once, plucking the correct notes without even asking for the key. While the rest of the group droned on, grotesquely flat, botching every lyric, Caroline invented a contrapuntal harmony as accompaniment.

Ben was in awe.

When Wilson and the rest of the party-going contingent noticed that they were no longer the center of attention, they lost interest. One of the girls invited the entire group to watch a movie in her room. This wasn't Wilson's most desired result, but it was at least a step in the right direction. The non-instrumentalists cleared out.

Ben hardly noticed them leaving. He and Caroline had long since moved on from playing pop songs, but he couldn't recall their transition to pure improvisation. All he heard were the high, sweet plucked tones she floated above his steady strumming. His eyes locked onto her fingers, followed them as they moved deftly up the strings. Her green nail polish shimmered in the fluorescent light of the hallway.

She began to sing. Her voice came as a clear soprano, warm and light. It danced on made-up syllables. *Dah nah nah . . . Lah nah nah . . . Hmm nah nah . . .*

Ben had just joined in—humming softly, so he could focus on *her* voice—when his partner suddenly decided it was time for the last chord. She strummed it three times, as if to emphasize its finality. She stood. Ben was too startled to really process what she said – something about a community service trip in the morning. He *did* remember to suggest they do this again. She smiled and walked back down the hallway, holding her guitar gracefully by its neck.

He had not seen her again until today, the first day of classes, and he was delighted to discover that she was sitting in his same lecture course, "International and Area Studies 101: Global Voices." It was a popular class, and the professor used the traditional roll call. Ben waited on his seat's edge, holding his breath in anticipation.

"Caroline Cooper?"

She raised her hand, and the professor moved on.

Ben hadn't waited long, obviously—alphabetical order does not conform to our dramatics—but it was enough to hear her name. *Caroline*, the girl with the Spanish guitar, the girl with the musical ear, the girl from down the hall, the girl who'd smiled when he'd suggested they play again . . .

Ben spent the rest of class thinking hard about what he should say when he approached her at the end of the hour. His task was difficult. He wanted to sound smart, funny, spontaneous, and cool, all at once, which is always a challenge to plan. Furthermore, her name kept echoing in his mind. *Caroline . . . Caroline . . . Caroline . . .* This,

14

combined with the professor's background noise, was disrupting his creative process.

On the other side of the classroom, Taylor Stuart was equally preoccupied, though with different concerns. As the professor explained the syllabus, workload, and reading list, Taylor knew that, as the course's Teaching Assistant, he should be paying close attention. The problem was a cappella. Whenever he tried to listen to the professor, his mind wandered back to his singing group. Recruitment was an extremely busy time for the president of the Chorderoys. There were fliers to put up, dorm performances to schedule, Facebook alerts to post. Moreover, tonight represented the peak of this "seasonal" stress—the pan-a cappella Recruitment Concert. It was the Chorderoys' only chance to make a strong first impression, and they were in direct competition with the five other groups.

Although graduation each May robbed every group of members, the Chorderoys had lost four of their strongest soloists and leaders. Taylor needed fresh talent to bolster the future of his group. Throughout the hour, the TA scribbled best-case a cappella draft scenarios in his notebook, engineering his ideal ensemble. They needed a dynamic soloist—preferably an alto, a true tenor, a soprano, a second vocal percussionist . . .

Taylor suddenly looked back and surveyed the class, searching for any familiar faces from Move-In Day, targets for a cappella recruitment. He spotted Caroline.

"Grades will be adjusted up to half a letter grade based on classroom engagement and participation," continued Professor Gruender. Taylor felt a pang of guilt. He turned and straightened in his seat, trying to be a little more present for his students. If there was one defining trait of the Chorderoys' president, it wasn't his generalized anxiety, his tendency to over-plan, or his fastidious attention to detail. It was a mostly private, very sincere sense of duty.

That duty was part of the reason Taylor was TAing for a political science class, although he was actually majoring in Architecture. Last semester, Taylor developed an interest in international issues by taking this class as an elective. When Professor Gruender asked him to TA for the course this year, Taylor felt a certain obligation to keep that interest alive. For him, discussing far-off nations was a bit like researching Deconstructivist Architecture, or singing passionately without instruments. He protected these perhaps less practical interests.

When the professor finally dismissed the class, both Taylor and Ben, for entirely different reasons, converged on Caroline Cooper. Taylor arrived first, of course. Faking nonchalance does not win many races.

"Hi there! Didn't you stop by our table on Move-In Day?"

"Yes, I did. You were in . . ."

"The Chorderoys," said Taylor, with a gigantic grin. "And you sang in show choir in high school, right? You should definitely come see us at the Recruitment Concert tonight." With this abrupt lead, Taylor launched right into his group sales pitch—friendly people, tight group, lots of fun, big plans for the year.

When Taylor took a breath, Caroline chimed in. "I'm not entirely sure I'm going to continue competitive singing in college," she explained. "Part of me wants to focus more on activities outside of campus. Community action, that sort of thing. But I'll absolutely consider it."

Caroline paused, and Ben thought he saw her smirking in his direction. (He had been hanging back a few feet, trying to look preoccupied with his smart-

16

phone.) "Ben here is a singer, not to mention a fine guitarist."

As Taylor registered Ben's face, he remembered that Dani had made first contact with this freshman during Move-In. Was "Global Voices" class providing Taylor with an opportunity to counterstrike?

"You sing?"

Ben thought back to his conversation with Dani Behlman. "Well, I sang in choir in high school. It was fun. Not show choir though. My high school didn't have the glee thing."

"Collegiate a cappella *isn't* glee club," said Taylor, perhaps too firmly. This was obviously a touchy subject. "But as for your music background, that's fantastic! An old-fashioned chorister and an instrumentalist! Pleased to meet you, Ben."

As they shook hands, Professor Gruender called over his TA to answer a question about office hours. Taylor frowned at the interruption, but excused himself quickly. "Gotta run, but I'll see *both* of you tonight!" He race-walked to the podium up front.

When Ben was finally alone with the raven-haired girl who lived down the hall, he remembered absolutely nothing of what he had intended to say to her. He improvised. "Show choir, eh? Were you um . . . the show choir diva?"

Caroline angled her head, surprised by the question. "I wouldn't say diva, but I did love group singing. It's very addictive."

Ben nodded. He found it hard to imagine the classical guitarist busting out show tunes. Then again, there was an air of mystery surrounding his new classmate. She was coy in the most charming way.

17

"Of course, I love playing instruments, too," said Caroline. "I mean, I had fun playing in the hall a few nights ago. We really should do it again some time."

Ben could not agree more, which was why he was absolutely determined to seem casual. "Yeah, we should," he said simply.

And they walked back to the dorm together, discussing favorite indie bands.

♫

Ben and Caroline arrived at the Recruitment Concert seconds before it began. They were running late after another guitar improv session in Caroline's room. ("No! That is *not* a euphemism," Ben informed his nosey roommate.) The auditorium lights dimmed just as they found their seats.

A dapper young man walked on stage, wearing a dark green dress shirt, a black tuxedo vest, and a bow tie. It was the uniform of his all-male group, the Dynamics, more commonly known by their nickname, the Dinos. When he spoke, his voice was extra bubbly. He was in his full-blown a cappella mode.

"Welcome to the ACUAC Recruitment Concert! ACUAC is proud to put on this event to showcase all six Brighton U. a cappella groups. With the performances tonight, we kick off the official a cappella recruitment season.

"Each year, a different singing group chairs ACUAC. My name is Greg, I'm with the Brighton U. Dinos, and I have the pleasure of being this year's ACUAC moderator and your host for the evening."

This was met with cat-calls, a "Hott-ie!" and a wolf whistle.

Caroline leaned over and whispered in Ben's ear. "Greg went to high school with me back in Kansas City. So much enthusiasm—the kid was a show choir beast!"

Greg smiled at the audience's reaction, although the color was deepening in his throat and cheeks. "As moderator, it's my job to introduce all of the groups and give a brief introduction to the auditions process. But first, a note about Brighton U. a cappella in general. All of the groups you'll see tonight are entirely student-directed and all of the songs you'll hear are student-arranged. There's no supervision whatsoever from university faculty or staff. We do what *we* want."

There were more cheers, including a "hear, hear!" The basic thrill of independence never gets old.

"I should also mention that tonight's concert order was chosen randomly, by drawing numbers out of a hat, and not by anyone in particular. So don't read anything into it."

Greg peered down at his note card. He had asked each group president to write a short introductory blurb. He recognized Dani's curly handwriting and red gel pen. "This first ensemble is the premier co-ed a cappella group at Brighton University."

Listening backstage, Taylor cringed. How he loathed when Dani used the word "premier" in her introductions! By definition, it simply meant "first." With a few semesters' head start on both the Chorderoys and La*chaim, the Harmoniums were, technically, the first co-ed group on campus. But the word premier implied so much more. As Dani was well aware, premier sounded like it meant *best*. What gave the Harmoniums the right to advertise themselves as the best co-ed group on campus?

19

Meanwhile, Greg continued reading the intro, which was chock-full of Dani's buzzwords. "This spring, they will release their seventh *studio album*. They look forward to *touring* high schools and universities across the country. They are thrilled to invite *hot* new talent to audition for their *nationally renowned* ensemble . . ."

Greg cleared his throat. She had underlined her favorite adjective once again. "Ladies and Gentlemen, please welcome Brighton's <u>premier</u> co-ed a cappella group, the Harmoniums."

During the applause, twelve singers walked neatly on stage. The men wore red shirts and black slacks, the ladies assorted red and black dresses. They quickly formed the customary arc of singers.

The Harmoniums' music director blew the pitch and brought his group in on a choral "ooh." Silence descended on the audience. Intrigued auditionees and seasoned veterans alike listened carefully, trying to recognize the chords.

The choral introduction faded and the soloist stepped slowly to the microphone at center stage, her strawberry blonde hair shining red in the spotlight.

The song was "I Can't Make You Love Me," originally by Bonnie Raitt. Dani had him immediately. Ben was transfixed, thoroughly impressed that the assertive girl he'd met by coincidence on Freshmen Move-In Day could sing so tenderly. Her every note came dripping with heartbreak and vulnerability. Part of him wanted to literally reach out and comfort her as she sang of her abandonment. In the chorus, she declared – in her most soulful belt – her determination to pick up her life's pieces and move on from this one-sided romance. Ben actually felt proud of her.

Most of all, Ben marveled at her extraordinary gift for eye contact. It seemed as if she was looking at him directly, but Ben knew that could not be. Everyone in the audience must feel the same. Still, he thought, only the most phenomenal soloists could seem so inclusive.

In fact, Dani *was* looking at Ben directly. Not for the whole song, of course, but every few seconds. The rest of the time she singled out and sang to the other males in the audience, fusing her gift for moving an audience with her calculating sense of strategy. As group president, she'd been reminding her members that this was a "man year" for the Harmoniums, meaning they needed to focus their energy on recruiting basses, baritones, and tenors. (Older members would recall that *every* audition season was a "man year," according to Miss Behlman.)

Dani pushed the high note of the bridge to the absolute end of the phrase, the kind of singing that's impressive because of the sheer physical challenge of breath control. Even Caroline, who thought Dani's tone a little forced, felt the effect. She found herself holding her breath, too.

And then Dani grew quiet, once again the dejected lover. She stepped back into the center of the arc. The background singers emulated a sad "piano" lilt. *Lu, lu, lu, lu— Lu, lu, lu, lu——*

Her last line was barely louder than a whisper. The silence was charged.

And the cheers were wild. The president of the Harmoniums smiled sweetly, and more than a little victoriously, as she absorbed the praise. *I can't make you love me*, she thought to herself. The irony of the lyric was not lost upon her: She did not believe it in the slightest.

Dani was still smiling as she came up from the group bow, and once again, Ben could have sworn she was smiling right at him.

"That was awesome!" said Ben to Caroline.

Caroline nodded. "There're still five more groups to go," she reminded him.

As Greg introduced the second group, Ben thought back to the words of the emcee's introductory speech: *All student-directed, all student arrangements.* In retrospect, Ben's high school choir seemed so lame. The only thing impressive about their director, Mr. Bruschearloepeghi, was his easily mispronounced last name. In chorus, he'd pushed the same recycled songs semester after semester —not because they were any good, but because it required less effort than teaching new ones. Half the kids in choir were only taking the class to salvage their GPAs. Most couldn't hold a tune to save their lives.

Not here, Ben thought, as he watched the Notabelles take the stage in their purple dresses. Singers at Brighton would know their parts. They might not all be as übertalented as Caroline – or have musical tastes which were uncannily similar to Ben's own – but they would all have passion. No more Bruschearloepeghi; no more musical rehash year after year; no more playing the system. This was college. This was original. This was real.

A cappella was freedom, and Ben was ready to join the cause.

♪ |

Chapter 3

Recruitment

After four singing groups had performed, the host announced a brief intermission. Greg came out into the audience to find Caroline. "Well, well, well if it isn't the infamous C-squared! The Original Care Bear! *La Guitarrista!* Koopa Troopa!" His hug was enormous. "Reunited again!" he cried. "Holly and the Coop."

"Look at you, Mr. Handsome Emcee," returned Caroline. She turned and introduced her high school choir classmate to Ben.

"Nice to meet you! And looking forward to your Dinos audition!" said Greg, with smiling self-assurance. He turned back to Caroline. "And you're auditioning for the co-ed and ladies' groups, aren't you?"

Caroline glanced at Ben, and said, "Yes, I think so. Everyone so far has been fantastic."

Ben smiled at the good news.

"By the way, Greg, what exactly is ACUAC?" Caroline asked.

Greg clenched his teeth. "Ooh, probably should've mentioned that earlier. Oh well, the details are more for current singers than for the auditionees. ACUAC is an acronym for the A Cappella United Administration Committee. It's the governing body for all of the singing groups. Our job is to keep things fair during auditions, so we make rules and attempt to monitor each other to make sure those rules are followed."

"What rules?" asked Ben.

"All kinds. Most of them are pretty intuitive, really." Greg took a deep breath and rattled off from memory:

"There's the 'Respect Provision' and 'Song-Staking' and the official policy against dirty rushing. That rule is called 'Limited Contact.'"

Ben was confused. Wasn't *rushing* a word from Greek life, an ordeal for potential fraternity and sorority pledges? But there wasn't time to ask—Greg's mind had leapt elsewhere. The emcee leaned in toward the slim soprano, his tone careful but filled with curiosity. "And how's Elliot? Are you still—"

"Yes, we're still together," replied Caroline. "He's at Berkeley this year, enjoying the sunshine. He's even designing his own major in music journalism."

The color drained from Ben's face. Somehow he'd neglected to consider the possibility that Caroline was already in a relationship. But it made so much sense. Of course, Caroline would be *taken*.

Lucky for Ben, Greg and Caroline didn't seem to notice his reaction, and he had a moment to recover from the sudden, overwhelming feeling of defeat.

"Good for him," said Greg, "Although I do wish he'd come to Brighton instead. I'd love to draft him for the Dinos." Greg glanced around at the mostly refilled seats, excited by the return of his audience. "Looks like I better get things going again. Later kids!"

As Greg bounded back onstage, Caroline shook her head. "So much enthusiasm. *All* the girls had crushes on him—not that he was interested."

Ben angled his head. "Oh, so he *is* gay. I wasn't sure if he . . ."

"Was gay or incredibly nice?" Caroline grinned. "He's both."

When the lights dimmed and Greg returned onstage, he was noticeably more serious than before. He usually enjoyed his moderator/emcee duties—guiding the show, charming the crowd. But Caroline's former classmate was only human. It wasn't easy for him to be impartial as he introduced the *other* men's singing group.

Greg cleared his throat and read from the scribbled print of the note card in his hand. "The next a cappella group was founded almost two decades ago by a group of guys who said 'F these instruments – we're gonna do it all with our mouths.' They've been making sweet, passionate, strictly auditory love ever since."

His voice was unusually firm and formal. "Please welcome Brighton's most eligible bachelors, the Gobfellas."

The group stumbled onstage, fake-panicking as if they had collectively slept too late and were all bolting for the shower. To say the Gobfellas had strange "uniforms" would be an understatement. The guy wearing a tie-dyed t-shirt stood beside a pink oxford, a tuxedo vest next to a ratty sleeveless tee. They wore slacks, a Go-Go dress, overalls, a speedo, steel boots, moccasins, tap shoes, no shoes . . .

They were letter jacket jocks, leather jacket rebels, thrift store junkies, and beach bums all at once, but Ben saw the unifying theme. The Gobfellas wore confidence, with none exhibiting more bravado than the "bro" who swaggered to the microphone.

Derek Ross was tall and broad-shouldered, with a blonde crew cut and a deep bass voice. His cut-off muscle shirt revealed the tattoo on his upper arm—in black Helvetica, the letters *GOB*. Rumor had it that he quit the football team freshman year to join the Gobfellas, telling his coach he was doing it for the ladies. Brighton athletics were only D-III, but this incident was often cited as clear proof of the (heterosexual) perks of being one of the "Fellas."

"First of all, let's have a big hand for Greg," announced Derek. "He has the very, ahem, riveting job of being *moderator* for this fantastic event. He's doing such an excellent job of it, too."

The audience chuckled.

Derek addressed the crowd. "You laugh, but it's a very serious matter. Hollis could have been like: Ladies and Gentlemen, the mother-fu**in Gobfellas are in the hizzouse! But, instead, he was like—" He paused to ready himself, and adopted his most sheepish monotone. "The Gobfellas are next. That is all."

Backstage, Greg's face burned with fury and embarrassment. The whole point of the emcee making the group introductions was to prevent exactly this type of grandstanding. Besides, what right did Derek have to pick on anyone in the a cappella community? The Gobfellas hardly ever contributed to ACUAC's pre-orientation planning.

Taylor, waiting with the Chorderoys backstage, shot Greg a sympathetic glance.

Meanwhile, Derek wore an enormous grin as he continued to work the crowd. "You laugh, but it's so hard, guys," said the Fellas' president. "Being *that* moderate isn't easy. And I just want Greg to know that we in the Fellas recognize what he's going through."

"You're the best, Greg!" said Derek's accomplice, a short high-tenor who barely came up to the president's shoulders. He was wearing Sponge Bob pajamas. "Let's give Greg a hand!" The audience applauded merrily.

"And while we're at it, let's clap it up for moderation in general. Most of you are freshmen, so you're new to this whole college thing, but I'll tell you a secret." Derek leaned forward. His smile was devilish. "The key to a successful college experience . . . is *moderation*."

No one believed it, which is why they laughed.

The shorter Fella smirked, pulled out a pitch pipe, and blew the starting note. Clutching the sides of his PJ pants, he sang the opening riff in his high, belting voice.

The vocal percussionist laid down a thick, steady beat. A small burst of spit flew through the air with every pulse.

Derek came in on the bass line, his voice husky and ultra-resonant. He rocked back and forth, pounding his fist to his chest.

The baritones joined him on a slightly higher note, pounding their chests with his rhythm. At this point, Ben finally recognized what song the Gobfellas were building—"Let's Get It Started" by the Black-Eyed Peas.

The second tenors joined in a little higher, followed by the first tenors in their falsettos. They all pounded their chests.

Derek spun in place and clutched the microphone. The muscled soloist beckoned to the audience, inviting them to join the rising energy. As the tempo rushed, the block of men behind him echoed his call.

The PJs-wearing tenor gave himself room, crouched his knees, and executed a sudden back-flip onstage. The crowd cheered. The Fellas pumped their first for the refrain: "Let's Get It Started!"

Ben barely heard the hidden word being sung by the chorus – the uncensored use of "retarded" instead of "it started." The freshman was at the edge of his seat, secretly hoping for more acrobatics.

As the song went on, the Fellas began shedding clothes, with little distinction between those who had more or fewer items to offer. Jackets, jeans, socks, a fedora, undershirts, and a giant-sized gag jockstrap all went flying into the audience.

Mr. Go-Go Dress danced as if he'd lost all bones. Tuxedo Man shook his booty for the ladies in the front row. Moccasins attempted "the Worm" onstage, seemingly disregarding the detriment to his man parts. Pajamas McSquarepants jumped on Derek's shoulders, signing "rock on!" to the sky with his pinkie and forefinger.

For the final note, the ensemble posed as not-so-classy strippers—modeling pale thighs, slapping bottoms, stroking furry chests—while Derek faded out with the bass line.

The audience ate it up, responding with applause and cheers and hysterical laughter. Girls screamed as if they might faint. From his corner backstage, Greg shook his head. The Gobfellas might not be the most musically sophisticated, but they *did* know how to entertain. Year after year with the same Black Eyed Peas' hit, yet they always kept the energy high.

The Fellas bowed—except for Go-Go Dress, who curtsied—and scrambled offstage.

As Greg tried to quiet the crowd for the last group introduction, Taylor paced back and forth. When the Chorderoys had drawn the final position in the singing order, the group president had been ecstatic. Every group wanted to be last so they could make a strong final impression. But following the Gobfellas was going to be more difficult than he'd imagined. When Taylor walked onstage with the Chorderoys, he doubted their classic song-with-a-twist would be at all memorable in comparison.

Unlike Dani's "I Can't Make You Love Me," the audience recognized the tune of the Chorderoys' number almost immediately. Smiles swept the crowd as they absorbed the familiar "string" bass, the light soprano "chimes," the feel-good Motown groove. Taylor's nerves led him to flub a little on the top note of his high tenor entrance, but he forced a smile nonetheless.

Watching from the back of the auditorium, Dani chuckled and shook her head. Her presidential rival had a weakness: He enunciated too much for Motown. She loved listening closely for him to over-pronounce the t's in "Ain't No Mountain High Enough." Back when they were on speaking terms, she'd teased him for singing with all the diction of an ESL teacher.

But Dani's amusement subsided when Olivia joined the song. The Chorderoys' recruitment coordinator sported her tightest white dress and blue stilettos. As she sang, she gently caressed Taylor's arm.

Dani hated just about everything about Olivia Goldfarb, but she especially resented her when she flirted with Taylor onstage. Dani looked on, disgusted, as Olivia put her hand on Taylor's chest, and stared up at him with wide, inviting eyes.

Taylor was careful not to publicize details about his personal life, probably because he knew how quickly news traveled in Brighton's a cappella rumor circuit. But Dani's powers of observation were astute. She had deduced on her own what she knew Taylor was trying to hide: He and Olivia were sleeping together. By Dani's estimation, they'd been hooking up for almost a year.

For the line about valleys, Olivia rubbed her hands on her hips and shimmied down suggestively.

Dani, whose knowledge of pop music bordered on encyclopedic, actually gagged. What an insult to all the classy performers who had sung that song! Sweet Tammi Terrell must be rolling in her grave! Diana Ross should sue for defamation! Dani searched the auditorium, but it seemed that no one else was appalled by Olivia's public display of promiscuity. The Gobfellas' full-blown strip-tease must have dulled their sense of decency.

But Dani's spiteful state was soon interrupted by an unexpected musical development. Suddenly, the Chorderoys were singing gentle *doo*'s, the revelry of Motown melting away into a heavenly major chord.

Dylan Genesius was a smooth-voiced high tenor with such a youthful appearance that he would have his ID checked for being at the mall past ten on a school night. In conversations, he was reliably sarcastic, but his singing voice was warm and calming. No one in the crowd had ever heard Maroon 5 sung so earnestly. His high notes for "She Will Be Loved" were golden.

Ben shot Caroline a quick, half-subconscious glance before refocusing his attention on the soloist.

The soprano didn't notice. Caroline would later mark that specific moment as the first time a cappella music gave her chills. This was precisely the kind of innovation she'd missed in high school show choir. Even before the mash-up, she'd loved the way the arrangement emulated the instrumentation of the original, how the background alternately echoed and challenged the melody line. She knew two things: She was now *definitely* trying out for collegiate a cappella, and her new group crush was the Chorderoys.

After this brief interlude, Dylan stepped back and the audience was thrust once more into the sweet buoyancy of "Ain't No Mountain High Enough." The final chorus stacked all the parts together: Taylor and Olivia's duet; a Diana Ross-style descant; swelling altos and tenors; a thumping bass; and a reprise of the hopeful anthem, "She Will Be Loved."

Taylor had been stage-grinning the entire song, but it was only when he heard the roar of applause from the

30

audience that he allowed a natural smile to stretch across his face. He glowed as the Chorderoys absorbed the praise.

After a few moments, Greg returned to the stage. As moderator, it was his responsibility to give the closing speech of the night, and he began by inviting each of the groups up for one last bow. It was an impressive sight as the six groups filed back on, the stage becoming a sea of colored uniforms: red-and-black Harmoniums next to white-and-blue Chorderoys; green-vested Dinos next to black-and-gold La*chaim—the Jewish music a cappella group; purple-wearing ladies of the Notabelles next to the eclectically-dressed Gobfellas.

After Greg finished his announcements, Ben and Caroline remained in their seats to discuss the show. Current a cappella singers, however, did not have the luxury of relaxation. The performers rushed to the outer rim of the auditorium to their various group tables, eager to sell CDs, distribute candy, and, most importantly, sign up auditionees. Other singers served as roaming representatives for their groups, going out into the crowd with clipboards, mingling and filling spots on their audition sign-up sheets.

These "grassroots" recruiters were selected strategically, especially in the co-ed groups. As experts in the recruitment process, both Taylor and Dani had a thorough understanding of the way in which physical attraction could aid them in enlisting new singers. Though their groups were rivals, their strategies were the same: Use attractive and congenial a cappella girls to lure potential male auditionees, who were always harder to come by than female auditionees. Indeed, there was some truth to Dani's assessment that every recruiting year should be guy-focused. Each fall, at least three girls tried

31

out for every boy, making testosterone a perpetually limited and precious resource in the a cappella world.

Further complicating the matter, co-ed groups also had to compete with the respective allures of the two all-male groups at Brighton. Neither the Harmoniums nor the Chorderoys could offer the same fraternal vibe as the Gobfellas or Dinos, that is, the prospect of hanging out with a fun-loving and rowdy group of dudes (who sang). The solution was to use especially friendly female sales-persons to emphasize the perks of being in a *co-ed* group. (Both presidents, of course, recognized that not every boy would respond to this method, but from a purely statis-tical perspective, the gay men in the audience often tried out with less coaxing.)

The circumstances gave Dani an advantage over Taylor. The president of the Harmoniums stood in a corner, talking to a group of mostly men about how much she loved singing that solo for her favorite ensemble. She peppered the "group love" messages she was spewing with reminders to sign-up for an audition before it was too late. "Make sure you write your e-mail address legibly so we can reach you!" she said, with a little laugh.

Luckily, Taylor had plenty of support from Olivia. Thus far, the recruitment coordinator had followed Taylor's instructions perfectly, from her clothing and general appearance to the choreographed flirtation of their duet. Now, however, Olivia relied on her instincts. She slinked through the crowd, clipboard in hand, honing in on potential auditionees. Olivia prided herself on having mastered the acaflirt. When a boy walked past wearing a Bears hat, Olivia exclaimed that she was a *huge* Bears fan! Suddenly excited, "the target" began to rant about the current team roster, the new management, the stadium. Olivia nodded when it seemed appropriate. She raked her mind – were the Bears a basketball team? – all the while smiling coyly and batting her eyelashes. She hid her ignorance well enough, however, and ultimately convinced the Bears fan, his roommate, and two other guys from his floor to sign up for audition slots.

It was not in Taylor's nature to stand idly by while others were hard at work. Instead, he instructed Gary, the Chorderoys' shy bass, to man the group table selling old albums while Taylor grabbed another clipboard and went after targets of his own.

Within seconds, he found himself talking to a petite freshman girl who told him that she had plenty of singing experience but was afraid of signing up. "I'm pre-med," she explained. "I don't want to *overextend* myself." Taylor hated that word and the annoying way in which Brighton U. students used it. Of course, he knew from experience that a cappella cutting into one's academic or social life was a legitimate concern. But the Chorderoys needed fresh talent! Despite her reservations, Taylor persuaded her to sign up for an audition time. She could make those pesky time-management decisions later.

Soon Taylor found himself talking to yet another nervous freshman. Her hand trembled as she signed her name. She informed the Chorderoys' leader that she was afraid of singing in public. Taylor resisted the urge to mouth off that she was without a doubt unique, that he'd never in his life heard of such a phobia, but instead, he smiled politely and urged her to sign up anyway. "What have you got to lose by trying?" he asked. His stage-grin had returned.

In truth, part of Taylor genuinely *envied* the freshmen, who were merely trying out. In a way, they had much less reason to be nervous. If a freshman auditioned and failed to make one of the groups, this simply meant that they were beaten out by other candidates, usually people they didn't know and perhaps would never meet. Generally, freshmen were resilient; they responded by joining Student Government, or the debate team, or any other of the multitude of student organizations on campus. There was always something else to consume an awfully high proportion of their time and energy.

For Taylor, however, the stakes were much higher. He couldn't simply jump ship and join the Anime Appreciation Club if the Chorderoys had a "humbling" audition season; not in his junior year, especially not as group president. And unlike the freshmen, he was very familiar with his competition. Losing now would make Dani's exceptionally self-assured smile even more unbearable.

And so, Taylor moved determinedly through the crowd, small-talking and goading and acaflirting until, at last, all the time-slots on his clipboard were filled.

Chapter 4

Dormstorm

Renee Murphy had a secret. It was a secret best represented by her "B-E-P" iPod playlist, a secret which explained—sort of—why the intense athlete, who had no formal singing experience, had just signed up for a cappella auditions.

The freshman member of the Brighton U. Diving Team was a coach's dream: an attentive student, a die-hard perfectionist, and a remarkably (competitors would say *eerily*) consistent performer. Renee's teammates suspected that her unnatural calm on the 10 m platform had something to do with her unique pre-dive ritual. As Renee waited for her turn on the block, she would sit alone against the back wall of the natatorium, holding her legs tight to her chest, resting her chin on her knees, listening intently to whatever music was streaming through her ear buds. It was Renee's facial expression while she listened, however, which had become the team's favorite subject of gossip, surpassing even discussion on team member hookups.

While waiting to dive, Renee glared at the top of the pool with steely brown eyes. The intensity in her stare was nothing short of murderous, as if she sought to assassinate the water with her perfect, splash-less entrance. Coach Bryce was a gruff old man, the type who believed that China's recent dominance in competitive diving was clear proof America's young people were growing soft. But even stern Coach Bryce was unnerved by Renee's stare. When the team captain brought up the subject once after practice, the coach smirked. "Murphy's

35

game face? You mean the look that could kill puppies?" The name stuck.

Her teammates assumed that the look coincided with Renee's choice of music, that the songs she listened to somehow encouraged her facial ferocity. But what kind of music could produce such a frightening expression was the subject of vigorous debate. Heavy metal was a front-runner, with one teammate suggesting Renee listened to Gorgonox, a fringe Satanic rock group. "She looks possessed!" insisted the diver, only half-joking.

When the team captain finally built up the courage to ask her about her pre-dive music, Renee refused to enlighten her. "Just your standard pop rock," she replied, and awkwardly changed the subject to calf exercises. The captain did not press further. Maybe whatever it was that possessed Renee before diving did not take kindly to questioning.

In a way, Renee was just as perplexed by the "B-E-P" playlist as her teammates. She had no recollection of consciously selecting her favorites, could not pinpoint the precise origins of her obsession with the three artists who helped her prepare for diving meets.

They had simply always been there: Billy Joel, Elton John, and Phil Collins. She'd grown up listening to them on car rides with her father. Today, they were her counselors before every jump.

Thus, when she stared at the clear, chlorinated water like the revenge-bent heroine of a Tarantino film, Renee might very well be enjoying Elton's catchy "Crocodile Rock." A particularly murderous look consumed her face when she prepped with Phil Collins' "You Can't Hurry Love." She had executed her first forward-somersault-pike with the tune of "Uptown Girl" still dancing through her head.

Wanting to protect her tough girl reputation, Renee kept her music tastes intensely private. In the event that the B-E-P playlist was discovered, however, Renee had already planned her response. She'd simply explain that these familiar songs had a useful psychological value and relaxed her muscles. Coach Bryce's suggestions about visualizing the upcoming dive made her too tense. Her silent sing-along sessions cleared her mind, the music freeing her body to do as she'd rehearsed. It didn't mean she was *actually* obsessed with these three artists. (Hopefully, any would-be snoopers would ignore the iPod's recorded play counts.)

But of course, the music was more than just a tool to take off the edge. Even Elton's "Sad Songs (Say So Much)" made her feel, somehow, better. The results-based, technical world of diving wasn't known for its sensitivity. As she'd advanced in the sport, Renee had relied increasingly on Pianoman, Rocketman, and Tarzan for their ability to uplift.

It was these sentiments that had made Renee's ears perk up when the all-male Dinos had come running through the halls of Delmar dormitory during the first week of school, shouting about a free concert in the lobby. For Renee, the announcement incited a quick internal debate. Part of her insisted on staying put—she still had hours to go on her physics problem set. But that other part, the part she kept alive with B-E-P, was restless. And so she went downstairs, to her first-ever a cappella performance.

In a cappella-speak, dormstorming meant touring the freshman residence halls and putting on free performances for the students. As Greg liked to say, "If the kids aren't coming to a cappella, we'll bring the a cappella to them." Although he enjoyed the idea of selflessly singing for the masses, even the cheery president of the Dinos was cynically aware that the free concerts were primarily a tool for recruitment.

Of course, the enthusiastic freshmen gathering in the lobby had no concept of the intergroup politicking which took place before the dormstorming performances. Dani had routinely insisted that the Harmoniums perform with an all-guys ensemble. The Gobfellas were out of commission, with Wednesday nights kicking off their weekends. That left the Dinos.

Dani's strategy in teaming up with a men's group was two-fold: From a marketing perspective, males were better at running and shouting through the dormitory halls to spread the word about the concert that was about to begin. (Dani, for her part, didn't believe in running, and, to protect her voice, she only shouted during debates.) In addition, partnering with an all-guys group allowed the Harmoniums to target guys who might initially plan to audition for men's ensembles only. During her group's last practice, she'd specifically instructed her singers to hit up any unrecognized male they saw conversing with a Dino and ask, "Have you signed up for your Harmoniums audition yet?"

Greg was not nearly so calculating when he accepted the Harmoniums' invitation to dormstorm together. He just hoped two groups would double the audience. Grinning, he watched the freshmen gather in the dormitory lounge, settling themselves on couches, chatting excitedly—some of the residents specifically eager for singing, others just pleased by the interruption itself, like children wishing for school fire drills.

Renee found a spot on the floor, leaning against an easy chair, and assumed her pre-diving pose.

The men's group assembled in an arc and began a familiar doo-wop chorus. Immediately, a sense of happy calm washed over Renee. Billy Joel's "The Longest Time" was a B-E-P standard, an old faithful for producing pre-dive optimism. At the state championships last spring, it was the melody which had been floating through her head as she nailed her triple tuck.

The Dinos' basses bopped their heads up and down with the jumps of the bass line. The tenors snapped with the syncopated nonsense syllables. *Bop! – Dop! – Dooahh, dooahh* . . . Greg sang the solo, stretching his musical plea for love to the top of his chest range. His curly brown hair bounced about in rhythm.

This particular Pianoman hit reminded Renee of riding in the car with her father. Professionally, Mr. Murphy was a tech writer for a science publishing company, a man regarded for his quiet expertise. But when he was playing parental chauffer, he and his daughter were duet partners. He'd crank the car stereo and they'd sing together as he drove her to and from practices. "My talented Renee. Part Lauren Wilkinson, part Carol King," he'd gloat. Even when Renee got her driver's license, she'd still ask her dad to take her to the pool. Car sing-alongs weren't the same without him.

After one jam session a few weeks before Renee started college, her father turned down the car stereo and offered some unexpected fatherly advice. "You know, honey, I realize you're into this whole diving thing. You're so determined, and that's . . . well, that's fantastic. But if you'd like to, you know, have some fun, try some new things in college . . . well, you should know that I—I mean your mother and I—well, we'd support you in that. You only get one freshman year, you know."

As she recalled her father's words, and listened to thirteen dudes belting classic Billy Joel, Renee had an epiphany. Like most big insights, it should have been fairly obvious all along, but at the moment it seemed downright revolutionary.

Renee realized that she loved music. Listening to favorites from the B-E-P list, her first rock concert with friends, a particularly loud singing session with her dad—these were some of her happiest memories. She just hadn't put it all together before.

Her father had suggested she "try something new." Could this new thing be singing in an a cappella group? Granted, there was the initial hurdle of making it in. Renee didn't have much experience singing in public, but she knew she had a decent sense of pitch. (That is, she could always tell how far her father was off.) And she knew how to read music. Long ago, before her mother had signed her up for the diving team, she'd been enrolled in piano lessons. In fact, before Renee demonstrated an aptitude for gymnastics, "the plan" was to be a competitive pianist.

Listening to Greg's warm voice in "The Longest Time," Renee thought a cappella might be exactly the breath of fresh air she needed. Based on the apparent cheerfulness of the Dinos, she couldn't imagine an activity *less* like diving. Compared to the cutthroat, every-point-matters world she was used to, a cappella was going to be a cakewalk.

Months later, Renee's father would have some explaining to do to his wife. "When I said something new, I meant go on some dates, kick back a few beers, something normal," he'd defend himself. "Not go off the deep end and devote her heart and soul to the college glee club." But these tense times were still far off; at the moment, Renee was enjoying the mere possibility that she could join a singing group. Imagine – music itself being the goal of an activity, not just the coping mechanism she used to survive it!

Of course, no one who was looking at Renee at the moment would have expected her to be enjoying such a pleasant daydream; in fact, the Dinos who had caught her eye were a little scared. Renee's unfortunate curse was that her default expression whenever she was listening closely to music just happened to look a tad violent. She could be enjoying herself, even having one of the most important realizations of her life, and still be wearing the glare that could kill puppies.

After the Dinos finished their number, the Harmoniums grouped together for Dani's power ballad. Renee continued to enjoy herself (and stare murderously) as the co-ed group sang, but she couldn't stop wishing that the Dinos would come back and sing another B-E-P staple. In Renee's view, the Dinos' all-male charter was nothing short of tragic. Without the gender requirement, Renee would have been so moved by her musical euphoria that she would have pledged herself to the Dinos immediately. Greg would have had one of the most driven a cappella singers in Brighton history.

As it was, Renee could only dream about joining an all-guys' group. "Girls cause so much acadrama!" she would later complain. And one name would be foremost in her mind.

♫

It was fitting that Dani Behlman should receive the news that night, with the adrenaline of dormstorming still churning through her veins. She sat in her ergonomic swivel chair, in front of her computer and efficiency desk, alone in her one-bedroom apartment. She read the email with steely concentration.

BRENNA NOBOKS, TREASURER AND CHAIR OF STUDENT GOVERNMENT TREASURY COUNCIL

TO ALL A CAPPELLA GROUP PRESIDENTS:

BRIGHTON UNIVERSITY'S SIX A CAPPELLA GROUPS CONSTITUTE A VARIED AND DIVERSE SINGING COMMUNITY; HOWEVER, *SIX* TOTAL GROUPS IS A LARGE AND ABOVE AVERAGE NUMBER FOR A STANDARD MIDSIZED UNIVERSITY.

THEREFORE, YOUR STUDENT ELECTED DEMOCRATIC REPRESENTATIVES OF THE TREASURY COUNCIL OF STUDENT GOVERNMENT HAVE DECIDED TO UNDER-TAKE A NUMERIC MODIFICATION. THIS WILL REQUIRE A CONSOLIDATING ADJUSTMENT TO THE NUMBER OF A CAPPELLA GROUP ALLOTMENTS INCLUDED IN THE PRIMARY UNIVERSITY BUDGET.

Dani actually felt nauseated as she read the e-mail's text. Deep down, the alto was as much an aesthete as a competitor. Her mind—nay, her very *soul*—cried out against Brenna Noboks' clunky use of synonyms. What-ever happened to precision of language? It was enough to bring Strunk and White to tears.

But despite the message's painfully inarticulate phras-ing, the Harmoniums' president got its gist. Reducing the budget meant defunding certain groups. And when a group was defunded by Brighton's Student Government, they lost their charter to exist on campus. No more permission to advertise, no more rehearsal space, no more performing on college property.

In her annoying, irritating, irksome, synonym-stuffed way, Noboks was writing about something truly horrific: a cappella group extinction.

At this point, Dani whipped out her cell and called up Joe. Back when Dani was a freshman, her Residential Adviser had been an extremely useful connection. Dani had adored throwing cocktail parties in her first-year dorm room. She selected the fancy cheeses and *hors d'oeuvres* on her own; being underage, however, she had needed a little help with the beverages. Luckily, she could depend on Joe to buy whatever she required in the way of wine and spirits. All she had to do in return was feign an interest in some show called *Firefly*. She promised they would watch episodes together "sometime" in the never-specified future . . .

Presently, Joe was a Master of Accounting student who was earning practical course credit for his graduate degree by helping Student Government organize their finances. Unfortunately, as it turned out, Joe wasn't nearly as accommodating in this new position of authority.

"Sorry, Dani, but with the economy like it is, the University's endowment really took a hit. The Dean is pressing hard on undergraduate student government to cut the activities budget across the board. All types of student groups are feeling the pinch – Diwali Dance Crew, improv comedy clubs, KBUR campus radio . . ."

With a sigh, Joe said, "There's really nothing I can do. I'm just a bookkeeper for this mess."

Dani didn't like the note of exhaustion she heard on the other end of the line. She briefly wished she actually knew something about these fireflies so she could cheer him up. When they disconnected, Dani sighed and forced herself to re-read the details of Nobok's dreadful email.

ENSEMBLE GROUPS WILL BE JUDGED AND EVALUATED ON A NUMBER OF FACTORS: RELEVANCY TO THE STUDENT BODY, CONTRIBUTION TO CAMPUS DIVERSITY AND CULTURE, MAJOR PERFORMANCES AT LOCAL, NATIONAL, AND INTERNATIONALLY SANCTIONED EVENTS.

Internationally sanctioned? In the context of a cappella, the bureaucrat could only mean one thing: the World A cappella Championships. Singers nationwide referred to it by its acronym, WAC.

Dani's familiarity with WAC was surpassed perhaps only by the extent to which she'd mastered the riffs in Mariah Carey's "Vision of Love." Each spring, WAC staged three different levels of competitions: quarterfinals, semifinals, and the finals in New York City. Because Brighton had so many groups, the University held its own six-group quarterfinal. The judges, a cappella experts of various stripes, scored each group's performance on musicality, choreography, showmanship, solo interpretation, etc. Only the highest-scoring group advanced to the next round.

Dani's intuition told her that Student Government would love using WAC as an evaluative standard. Since it was a contest judged by outside parties, it had the semblance of objectivity. If SG was looking for an allegedly unbiased—and highly oversimplified—way of differentiating groups, WAC presented an easy answer.

The alto was also a realist, and bitterly concluded that *certain* a cappella groups would no doubt have an easier time protecting their existence on campus. The extensive

44

alumni network of the Gobfellas could fight cuts by threatening to stop all donations to the school. The administration wouldn't be happy about this, giving the singing frat what amounted to a free pass in the survival game. The Notabelles were noteworthy for being the only all female group, whereas La*chaim's religious tradition spoke to the "diversity and culture" of campus. Bad press alone would make SG hesitate before cutting either of these groups. The *Student Times* columnists would have a justifiable field day. Dani imagined the headlines— "Ladies' Voices Silenced!" "Harmony Squashed by Anti-Semitism!"

No, the Harmoniums' president knew which groups were truly vulnerable. First, the Dinos, simply because they were the younger, less-established men's group. Then, the Chorderoys and the Harmoniums. To the ignorant – in other words, the SG Treasury Council – the two groups must look the same. Contemporary, pop rock, secular, co-ed.

Dani read on:

THE COMMITTEE WILL MEET IN APRIL TO DETERMINE WHICH GROUP(S) SHOULD BE DISSOLVED. WE ARE ASKING YOUR GROUP EXECUTIVE PRESIDENTS TO PLEASE DOCUMENT AND RECORD YOUR GROUP'S ACHIEVEMENTS THROUGHOUT THE YEAR FOR THE COUNCIL COMMITTEE'S EXAMINING REVIEW. THANK YOU FOR YOUR COMPLETE COOPERATION & TOTAL COMPLIANCE WITH THIS SIMPLE REQUEST.

ALL BEST!

BRENNA

Even the salutation sucked. Dani stared at the screen, fuming.

Of course, Dani loved her group. She knew it would be tantamount to tragedy if the red-and-blacks could no longer show off their pipes around campus. But in fact, Dani had a more *personal* stake in the Harmoniums' survival. Dani liked to think of the academic portion of college as a sort of necessary evil. The college degree, her major in English Literature—this was the fallback credential. Her real goal was to make a living from her voice. She intended to be a professional singer.

But if Dani were to become the next Sara Bareilles— the college a cappella singer turned pop sensation, not to mention Dani's life model—then her singing group needed to be much more than an "extracurricular." The Harmoniums had to be her platform to discovery. She needed them to be crowned "Best of Brighton," and propel her big voice all the way to the WAC championship round in the Big Apple.

It wasn't just that the Harmoniums needed to survive for the next two years; they needed to be gloriously successful. They needed to win WAC so that Dani could finally reveal her voice to the world. And the fewer groups singing at Brighton, the more likely she was to come out on top.

Dani's mind raced. She had so much work to do before the spring competition. There were talented voices to recruit, gigs to organize, new community contacts to make, plans to sabotage . . . For personal reasons, Dani knew which of the other two vulnerable groups she wanted eliminated. Pretty boy Taylor wouldn't know what had hit him.

Thinking about her rival made Dani's competitive flames burn all the hotter. She hurried to work creating a new document on her computer and began typing away furiously.

She named the file STRATEGIC OBJECTIVES—*her* synonym for "War Plan."

♫ |

Chapter 5

Auditions

96 . . . The number hung heavy on Dani's mind as she walked to the music school the next morning, simultaneously balancing her purse, a stack of colored fliers, and a tray of gourmet homemade cookies. Four maddening sign-ups short of her personal goal: 100 auditionees. While 96 was still impressive, given the decreased size of this year's freshman class, Dani was not giving herself any slack.

Taylor was already taping Chorderoys posters to the hallway walls when she arrived. His sheets for this morning were basic black and white—"Chorderoys Auditions This Way" with the group's circular *C* logo and an arrow indicating the direction. He was saving their group's small, Student Government-funded color copy allowance for the spring concert.

Setting the baked goods aside, Dani posted her first flier. Her signs were full-sheet color pictures of group members in various social poses—laughing, eating, chatting, dancing—all the while wearing their Harmoniums tees, coincidentally. In each photo, Dani posed, smiling and pointing outside the frame of the picture, leading auditionees to the Harmoniums' tryout room.

Dani held her flier up next to Taylor's most recent posting and taped her own poster so close their edges overlapped. Stepping back, she admired the contrasts: Black and white versus *red*. Informative but plain versus fun. She liked the message.

Taylor gulped. "Shouldn't we space them out a little?"

"Oh, but this makes it easier for them to navigate," said Dani. Her green eyes sparkled.

Armed with fliers and painter's tape, the two group presidents made their way down the hall. Taylor tried to move quickly, but Dani never allowed him to move more than one space ahead of her. Side by side and silent, they taped up a long stretch of postings. When they'd finished the first corridor, Taylor cleared his throat.

"Wasn't that—that was an interesting e-mail we received from Student Government."

"Was that a question, Taylor?"

"Um . . . er—"

Dani shook her head. "Never mind. Have you told your group yet?"

Protective as always, Taylor had been waiting for a safe moment to share the news, not wanting to set his group on edge just before auditions. Still, he knew he needed to hurry if he wanted the message to come from him. While the six groups were all more insular during auditions season, acatypes were talkers by nature.

"Well?"

The Chorderoys' president shook his head.

"Interesting."

Taylor stared directly at the wall so as to avoid what was, no doubt, an intentionally judgmental look from his rival. "I understand the University is in financial straits. But I don't see how the a cappella groups really have an impact on the problem. All we ask of Student Government is a little rehearsal space, someone to run the sound system at gigs, a handful of color copies . . ."

Dani smirked. This morning, she'd presented the student tech worker at the copy center with a half-dozen homemade cookies and some friendly flirting. She'd printed her color fliers free of charge.

" . . . Relatively speaking, the a cappella groups are very inexpensive. We're a drop in the bucket. I don't see how SG thinks cutting back singing groups is an effective solution to the University's real money problems. This 'cut everything' mentality is extremely impractical."

Dani laughed, as if the subject of hardship made her downright bubbly. "Oh, come on now. Across-the-board cuts are standard procedure when times are tough. It wouldn't be fair if the a cappella community didn't take a hit, the same as everyone else. Perhaps SG is onto something intelligent for a change. After there's been this cut, the remaining groups will be far more appreciative of their right to sing." She pressed out the wrinkles in her final strip of tape. "Well, may the best man win. Enjoy today!" She turned and walked smartly down the halls, her red heels clicking with each step, Taylor gaping after her.

Dani located the Harmoniums' home base for the day and entered, grasping her cookies and remaining fliers in one hand as she opened the door with the other. During auditions weekend, each group staked out one of the classrooms in the music school, all of which were furnished with a piano. Auditioning for multiple groups was widespread practice, and students who signed up for back-to-back tryouts usually discovered that their audition rooms were just a few short steps apart.

One by one, prospective a cappella singers came through the Harmoniums' audition room to be heard by the entire ensemble. At the start of every audition, Charlie, the Harmoniums' music director, led the singer through a few singing exercises. "On the syllable 'la,' let's sing up and down this major chord. Repeat after me: *La- la- la- la- la . . .*"

They were called "vocal warm-ups," but of course, they weren't warm-ups in the traditional preparatory sense at all. Quite the contrary; they were a performance. From the moment the singers opened their mouths and let fly their first unaccompanied notes, they were being judged—on their pitch, on their tone, and on that most subjective trait, their overall fitness for the group.

Generally, Dani made up her mind about offering a callback by the time a person had sung just three notes. Moments into the "warm-up," she would make a little mark – yes or no – on the paper record she kept for each singer. Regardless of her decision, Dani continued taking copious notes in her curly red script, dutifully offering everyone her full attention.

For the ten minutes each singer was in the room, singing scales, reading out rhythms, and performing brief solos, Dani revealed no inkling of her true intensity. To the auditionees, she was all smiles and homemade sugar cookies.

"Incredible! What an amazing take on that!" Dani exclaimed, after a particularly atrocious rendition of "Think of Me" from the musical *The Phantom of the Opera*. It was only "incredible" because it was so hard to believe how truly awful it had been. The Harmoniums all wished they could expunge the trauma from their minds.

After the poor singer had selected her cookie and left the audition room, Dani chastised her group for not showing a similar degree of enthusiasm.

"Who cares? No *way* she's making the group," snapped Shelby, the Harmoniums' shrill, irritable soprano. (In a cappella, as in life, there's always an irritable soprano.)

Dani frowned. "Remember, SG is looking to cut groups. And who actually votes for those representatives? Who considers running for Treasury Council?"

Experienced performer that she was, Dani knew to hold her pause—

"Motivated people," she said, finally answering herself. "People who care enough to try new things. *Gunners.* Talent or not, they run this place. So yes, it matters. It matters how we treat each and every person who walks through that door. Sure, many will be disappointed when they see the callback lists. But we can only hope they'll like us anyway. If the gunners like us, the ones who end up in SG might still let us sing. But if they resent us, we're already dead in the water."

Her words were met with thoughtful silence. If any seniors in the Harmoniums suspected that Dani might have more personal reasons for her adamant auditionee-friendly approach, they did not mention them.

Late that Saturday afternoon, the Harmoniums were experiencing something of a drought. The last few hours of auditions had been unremarkable: lots of people who could only sort of sing, with very few truly impressive talents. (In spite of this, Dani continued to pronounce solos "fabulous!" and "amazing!" with the same cheerful inflection.)

So when the golden-haired boy she'd first met on Freshmen Move-In Day came through the doors of Music School Classroom 203, Dani was hoping for a standout.

Ben Jensen was auditionee 22 of 96. He looked straight ahead as he sang.

La- la—

Dani approved his callback in record time, making the subtle mark after just two notes of "warm-up." By note three, she'd decided he ought to be a Harmonium.

As Dani listened to Ben ascend into his high tenor range (had the solfège *do-mi-so-mi-do* ever sounded so sweet?), she considered his physical and vocal traits in unison. To her, Ben's warm, energetic tenor timbre came *with* his fantastic head of hair; his perfect pitch *with* his thin athletic frame.

It had been a long time since Dani had felt the stirrings of an a cappella crush, an attraction inspired by someone's raw singing voice. Her last such crush had not ended well. Since then, Dani had forgotten just how strong the attraction could be—how a human singing voice, alone and unprotected, could completely capture her attention.

When the music director led Ben through the rhythm test—the only part of the audition which was clapped, rather than sung—Dani felt as if she'd been jerked from a happy daydream. Who cared about those cold, mathematical rhythms? She wanted that voice again!

At last, all that remained was the solo. Traditionally, this was the hardest part for prospective singers (and, at times, for current group members as well). Auditionees chose their own songs, but they were required to sing them a cappella. For young singers, so accustomed to the guidance of a piano or guitar, this was often the moment they feared most.

Ben cleared his throat. He straightened a little, repositioned his feet, tugged at the collar of his button-up, and said what was so utterly obvious to everyone in the room: "I'm sorry, I'm a little nervous."

Dani beamed. "Don't be."

When Ben began singing the Beatles' "Got To Get You Into My Life," Dani ignored the anxiety-induced shaking in his voice—didn't even make a note of it. She was too much in love with his little bouncing dance, his swaying side to side. And when at last he came into his full voice, she heard only the electricity beneath his high notes, the pure energy of his tone.

Gazing upon this younger, cuter, and blonde Paul McCartney, Dani lost all objectivity. Fantastic visions filled her mind. She pictured Ben in their red formal uniforms; imagined the spotlight shining on his perfect golden hair. She heard their voices singing together, his youthful timbre complementing her naturally soulful alto.

The more Ben sang, the more Dani saw him as her opportunity. They could sing duets together—*power* duets. They could be Brighton a cappella legend. More than that—they could make group history together at the World A cappella Championships! Gunner though she was, it was impossible for Dani to advance the Harmoniums from this scholarly Midwestern college to the spectacular WAC finals on her own. True, the judges were looking for an ensemble cast of talent. But perhaps adding Ben would be enough. The golden tenor just might be her golden ticket to the international stage.

When Ben finished his solo, all the Harmoniums offered him enthusiastic applause. The tenor smiled downward, sheepish and adorable. Dani stood and personally walked the cookie tray to her new musical *amore*. "Take two! Three! I can always bake more!"

After Ben left the room, the Harmoniums continued buzzing their approval. Standard procedure after an audition was for each group member to gesture a quick "thumbs up" or "thumbs down," an instant poll to be used in later decisions. Dani normally insisted on the custom, trusting the individual thumb votes more than any group wide discussion.

But in this case, Dani abandoned all pretense of protocol. "We *must* have him," she declared, and no one argued against her.

The group had barely settled down again when the next singer entered. Despite her growing excitement about Ben, Dani was determined to give everyone a fair evaluation. She began taking copious notes, starting as always with the superficial: cute skirt, simple pony tail, tasteful application of make-up, etc.

Again, Dani marked the 'yes' on her sheet early into the "warm-up." Two good ones in a row! The drought was finally over. Her ever-present smile lengthened.

As she listened, the Harmoniums' president found herself increasingly fond of this girl's tone. She had a voice that floated—a feat, Dani knew, which was harder than it seemed. *A true soprano*, the group president jotted down. Above the word "true," Dani drew an arrow and wrote, *Useful for WAC*.

When the auditionee began singing "Here Comes the Sun," the coincidence of two back-to-back songs by the Beatles did not immediately strike Dani as unusual. She was too busy listening. Notwithstanding the upbeat lyrics, Dani felt a distinct hopefulness behind this girl's singing. This was an unusually *supportive* voice. And it struck Dani that it might blend perfectly into her own.

When it came to divas with genuine talent, Dani was an expert. Patti Labelle had her Bluebells. Beyoncé had Destiny's Child. Adele had her soul sisters. In every generation, backup voices were essential.

Dani imagined this girl's voice harmonizing behind her in the block, adding a subtle aural halo to each of Dani's solos, creating a "glow" effect. She wanted this soprano. (Of course, it certainly didn't hurt Dani's assessment that she and this auditionee had such different voice types. A "true soprano" would never be direct competition for the big-voiced alto.)

"Gorgeous!" Dani cried, when the girl had finished. "What a gorgeous solo! And what a pretty name you have, Caroline! So fitting! Have a cookie, please."

When Caroline was gone, the Harmoniums conducted their thumb poll. The result was unanimous: Callback.

The Harmoniums' president checked their schedule and saw that they were finally on their break. She leapt up. "Diet Coke time! Even the best of us need our caffeine and pseudo-sugar!" As she left, she heard the irritable soprano grumbling about cancer and brittle bones.

Dani was just turning the corner to the vending machines when she saw them: Ben and Caroline, chatting excitedly. Instinctively, Dani stopped in place, standing behind the opposite wall. She listened in silence.

"I was so nervous, but they were really nice in there! Thanks for waiting around for me to finish."

"Of course!" said Ben. He looked quickly down at the floor, bashful about seeming overeager. "It wasn't any trouble. Thanks for your song suggestion."

Caroline shrugged. "You pretty much can't go wrong with anything by the Beatles. Well, 'Why Don't We Do It In The Road' might have been a risky move, but you're always safe with the classics."

Ben proposed sharing a candy bar—his treat. As they strolled off, they argued playfully about who should have dividing power, each suggesting the other.

The exchange wiped away Dani's happy frame of mind. Her foul mood did not dissipate when she was alone and at last had that Diet Coke in hand. It wasn't just that the twosome had supplemented her cookies with candy, although this, too, was offensive. The wholesomeness of their entire interaction made her blood boil! Could Ben—her Ben—really be romantically interested in Caroline? The thought made her want to march back into the audition room and reverse her most recent vote in the thumb poll.

Whipping out her iPhone, Dani began strategically Facebook-stalking. She sighed in relief. Thankfully, Caroline was already "in a relationship" with some guy named Elliot. But the news was not all good. Ben and Caroline were neighbors on the same freshmen floor. Someone had recently uploaded a mobile pic of them playing guitar together in the dorm hallway. It was far too cute for Dani's peace of mind.

Dani stowed her phone away and forced herself to think more optimistically. Why should she worry about a hypothetical Ben & Caroline? This was entirely preventable. The critical first step, for her purposes, was getting Ben *into* the Harmoniums. With this in mind, the two freshmen's current proximity to each other was not a tragedy, but another opportunity.

As Dani walked by her group's colored posters—posters with herself, pointing and cheering herself on—it became increasingly clear to her that Caroline was the key player. After all, Ben had hung around for Caroline's audition, used her song recommendation, shared his stupid candy bar—

It was the thought of food which triggered it. Dani smirked, suddenly imagining a very *useful* girl-to-girl talk.

By the time Dani returned to the audition room, her next move was obvious: Win over the girl, and convince her to bring Ben Jensen with her.

In Dani's view, Ben's future in the Harmoniums was non-negotiable. She was simply going to make it happen.

♫ |

Chapter 6

Acting

Although he had yet to sing a single note, Akash was already facing the most difficult part of his a cappella auditions process. He'd just arrived at the music school building and followed the signs leading to the Gobfellas' tryout room. On the other side of the door, he heard a husky-voiced baritone belting a scale.

There was a small table with instructions to complete a questionnaire while waiting. Predictably macho, the Gobfellas' audition form had an "essay" question involving a hypothetical duel to the death between Chuck Norris and Jack Bauer. Akash's answer pitted Bauer's ability to dodge sprays of bullets against Norris' fatal roundhouse kicks.

The humor questions were easy for him, and yet the freshman stared at the sheet, struggling. Akash was unsure what to put for the first blank—his name.

Akash was what his father jokingly referred to as a "dasher," meaning he had a hyphenated surname: Akash Sheffield-Patel. Lately, he had been wanting to drop the pre-hyphen portion entirely. Akash was accustomed to the occasional confusion brought on by juxtaposing Gujarati Indian with the traditional WASP. But passing the Sheffield Athletic Center on the way to Psychology class was a whole new level of uncomfortable. The Sheffield Central Campus Library was even worse. Students were already complaining about their need to "pull all-nighters in Sheff."

Akash's worst fear was that he would be thought of as just another of Brighton's legacy students. No matter how high his GPA or SAT score, if he revealed himself as a Sheffield, people would assume he'd received preferential admissions treatment because of his last name. (*Half* his last name, that is. The Patel portion hadn't worked to his advantage.) Thus, as much as he loved his rich Texas grandfather, Akash was determined to downplay his connection to the esteemed alumnus.

The difficulty was that just before Akash was born, another Sheffield legacy student had left his mark on the University. John Sheffield was a founding member of the Gobfellas, the first a cappella group at Brighton and one of the leaders of the modern a cappella era. All his life, Akash had heard hilarious tales from his uncle's years as a Fella: pranks on professors, pledging traditions, shows at the student bar, philandering with their acagroupies, the Gobgirls. Uncle John's tales were always heavy with nostalgia. The Fellas were the highlight of his youth.

Although Uncle John was not as wealthy as his father, he nevertheless managed to send a substantial donation each year to his old college group. Write down the Sheffield name, mention John "Bro Montana" Sheffield in his audition, and Akash knew his chances shot through the roof. The logic was so tantalizing: Akash really wanted to share the Fella connection with his uncle. Why not increase the odds?

At the same time, Akash knew this a cappella audition was his first chance to prove himself at Brighton without assistance from the Sheffield family name. The Gobfellas wouldn't know he was a Sheffield simply by his appearance. Thanks to his father, Akash didn't have typical Sheffield features. (This, too, resulted in some confusion. He was often mistaken for Serbian or Greek, and sometimes strangers asked his help in Spanish.)

Through the door, Akash heard deep-voiced laughter. Had the auditionee said something funny? Uncle John said the Fellas considered personality almost as much as singing ability. Akash frowned down at his questionnaire, still undecided.

"Which question is giving you trouble?"

The girl across the hall from him had a giant purse in her lap, an oversized tote which was bedazzled with fake jewels and multicolored mini pompoms. She stared at Akash with big light blue eyes, the kind which always appear clear and a touch fanatical in old black and white photos.

"You look stressed," she said. "Tough question? With the Gobfellas, I'd expect funny questions." She leaned forward. "Need any help? I'm funny sometimes."

Akash shook his head. "It's not a question, really," he explained. "I'm just—just generally nervous, I guess."

"Oh. I see."

"Thanks though." Akash went back to staring at the empty blank.

"Say, if I was the lovechild of two famous singers, who should I pick as my parents?"

"Excuse me?"

She showed him the sheet on her clipboard. "It's one of the 'just-for-fun' questions on the Chorderoys' form: If you could be the lovechild of any two musical celebrities, who would you pick?"

"Hmm . . . that's a tough one."

"I know, right? There're just so *many* to choose from. At first, I was thinking Celine Dion and John Legend— talk about a power couple. Besides, I've always thought biracial children were the most attractive. But then I got to thinking what a good father Tim McGraw would be. And if I were to have Tim as my imaginary lovechild father, perhaps I should have a mother who was more edgy. Christina Aguilera, maybe. Then again, it'd be nice to have a singer-actress, one of the old inspiring ones, a Julie Andrews or a Barbra. And there are all those singer-songwriters out there, too, such creative types, I'd bet they'd make great parents . . ."

When Akash had the opportunity to successfully interject, he said, "Maybe you should just put whatever combination you liked first."

A wide smile stretched across her face. She had a slight overbite, but it was a very friendly smile. "You're right! Gut instinct. That's the most natural thing to do." She jotted down her selection. "Thank you very much, kind sir."

"No problem."

The silence was brief.

"Okay, excuse me. Again. I really can't help dispensing free advice to nice people." The loquacious girl reached into her mega-purse and removed a large hardback book. It was tabbed throughout with yellow highlights, and extra-thick from all the dog-eared pages. She flashed the cover: *Psychology and Theater: A Practicum.*

"You mentioned that you were feeling 'generally' nervous. Well, Dr. Lund here says nerves are a natural part of the body's preparation for a performance. But there are good nerves and there are bad nerves. Good nerves stem from excitement – feelings of intimate connection between self and the role which is about to be played. Bad nerves stem from falseness – a sense of disconnect between self and role. In other words, it's all anticipation versus angst."

Her eyes were extra wide as she made the many distinctions. "Thus, the key to good acting isn't acting at all, at least not in the 'faking' sense of the word. It's really about authenticity. Being the role, instead of pushing it; living the song, instead of merely singing it."

"Oh, by the way, I'm Nicole McLain." As Akash leaned in for their introductory handshake, the smell of pear perfume wafted toward him.

Nicole pulled a peppermint from her purse to soothe her throat. "I should mention that I actually added the singing part. The book itself is just about theater—not that there aren't overlaps between the forms. But my apologies for rambling."

"It's okay." Akash was concentrating on the voice on the other side of the door. Whoever it was in there was succeeding—or failing—on his own merits. And while it wasn't really the point of Nicole's unsolicited diatribe, her words had nevertheless persuaded him that, in fairness, he should, too.

Akash scribbled down his decision: No hyphen. No special treatment. Just 'Akash Patel.'

The door opened. "Next douchebag!" they called.

"Good nerves, Akash!" whispered Nicole. He disappeared inside.

When the representative from the Chorderoys came to bring Nicole into her co-ed group audition, she was prepared. She handed him her nine headshots—nine exactly, for the group's current membership. In the other hand, she held her bottled spring water, room temperature for optimal lubrication of the vocal chords.

She recognized Taylor's face from his duet during the Recruitment Concert. The group president read from her sheet. "Nicole McLain. Hometown: Garland, Indiana. Can't say I've heard of it."

"It's very small," Nicole explained. As she spoke, her shoulders rocked back and forth at the front of the classroom, refusing to be still. It was as if her whole body were about to burst from want of singing.

"Celine Dion and John Legend," read Taylor. "Fantastic choice." It seemed to Nicole that it was a very long time before the small talk ended. When it was at last time for her solo, she remembered what she'd practiced:

Nicole cast her blue eyes downward, mentally returning to what was mostly an unhappy period, her first years of high school. Extra weight clung to her hips and thighs, cruelly refusing to burn or diet off. Popular girls deliberately looked the other way as she walked down the halls. Her whole life was burdened by the horrible feeling that in order to be accepted by her classmates—or anyone else, really—she needed to hide her hobbies, her brains, her enthusiasm, her eccentricities.

And with that meditation, Nicole was at last ready to sing. Mariah Carey's "Hero" was about finding one's inner champion when times were especially bad. The beginning was tender, and Nicole's voice came soft and vulnerable.

In the chorus, she began to flex her belt. Her notes hung longer in the air. Nicole raised her palm, pushing aside the popular girls, the cynics, the "realists," the intolerant, and any other of her dream-opponents in the near-vicinity.

It is, of course, both a cliché and a scientific inaccuracy to speak of emotions emanating "from the heart." But *singing* "from the heart" is almost accurate, and it was an especially close descriptor for Nicole McLain: Her power-gospel voice originated from a pounding red-hot core of feeling inside her chest.

Long strands of caramel-colored hair bounced with each punctuated lyric. The whole room shook with the volume of her soulful riffs. As she sang, Nicole was in communion with her primary dream—to someday be an inspiration to many, many others—melodramatic and unlikely though it seemed.

In the final chorus, Nicole was quiet again, but it was the dynamite form of quiet: all of the feeling from earlier, just compacted. She closed her eyes, head raised like a soulful Amy Grant. Her voice trailed off.

As the Chorderoys applauded, Nicole wiped her red eyes and cheeks with tissues from her purse, while mouthing "thank you, thank you."

"No, thank *you*!" said Taylor, whose eyes were glistening, also. "Do you have any questions for us? Anything at all?"

Nicole fanned herself, still cooling from her self-induced fit of emotion. She spoke between gasps for air. "I do—actually—I love ballads—as you might—have guessed."

"Don't we all?!?" said Taylor. He searched the room for approval from his fellow group members.

"I saw on the Chorderoys' website—that you guys had listed some songs for this year. I loved the pop songs you picked—very fun. But I didn't see many true ballads. So I was wondering, how do you determine your song mix each year?"

"Well, we can always arrange more songs! Anything you'd like, really!" blurted Taylor. His face reddened. "I mean—er—why don't you take this one, Sid?"

The Chorderoys' music director explained that the group had already pre-selected some songs for this year, but they would be choosing more once they had their new members. The final song list was decided by group vote, and was heavily based on the musical tastes and talents of their singers for that year.

It was a very judicious answer. Nicole listened carefully, although her heart was still pounding, her fingers still tingly and warm. When Sid had finished, Nicole had one more question. "Can I request a group hug from you guys?"

The ballad-loving alto left the audition room smiling. She went directly to the ladies' restroom and stared into the mirror. She'd done it! Four successful a cappella auditions. Assuming she received multiple callbacks, Nicole predicted some difficult choices. Currently, she was leaning toward the Harmoniums because of the ballads issue, and the fact that Dani Behlman had absolutely nailed "I Can't Make You Love Me." But the Chorderoys were a very close second.

Nicole walked out of the bathroom, still basking in her post-performance glow, and not at all looking where she was going. She barreled into another young woman in the hallway, a short-statured girl with ear bud headphones and a curiously intense expression on her face. They hit hard.

Renee Murphy had been listening to her "B-E-P" playlist and walking purposefully to her audition for the Chorderoys. When they hit, Renee lost her grip on her iPod. At the same time, Nicole's supersized purse slipped off her arm, spilling its contents across the floor.

"Oh, my goodness! I am so sorry!" cried Nicole. "Are you okay? I can't believe I hit you. You're just so—so *petite*. I don't think I even saw you coming. Please, you don't have to help me. I can handle it. Are you okay?"

Renee assured her that she was free from injury and perfectly willing to help.

Nicole hurried to help her collect her iPod from the corner. "Looks like it didn't break," she announced. She read from the display. "Ooh, Tiny Dancer. Elton John.

Smart choice before an a cappella audition. Such a warm, uplifting melody."

Renee snatched back her mp3 player. "Thanks." The diver proceeded to help Nicole collect her things: nutritional bars, spring water, vitamin water, make-up accessories, lip balm. She stacked the extra B&W head-shots.

"As you might be able to guess, I was one of those theater kids in high school."

"Yeah, I guessed," muttered Renee.

"And you were . . . a swimmer? A diver?" Nicole motioned to the Brighton Swimming & Diving tee shirt.

"Diver." Renee glanced at her watch. "Actually, I should probably get to my audition. But—um—sorry about this."

"Don't be silly!" cried Nicole. "It was my fault entirely."

"Well . . . yeah . . . you weren't really looking . . ."

"Go, go! I don't want you to be late because of me! Good luck in there! Or, as they say, good nerves! If you've been listening to Elton this morning, I'm sure you'll be just fine."

Nicole spent a few more minutes re-layering her purse after that fateful first collision before starting back across campus. On the way, she kept thinking about the girl she'd accidentally rammed into. She'd seemed very serious to Nicole, wearing her team shirt, the smell of chlorine lingering in her hair. A college athlete was not the first person one would expect to audition for a singing group. It was very unorthodox; Nicole loved it!

Still glowing, Nicole mused about 'power couples' and 'Mariah Carey' and 'independent spirits'—some of her favorite subjects—as she trekked up the stairs to her dorm room, which of course, was on the third floor of Arthur C. Sheffield Hall.

♫ |

Chapter 7

Limits

The callback announcements were posted early— seven A.M. on a Saturday was a brutal hour by college standards. Sporting PJs and flip-flops, Caroline and Ben stumbled over to the student activities center to see if they were among the listed names.

Lo and behold, they'd made the first cut! In fact, both Caroline and Ben had been called back to all of the groups for which they'd tried out. Caroline stretched out her arms and gave Ben an enormous hug, which the tenor found thrilling, though puzzling, after its approximately second-and-a-half duration.

The speediness with which she pulled away reinforced what Ben was already reminding himself constantly: Caroline was *in a relationship*. Halfway across the country, there was some guy named Elliot who was studying music journalism at Berkeley, and Skyping with Caroline on an almost nightly basis.

For her part, Caroline had noticed a boy out of the corner of her eye who was *still* scanning the board for his missing name. It was clear that the poor guy, rejected from every group, was either already devastated or soon would be. Respectfully, Caroline had cut short her celebratory embrace with Ben. Without the benefit of this explanation, though, Ben merely felt extremely confused by the flash hug.

He wondered if his name had ever been mentioned in Caroline's video-chat sessions with Elliot. They'd been spending a lot of time together, walking to and from their "Global Voices" class discussing favorite authors, inventing new melodies late at night on their guitars, rehearsing their a cappella audition solos—just the two of them, in a tiny, glass-walled practice room in the music school.

Ben worried—had Caroline pulled away just now because she thought he was getting *uncomfortably* close? How could he convey that he would never encourage her to cheat (even if the thought had crossed his mind)?

They turned, and Caroline shot a sympathetic glance to the sad guy who hadn't received any callbacks. (Later that day, the poor fellow would send a heartbreaking "why did you reject me?" email to the groups' presidents, and would receive a carefully worded, but exceptionally frank, response from Dani Behlman.)

As they walked back to their dorm, Ben was preoccupied thinking about the dangerous terrain that lies between "close" and "inappropriate." Ben did not even consider that they were quite unintentionally ignoring another rule on closeness: Neither remembered that ACUAC's "Limited Contact" rule had already taken effect.

♫

Dani's morning had been productive: Another talent locked down for the Harmoniums. Another masterful skirting of the law.

In addition to banning contact among auditionees during callbacks, ACUAC's Limited Contact rule prohibited singers from speaking with auditionees who had been called back to multiple a cappella groups, the purpose being to prevent bribery, lying, or "dirty rushing," among ensembles competing for the same singer. The single exception to the restriction was if the auditionee initiated the conversation with a current group member; then, that singer could respond to any questions asked.

In practice, auditionees rarely struck up conversations with older students who they barely knew. As a result, "Limited Contact" usually meant "*No* Contact" with prospective singers. But the president of the Harmoniums was exceptional. She had her methods for encouraging conversations which were, seemingly, legal.

Philip Eason thought it was fortuitous that he'd happened to bump into Dani at the library coffee shop that morning, but of course her encounter with the freshman auditionee was entirely *non*-coincidental. Dani jumped to refill her chai the moment she saw that her target happened to be standing in line. She was extremely proud of her physical maneuver: part strike, part "boxing out" the other customers. When Philip turned at the counter, Dani was right there, smiling.

"Oh . . . hi," he muttered, in his masculine bass. "How're callbacks?"

It was the crudest of initiations, but it was a question, and therefore, was enough.

Dani acted flustered. "What was that again? Oh yes, a cappella callbacks. Pardon me, I'm about to spill this hot tea all over myself. Would you mind if we sit down for just *one* minute?"

By the time Philip had finished his Americano, Dani had "answered" his question by insinuating that the currently small-numbered Chorderoys were probably going to tank next year ("Shame," said Dani, "They *try* so very hard"); that the Gobfellas would ruin him professionally ("Remember Enron? All Fellas alums"); and that joining the "really nice," "super sweet" guys in the Dinos would forever shatter his heterosexual image.

(This last attack was the most absurd: Anyone so uncomfortable with society questioning his sexuality has no business joining an a cappella group to begin with.)

But we all have our treasures, and Philip's was his reputation. He left the coffee shop a Harmonium for life.

Despite these and other successes, Dani remained unsatisfied. She'd yet to make contact with target number one: Caroline Cooper. Caroline was her key to securing both the ideal back-up singer and a handsome tenor heartthrob. Dani had spent the entire week camping out in the usual freshmen haunts, coordinating the coincidence.

That afternoon, Dani was in the Central Campus Cafeteria, which was further proof of her dedication: She *despised* cafeterias. Even as a freshman, when purchasing the University dining plan was required, Dani had prepared most of her own meals. Mass food distribution centers offended her militant sense of independence. The salad bar didn't even have sprouts!

Dani wasn't happy about her lunch partner, either. Melanie Hughes was an idealistic Harmoniums sophomore who apparently relished the cafeteria's macaroni and cheese. Dani was mortified as she watched her companion gobble down the clumpy yellow side dish.

At that moment, Caroline rushed into the cafeteria. She sighed when she saw that the line for vegetarian entrées, normally the shortest, had more than a dozen people. Thinking quickly, she grabbed a bag of pretzels, an apple, a ready-made muffin, and a bottled tea from the "Grab & Go Station." The lady at the check-out scanned the bag once, then again, then again . . . Only when Caroline desperately offered to return it to its cart did the cashier give up and type in the numerical code.

By the time Caroline had finally made it through the lunch line, she felt feverish. She *hated* being late. It was in this anxious state that Caroline spotted Dani's familiar face from across the lunch room. She rushed over to her table.

"It's Dani, right?"

"Yes. Yes, that's me," Dani replied. The Harmoniums' leader was stunned, having been momentarily distracted by those mysterious, grotesque pasta clumps.

"Sorry to bother. It's just that you're the only upper-classman here I recognized, and I was wondering if you could help."

Dani was of the sensible opinion that lucky circumstances were largely created by the individuals who enjoyed them. But that afternoon, even Dani questioned the role of self-determinism in her unexpected fortune.

Dani beamed. "How can I help?"

"I'm starting lessons today," Caroline explained, gesturing to her black guitar case. "And I thought they would be in the music school, but I just looked at my schedule, and it says Sheffield Multipurpose Room. I can't tell if *this* Sheffield is the one in the library or the one that's all the way on North Campus."

Dani bristled in her seat. North Campus was so far that Brighton students, able to walk to most other classes and campus activities, had to take buses to the satellite campus. The president of the Harmoniums hated public transportation almost as much as she did cafeterias.

Melanie swallowed a mouthful of gluey cheese before contributing. "Strange how they name everything around here Sheffield, isn't it? Sheffield Science Center, Sheffield Library, Sheffield Sports Field, Sheffield Performance Hall, Sheffield—"

Dani interrupted with a machine-gun burst of laughter. "You're so funny, Melanie," said Dani, in her perkiest voice, "But it looks like she's in a hurry, and needs to know where to find *her* Sheffield. Now."

Melanie's friendly dimples showed as she smiled. "Oh right. Of course. Sheffield *Multipurpose*. That's just next door. Two buildings down, in the basement of Hanforth Hall. It's only about a minute away. I'll walk you there."

The color rushed back into Caroline's cheeks. "Ah, thank you! That'd be great."

Dani checked her ruby-faced wristwatch and glanced up hopefully. "Your lesson starts at one?"

Caroline nodded. "I thought I was going to have to take the bus."

"Then you've got some time," Dani observed. "Would you like to join us?"

Caroline hesitated. Sitting with one of the group presidents the day before the A Cappella Draft seemed awkward. But, as she looked around the crowded dining hall, Caroline didn't see a single empty table. It *would* be nice to sit for a few minutes.

Caroline accepted, and Dani removed her purse from the extra seat she'd been saving. The freshman soprano set out her "lunch" and began eating hurriedly.

Dani grinned and pointed to the black instrument case. "That's right! I remember from your callback questionnaire that you played . . . cello?"

Caroline covered her mouth as she swallowed a mouthful of apple. "Just guitar, actually. Classical guitar."

Melanie's face lit up. "Wait—I just remembered! Caroline Cooper – you're signed up for the Harmony Halls program, right?"

She nodded.

"Well, I'm on the exec committee!" And with that, the alto began discussing the new initiative. Harmony Halls offered free music programs in local inner-city high schools that had lost their music curriculum funding.

For Caroline, it was just one of her new volunteer groups. She was also helping with the local Big Brothers, Big Sisters mentorship program, the St. Francis Center for the Homeless, and Habitat for Humanity's alternative service spring break.

As Caroline referred to these plans, Melanie ate it up like macaroni. Community service was the sophomore's true passion and primary time commitment— outside of a cappella, of course.

Dani had no specific problem with do-gooders. She was just frustrated that the one sitting across from her didn't know how to *use* her passion strategically. Finally, Dani saw her opportunity.

"As you can tell, Melanie's really involved with service . . . *things* here on campus," interrupted Dani. "And the Harmoniums, of course, are completely supportive of that." She paused to smile, before suddenly becoming very serious. "But frankly, Caroline, that's not the case with every group."

Caroline frowned. "What do you mean?"

Melanie was looking cross-eyed at her group president. She, too, was confused.

"The Chorderoys, the Notabelles—well, I shouldn't name names. There's just this misconception among certain ensembles that students don't have the time or stamina to do several other activities along with a cappella. But in the Harmoniums, we like to leave that choice to the individual singer." She smiled at Melanie. "Over the years, we've attracted several of the most musically talented *and* community-caring auditionees."

Caroline looked at the table. "That's . . . interesting."

"But I digress," said Dani, picking up steam. "Any idea about your major?"

Caroline deposited the apple core in her empty bag of pretzels. "Well, don't laugh at me, but my academic plans are kind of intense."

It was Dani's experience that defensive lines like "don't laugh at me" were often followed by personal information, and personal information was always the most useful. She leaned forward. "Tell me."

"I want to get a triple major: Music – Instrumental Performance, International Relations, and Urban Studies."

Dani held back a laugh. So Caroline's big revelation was simply that she was a big nerd with a bleeding heart. As if that were a rarity! This was Brighton University, after all.

"That's brilliant," cried Dani. "I'm so impressed!" She extolled the benefits of such a plan: Why limit yourself to one particular field? Why not take the best aspects of *all* of Brighton—music, humanities, sociology, art! "If I could start college again, I would definitely do it your way," Dani declared.

The freshman's expression was a mixture of relief and pride. "Really? You think it's a good idea? Because lots of people have said it's too much."

"Forget the naysayers," said Dani with a dismissive wave of her hand. "Personally, I think it shows that you're a determined, well-rounded, *fascinating* woman."

Caroline smiled. Even the humblest are moved by flattery. "It *was* one of my interesting personal facts for the Chorder—I mean, another a cappella group's questionnaire. At the time, I thought it was kind of lame."

Dani hated the fact that a rival group knew any information about a candidate before she did, until she realized that the revelation had just presented her with another opening. "You said you put the triple major detail on the Chorderoys' audition sheet?"

Caroline paused. "Yes. Why?"

"Oh, it's nothing important, really," said Dani, with a little laugh. "It just makes sense now why Taylor was talking about multiple majors yesterday." She followed Caroline's eyes closely, wanting to make absolutely sure that the soprano made the desired connection. "You know, Taylor Stuart. President of the Chorderoys."

"I know him, kind of," said a still-confused Caroline. "What did he say?"

"Well, Taylor's a very serious guy, especially when it comes to a cappella, and I just heard him mention something about it being too difficult to accept a singer who was taking coursework in more than one or two areas. As the group's leader, he expects a cappella to be everyone's number one priority, even over academics."

Caroline was shocked. "Really?"

"Yeah," said Dani with a solemn nod. "I wouldn't take it personally, though. He's not really a fan of liberal arts education in general. He thinks people should get 'practical degrees.'"

"Sounds like my father," muttered Caroline. The resemblance clearly distressed her.

Dani noticed that Melanie was silently shaking her head and giving her a look, as if she'd just now crossed some line. It was truly terrible luck that the most self-righteous member of the Harmoniums was Dani's lunch partner that day. Why couldn't Melanie understand that "Limited Contact" was a rule which was lenient by its very definition? And so what if Taylor had never said anything about Caroline? Didn't Melanie recognize that she was acting for the good of the group?

But it seemed this sort of moral flexibility wasn't Melanie's strong suit. She ended their conversation prematurely, turning to Caroline. "It's time to go, I think," said the sophomore. Caroline gathered her things and began to follow Melanie away from the table.

Dani leapt up. "Wait! Before you leave, I'm curious. Have you been speaking with any other auditionees?"

Caroline hesitated. "A little."

Dani nodded. "That's good to hear. You know, back in my day, all of us freshmen were too shy to communicate amongst ourselves. But it's good to talk about such things. It seems obvious, but if you don't the consequences can be . . ." She paused, pretending to search for the right word. "*Regrettable*."

"Okay! Off we go!" said an over-eager Melanie.

Dani touched Caroline gently on the arm. "You have a gorgeous voice, Caroline. I'm so glad we were able to have lunch together."

"Um . . . thank you. Me, too."

Dani was still smiling as she crossed the quad and trekked across the parking lot fifteen minutes later. She'd decided to reward herself.

Although she felt a little guilty for skipping class so early in the semester, the feeling was quickly superseded by the pleasure of strolling into Whole Foods Market. Dani rarely cooked for anyone other than herself, but she was quite the chef, and her mind raced with ideas for tonight's victory dinner—wild Alaskan salmon, steamed asparagus with freshly grated Gouda, red pepper brochette, spinach and goat cheese salad, her favorite Sauvignon Blanc. She laughed a little as she grabbed her shopping cart. After all those cafeteria lunches of strategic self-sacrifice, this meal was going to taste even more delicious.

♫

Ben Jensen sat on the edge of his raised twin bed, strumming random chords on his guitar. Like so many on the night before the A Cappella Draft, he was thoughtful.

The group preference cards, which were used to place auditionees into their new a cappella homes, were due tomorrow. Ben had narrowed his top choice down to two, but he had yet to decide which group to rank first. If he hadn't been rehearsing so much with Caroline, he might have given more thought to the men's groups. But that week in particular he was leaning towards co-ed ensembles, specifically the Chorderoys and the Harmoniums. He thought he would be happy in either of them.

There was a knock at the door. When Caroline walked in, he could tell she was frustrated. "Bad guitar lesson," she explained. She plopped down on his giant bean bag chair. "Something felt off. I kept missing my frets."

While Ben tried to cheer up Caroline, inspiration struck him: Since he couldn't decide between the top two groups on his own, why not let their friendship be the tie-breaker? In fact, he could think of several reasons why this was an excellent idea . . .

But then he hesitated. The problem was that a cappella group preferences were a somewhat uncomfortable conversation topic. What if Caroline's favorite was the all-girls group, the Notabelles? He couldn't exactly tell her she should change her mind.

Nevertheless, Ben desperately wanted to know Caroline's leanings, even if it meant an awkward conversation. Mustering his courage, he broached the subject head-on: "So, um . . . I was wondering . . . what group are you er . . . ranking first or . . . you know, considering?"

People have odd ways of expressing feelings. For Ben Jensen, asking Caroline about her favorite a cappella group was his first attempt at saying something more.

"Well, I've liked the Chorderoys from the beginning," began Caroline. "They've got this really great energy about them. It's fun watching them sing! On the other hand, the Harmoniums are strong performers. Classy and sophisticated, very driven, but . . ." She frowned, but didn't elaborate.

With a deep exhale, Caroline said, "I guess I'm still leaning towards the Chorderoys. They've always seemed so nice and creative. Quirky in a good way."

Ben grinned, very relieved. "That was my impression, too. Musical qualities aside, you just kind of *like* them."

"Exactly!" said Caroline. "That's what I felt, even as far back as the Recruitment Concert. And aren't first feelings always the most natural?"

Ben stared into her eyes, which were brown and bright and lively. "Yes. I think so."

There was a long moment of silence.

"So . . . just to confirm . . . Chorderoys?" Ben finally asked.

Caroline nodded. "Chorderoys."

They smiled at their secret pact. Then, Ben quickly changed the subject to the surprisingly delicious burritos in the campus cafeteria—an unimportant segue which he wouldn't recall even a few hours later.

It's funny how some bits of dialogue stick out, and how certain exchanges are remembered in extraordinary detail. For Ben Jensen, the short chat he and Caroline had about group personalities and preferences was one of those infuriatingly crystallized memories. He would flash back to it periodically for the rest of his college career.

♫ |

Chapter 8

Chords

Three people sat waiting on Taylor Stuart's olive green couch. Tiny Violet Hennings had laced her fingers together. Her small eyes darted about, examining and reexamining the quiet living room.

Tall, curvy Olivia sat on the middle cushion, wearing a low-cut sundress and high heels, staring with boredom at her woven ankle bracelet.

To her right was Sid Davis, the Chorderoys' humble musical director, reading Taylor's latest copy of *Architectural Digest*. With his long spine hunched over and his chin resting between two slender fingers, Sid seemed already to be in a philosophical mood.

Taylor stood facing the couch and, like Violet, stared around taking in the emptiness of the room. He glanced at his watch. He was trying very hard not to pick at his eyebrow, but tardiness was never good for his nervous tic. "Where is everybody?"

"*Relax*, buddy," said Olivia, in her sultry alto voice. "It's only five after."

"But we're on a time crunch. I've got to go to the Music Building to collect the auditionees' preference cards along with the other presidents soon, and our group hasn't even decided—"

"*Gorgeous* curtains, Taylor!" Violet exclaimed suddenly. The soprano had a very peculiar social reflux: Whenever she was uncomfortable, Violet felt compelled to throw out a compliment, the very first positive thing that came to mind.

Taylor cocked his head, puzzled. The curtains themselves were pretty ordinary. Taylor was struggling to come up with a response to Violet's outburst of politeness when there was a sharp rapping at the door.

In walked Joanna Norwood, a tall African-American soprano. Confident and organized, Joanna hated being late almost as much as she did apologizing. "I drove as quickly as I could after volleyball," she explained. "He needed a ride."

He was Gary Abrams, the third junior in the group. Gary was short—he barely came to Joanna's shoulder as they stood side-by-side—with an unfortunately receding hairline. Not much of a talker, Gary nodded silently.

"It's cool," said Taylor. Joanna had warned him in advance about her practice, and Taylor was compulsive, not totalitarian. "Any idea where the sophomores are, though?"

There was silence.

"These walls are beautiful!" exclaimed Violet. The group stared at her, bewildered. Violet struggled to justify her spur-of-the-moment aesthetic opinion. "The gray shade is . . . it's very modern."

Because it made more sense than talking about plainly painted walls, Taylor said something about the neighborhood surrounding his apartment. "The rent is a little more expensive out here, so I'm looking for a roommate to cut down on the cost. Do you guys know anyone who's looking?" He laughed awkwardly. "I guess I could cut a special deal for someone in the group, if anyone's interested."

There was another lengthy silence as Violet, Olivia, Sid, Joanna, and Gary avoided Taylor's eyes.

"Taylor, I *love* your coffee table!" cried Violet. "Small, but efficient . . . and it has such nice . . . angles, and . . ."

Fortunately for everybody, Violet was interrupted before she could continue fawning over Taylor's Ikea furniture. The door creaked, and in walked the group's three sophomores. Guillermo came first, his face red-brown and glistening with sweat. He was carrying several grocery bags.

Behind him walked Dylan, grinning devilishly. He plopped more bags on the counter. "Sorry, sorry. We went on a little morale-boosting run."

Erin came in behind them with a jug of cranberry juice cocktail. It was her unofficial job to keep her more mischievous classmates out of serious trouble. Although the folksy alto didn't actually drink alcohol, she'd assisted with their sophomoric mission today: Using fake IDs fit right in with her antiauthoritarian leanings.

Guillermo pulled a case of beer out of his bag. "Get it? A little *draught* for the A Cappella *Draft*." His laughter was exceptionally jolly.

Taylor was not amused. "Not happening."

"We're not going to get *wasted*," clarified Guillermo, obviously believing this to be an important distinction.

"No! Absolutely not!" yelled Taylor. "We've got important decisions to make and we shouldn't . . . we shouldn't be under the influence!"

"Come on," pled Dylan. "You know the Gobfellas are going to show up to the Draft completely smashed."

"We're *not* the Gobfellas!" Joanna chimed in firmly. The volleyball player was wearing the same intimidating expression she used when she leapt up to spike the ball down on an opponent.

But the sarcastic and easygoing tenor wasn't giving up. Dylan walked to the couch and leaned forward. "Olivia?"

"I'm not drinking beer," insisted the alto. "That's disgusting."

"Of course not!" Behind Dylan, Guillermo held up a handle of top-shelf vodka and a liter of Diet coke.

"You know me so well, *boys*," said Olivia, in her sexiest voice. She shifted in her seat and re-crossed her legs. "I *like* that."

"We didn't forget you, Miss Violet," said Dylan. He brandished a second bottle and read from the label, "Strawberry Explosion and Passion Fruit Margarita Mix!"

"You can share, Taylor," quipped Guillermo.

The Chorderoys' president went bright red in the face as his stressed boiled over. "I can't believe this is even being discussed! People, tonight is crucial! We've got to make good choices—no mistakes! Student Government is planning to CUT a cappella groups!"

As soon as the words came out of his mouth, Taylor regretted his timing. The whole room went silent with shock from the news. Taylor knew he had to speak quickly, or Violet would become a veritable volcano of random compliments.

"SG is shrinking the student activities budget so that there will be fewer singing groups next fall," muttered Taylor, his voice faltering. "We've got to get good people because this year—" He gulped, "This year is the evaluation period."

Everyone waited on edge for Violet to say something painfully awkward.

Luckily, Sid spoke first. People were rarely surprised to learn that Sid was a singer; his speaking voice was naturally calm and soothing. "It sounds, then, like we've got an entire year before SG makes its decision," said the music director, reasonably. "Let's focus on tonight, and save those worries for another day."

Sid flashed the sophomores a wry, but sympathetic, grin. "And how about we save your 'groceries' for later?

After the Draft, we should all be in a more celebratory mood."

Nodding reluctantly, the sophomores placed their items in the refrigerator and took their seats by the olive green couch.

Taylor took a deep breath and examined the circle of faces around him. The nine disparate voices of the Chorderoys had finally arrived. It was time to have their talk.

The group president directed his explanation to the sophomores, who had not yet been on this side of recruitment. "Okay, here's how this works: We'll decide our favorites first. After that, I'll go meet with the rest of the presidents to collect the auditionees' personal rankings, so we can see who preffed us. Then, tonight, we'll all go to the Draft with the other a cappella groups, where the auditionees' preferences will be matched with the groups'."

"And then we'll go welcome the newbies personally!" said Guillermo, remembering this part fondly.

Taylor nodded and peered down at the notes on his clipboard, on which he'd recorded the "thumb-votes" of the group members after callbacks. "We'll start with the ladies. First: Bree Abbott. I recorded three yeses and six nos."

Violet's hand shot up. "Ooh, I was a yes! I thought Bree might simply have a more latent talent than the others. She was probably really nervous." Since declaring her major in Elementary Ed, Violet had been describing people in terms of potential more frequently.

Gary shook his head vehemently, as if to say 'not that nervous, just off-key.' Like the low bass notes he sang for the Chorderoys, Gary's opinions were sometimes more felt than heard distinctly.

"Who else was a yes?" interjected Dylan, who was rather blatant in his desire to accelerate the draught/ Draft.

"That would be you and Guillermo."

"Ah, then, let me refer to my notes." Dylan pulled a few crumpled evaluation sheets from his jean pockets. "Let's see . . . what could have impressed me about Bree?"

Joanna stared over his shoulder and cried incredulously, "You gave her a PERFECT TEN for 'pitch?!' And you added new categories for 'face' and 'body!' This is SUPPOSED to be about her singing voice, not how hot she was!"

Dylan, whose devilish grin always perfectly contrasted his baby face and clear high-tenor voice, retorted, "I like to be *thorough* in my evaluation."

"Ugh, you're like a horny Justin Bieber!" snapped Joanna. The tough soprano never ceased to give him grief for his extra-youthful appearance.

"Well, I gave her tens, too," chimed in Guillermo. "But I sort of like everybody." This was true; the pudgy vocal percussionist seemed incapable of disapproval. He'd given a thumbs-up even to the guy who had sung "Twinkle, Twinkle Little Star" all on one note.

While the rest of the group offered arguments against Bree, Guillermo and Dylan's eyes met, and they shared one of their silent best friend connections. After a moment, Dylan announced, "Guillermo and I have decided to pass on Bree." Hot freshman though she was, they knew Bree was consistently off-pitch. They had to pick their battles.

"Next is Caroline Cooper." Taylor straightened with pride. "She was my personal recruit from the class I'm TAing. Eight yeses and one no."

"Great stats!" cried Guillermo, happy to be in the majority again, which of course happened whenever the majority voted yes.

Olivia re-crossed her legs. "I was reluctant. We already have plenty of your traditional good-girl voices in the group, and I hoped we might be a bit more *experimental*."

"Caroline's my number-one pick," said Sid, in his evenhanded baritone. "Fantastic pitch, technique, energy. If her ranking of us allows, we have to take her."

Gary agreed, nodding decisively.

With a strong majority and the music director's own endorsement, the Chorderoys were ready to move on. "Okay, that's a *yes* for Caroline. Now, Nicole McLain. She was more controversial: five yesses and four nos." Taylor's eyes darted about nervously. "Before we begin, I'd like to remind everyone that Nicole was a very effective performer. No matter what people think about her personality, she can clearly rock a solo, and that could help our case this year with SG."

"But—she's nuts!" cried Dylan frantically.

Olivia flipped back her shiny black hair. "Tension! *Fire!* She's exactly what we need!" declared the alto.

"Nicole does have a powerful voice," said Sid, with a pointed glance towards Taylor. "But quite frankly, I'm concerned about her ability to blend in with the group. She won't be singing every solo, and we don't want anybody's individual part sticking out in the background."

The group president sighed. This, Taylor knew, was the great a cappella debate in a nutshell: The *choir* camp versus the *theater* camp. In high school, the choir camp sang chamber music, learned solfège hand signs, attended All-State Chorale, and religiously used diaphragmatic breathing exercises. The theater camp, by contrast, embraced the performance aspects of a song: acting, showtunes, musicals, and choreography.

Collegiate a cappella required both theatrical and "pure" musical skill sets, but there were often conflicting views on the relative importance of each. During the recruitment season, the choir camp and the theater camp faced off head-to-head.

"We could use her spunk!" squeaked Violet – theater camp.

"At the risk of our entire group's blend?" pressed Joanna – choir camp.

Dylan, meanwhile, was fixated on Nicole's personality. "She brought a million headshots with her! She's majoring in Theater! Don't you guys see how much *drama* she'll bring to the group?"

"Not everyone who does theater is a real-life drama queen!" countered Erin, who was herself a frequent victim of stereotyping. With her extra long ponytail, hippie jewelry, and the occasional left-wing political tee, people sometimes made additional assumptions about her. ("For the last time: I'm an ethical eater, not a *vegetarian!*" she'd complain. "It's not the same!") "We shouldn't make judgments based on stereotypes!" said Erin firmly.

"Oh please, it's not a stereotype if it's so *obviously* true!" said Dylan.

Taylor was getting desperate. He knew the group needed more female soloists; Olivia was their best, and this was her last year! "Couldn't you work with her, Sid? You're such a good coach, and she seemed like she was already learning how to blend with the other altos during callbacks."

"The vowels did improve somewhat when she was concentrating," conceded the music director. "And she

92

would be a strong soloist . . ." Sid stared profoundly at the ceiling, as if he were pondering a far loftier question than whether to admit another alto.

Taylor hesitated before adding, "And five to four is still technically a majority."

At last, the music director agreed: The Chorderoys should take Nicole if they could. "She's got a good belt voice," Sid reminded the opposition. "I think she can learn to control it."

"Okay, but I swear she'll be a crazy!" said Dylan, as if he had definite authority in this matter.

Taylor read the next name: "Renee Murphy. Also controversial: Six yeses to three nos. Personally, I didn't think she'd be a very strong performer. Seemed a little icy and—" The president stopped when he saw Sid's stare: Taylor owed him one.

"Renee's a natural singer," began the music director, who seemed to prefer the underdog candidates. "I don't know if she has much training, but she has great musical instincts. We could use someone like her to balance out our slower learners." No one asked to clarify who those might be.

Guillermo peered around cautiously before speaking up. "I still voted yes, but does anyone else remember that Renee had this sort of er . . . *scary* look on her face as she sang?"

"Like a serial killer?" said Dylan. He faked a shiver. "That look haunts me still."

Sid took a deep breath, and spoke with a Yoga instructor's serenity. "She had a serious expression, yes. If she joins, we'll have to remind her to smile during performances."

Despite his debt to Sid, Taylor wasn't sold on the idea of taking Renee. He'd gleaned some new intel from his

Facebook stalking. "I read . . . somewhere . . . that Renee is on the Diving team."

"And that somehow diminishes her desire to sing?" asked Joanna, who for obvious reasons was sensitive to the scheduling conflicts of student athlete-singers.

"Well . . . um . . . singing and sports . . . not everybody can handle so many activities at once . . ." Taylor sputtered.

Joanna, who was also pre-law, dove right in. "Can't handle it? Shouldn't that be her choice—as a fully competent, adult young woman?"

"Um . . . uh . . ."

"Agreed, Taylor's a big sexist," said Dylan sarcastically. "But let's focus on what matters—her stare! She was a singing Hannibal Lecter! Except very petite, and you know, with tiny little boobs—"

"Don't talk about her like that!" begged Violet. Tears were welling in her eyes. "Renee . . . Renee was my favorite auditionee . . . 'Tiny Dancer' was . . . so adorable . . . we have to get her . . . She's already like—" she wiped her eyes, "like a *little sister* to me."

The group was silent, completely bewildered. Two short auditions and Violet was already calling Renee her little sister? Sid shook his head. Why was he surrounded by so many people from the *theater* camp?

Since not even Dylan was willing to challenge the fiercely maternal soprano again on this subject, Renee was quickly decided as a *yes*. The Chorderoys progressed through the rest of the female candidates, who all seemed to move more quickly after Violet's emotional outburst.

When it came to the guys, there was generally much less debate. There were never as many, and most of those who auditioned were easily sortable.

"Russell Sterling?"

"Fellas!" cried the group.

"Daniel Schwartz?"

"Dinos!"

"Chaz Johnson?"

"Fellas for sure!" declared Dylan. "That guy *screams* 'singing frat.'"

When Ben Jensen's name came up, there was more hope that he would choose a co-ed group, but Taylor grimaced. "We *all* voted yes, which means she'll want him, too. Dani always finds ways to break 'Limited Contact.' She's probably already won him for the Harmoniums with her flirting."

"Hmmph!" said Olivia, rather upset. A Gender Studies major (with a minor in Marketing), Olivia was the kind of feminist who believed a woman's sexuality was her *power* to wield. Throughout callbacks, Olivia had worn her shortest skirts, her highest heels, her finest push-up bra, and her coyest smile. She took offense that anyone could think Dani was the superior seductress. "Have some faith in my *abilities*, Taylor," chastised the alto.

The last male on their list was Akash Patel. "Seven yeses and two nos," recounted Taylor.

"Akash is another of my favorites," said Sid. "The solo was stiff, but his natural tone is deep and warm."

"We'll have to see where he ranks us," said Taylor, gathering his things to leave. "If I remember correctly, Akash only tried out for us and the Gobfellas."

"That's funny," said Erin. "He seemed humble, friendly—didn't *seem* like a Fella."

"Hey!" said Dylan. "What happened to no stereo-typing?"

"Oh, I think it's allowed if you do it in a positive, encouraging way!" chirped Violet.

The Chorderoys were still arguing this point when Taylor left to meet the other group presidents. He was about to discover what the auditionees thought of his singing group, whether all of his hard work during the recruitment season had been for nothing. His nerves were setting in with full force. As Taylor drove to campus, he held the wheel with one hand, and subconsciously tugged his eyebrow with the other.

♫

Half an hour later, Taylor called the remaining Chorderoys, still waiting at his apartment, with the results. Sid put him on speakerphone, so that Taylor heard the excited reactions as he relayed the auditionees' preferences. With each announcement of a first-choice ranking, Guillermo's voice was especially boisterous; Taylor deduced that he'd already broken into his "groceries."

"Newbies! Newbies! NEWBIES!" Guillermo cheered.

Yet Taylor could not join in on the audible merriment of his fellow Chorderoys. He felt heavy and tired and . . . dirty.

The feeling stemmed from a private conversation he'd just concluded with Dani. Even then, Taylor understood the gravity of their agreement. He understood that they'd forever changed the course of two a cappella groups.

And even then he knew it was irreparable.

♫ |

Chapter 9

Drafted

When the rest of the Chorderoys joined Taylor at the Business School just before the A cappella Draft, the president found Guillermo wasn't the only group member who'd been drinking. Violet greeted him with an enormous hug and a brand new nickname: "*TAY-TAY!*" The spirited soprano's second passion fruit margarita had hit hard.

"*Tay-Tay.* Dear. Old. Tay-Tay. Why don't we skip this Draft thingy and go contact the newbies now?" Violet laid a drunken hand on his chest. "Tay-Tay. It's *time*."

Taylor shook his head. "There're still decisions to make." He watched nervously as the other singing groups slowly arrived, filling the chamber with their excited voices. At the moment, the group president was so anxious that not even a drunken Violet could make him crack a smile.

He motioned the soprano to a seat with the rest of the group, who were settling in halfway down the auditorium. The Music School had long ago made the determination that late night gatherings of a cappella singers were dangerous, and thus, forbidden. As a result, the official A cappella Draft was held in Brighton's Business School, which was predictably more *laissez-faire*. The high-tech MBA Auditorium was available without supervision for just thirty bucks a night.

Taking a break from keeping a close eye on her fellow sophomores, Erin gazed about at the familiar faces filling the curved, amphitheater-style seating. She spotted representatives of every group but one. "Is it true that the Gobfellas always show up late?" she asked.

"Every year," sighed Taylor. While he waited for the Gobfellas to finally make their grand entrance, the group president began picking at his brow. Even normal Drafts made him nervous—all the speedy actions and reactions, so little time for deliberation. With the added stress of his earlier talk with Dani, it was almost too much to bear.

At last, the Gobfellas stormed in with cheers and hooting. Their dress for the evening was "Fellas formal," which included oddities such as a tuxedo with clown shoes, a lilac pinstripe suit, and a sports coat made entirely of electrical tape. Brighton's singing fraternity had thoroughly "pre-gamed" and was in top form: Ready to claim their brothers, blow off the a cappella establishment, and get on with kidnapping the pledges—that is, their new singers.

Derek Ross was the Gobfellas' president. The former-footballer-turned-aca-stud strutted to the front of the auditorium.

Dani was already on the stage, chatting with a few of the other group presidents, when Derek surprised her with a spontaneous kiss on the cheek. "Can't make anyone jealous!" crowed the head Fella, his breath reeking of cheap beer. He proceeded to give the female leaders of La*chaim and the Notabelles similar kisses.

Greg Hollis gave him a threatening glare. "We're ready to start," said the Dinos' president, firmly.

"Fantastic!" returned Derek. With his pink button-down and dark brown sports coat, Derek looked like a fortuitously nonexistent candy: chocolate-wrapped bubble gum. "We'll go first. Chaz Johnson—"

"No," interrupted Greg, exerting his authority as ACUAC chairman. "We have a pre-set recruiting order."

Derek relented. "Fine." He instructed his fellow bros to hang tight. The Fellas plopped down in the auditorium seats. With their sloppy dress clothes, they looked like a bohemian pack of businessmen or a bizarre boys' club.

"First, the lovely ladies in the Notabelles," announced Greg, gradually returning to his more cheerful self. Their group president stepped forward.

Taylor thought of Kara Abingdon as an "old-school" Notabelle. The leader was fond of quoting the all-female group's founding motto, "Sisterhood through Song." It was a creed which dated back to the '80s, the heyday of Madonna, big hair, and "girl power" music.

More recently, it seemed that this more traditional brand of girl power was not as popular as it used to be among Notabelles auditionees. Each year, their group lost plenty of talent to the co-ed ensembles. It seemed young women no longer saw this integration like Kara did: as a betrayal to their gender.

Taylor, too, had noticed this trend during his years at Brighton. He'd also seen the Notabelles' rankings for this fall, and they weren't great. He wondered how the all-female group's choices would take them into account.

"We'll take Margaret Samuels," said Kara. Her voice was proud, despite the fact that Margaret was the only girl who'd ranked them first that year.

"WOOHOOOO!" shrieked the Notabelles in the audience. There was a round of hugs and cheerful high-fives.

Kara stepped back in line with the other group presidents, where she would wait to see if additional singers were passed down for the Notabelles' drafting from higher-ranked groups.

"Next up, the Harmoniums," Greg announced.

Dani Behlman walked confidently to the podium, her hips swaying, her red heels clicking on the stage. The Harmoniums' president believed notes were for amateurs. She recited each name from memory: "Amber Birch, Phillip Eason, Max Lerouge, and—"

She paused, and said the final name with extra relish— "*Caroline Cooper.*"

The Harmoniums cheered and applauded. Further back in the Chorderoys' section, Taylor saw Sid frown, but nod with understanding. He knew his music director was disappointed, but understood that the Harmoniums would be foolish to pass on such a strong vocalist, and since Caroline had ranked the Harmoniums first . . .

"Wait!" said Kara suddenly. "I think there might be a mistake."

When Kara interjected, Taylor began frantically tugging at his brow.

The Notabelles' president consulted the notes on her clipboard. "I wrote down that Caroline ranked the Chorderoys first, *followed by* the Harmoniums, followed by us."

"I have it flipped for the top two groups!" said Dani, quickly. "How about you, Taylor?" she asked, giving him an intense stare.

"Um . . . yeah . . . my notes . . . same as yours," Taylor stammered.

During the earlier meeting, the leaders copied down the information that the auditionees had listed on their individual preference cards. Using each president's notes, the ACUAC moderator inputted these rankings into his computer for "safekeeping."

"Let's see here," said Greg. He opened the spreadsheet on his tablet computer. "Caroline Cooper:

Harmoniums – 1, Chorderoys – 2 . . ." Softly, he added, "Notabelles – 3."

Kara frowned. "I guess I made a mistake."

"I could check Caroline's actual preference card if you'd like," Greg offered, eager to please. He motioned to a black canvas bag in the corner.

At this point, Taylor was pulling his brow so hard the skin lifted up with each tug. Out of the corner of his eye, he could see Dani glaring at him.

After what seemed a long time, Kara finally relented. "No, that's okay." Either way, the disappointed president knew that the Notabelles wouldn't be drafting Caroline that night.

Derek slipped his arm around Kara's waist. "Tell me the truth, have you been drinking?" he asked. His breath stunk from several shotgunned beers. "I promise not to judge."

Kara rolled her eyes and pushed away the drunken flirt.

"And now, the Chorderoys," said Greg.

At the podium—standing before the entire a cappella community—Taylor was so nervous he could barely speak. Finally, he eked out the names of those singers who had ranked his ensemble first, and who were also his group's top choices:

"Renee Murphy, Ben Jensen, and . . ." His voice was especially light and shaky as he said the third name. "Nicole McLain."

Violet squealed! Even knowing in advance that it would happen, she was thrilled. Renee was actually going to be her baby soprano!

Guillermo and Sid began chanting, "CHOR-DER-ROYS! CHOR-DER-ROYS!" Sid let them go for a few rounds before asking them to calm down.

101

As Taylor stepped back in line with the rest of the presidents, he saw another confused look cross Kara's face. He knew that, once again, she'd written the singer's order differently. Luckily for him, this time she didn't challenge the record.

When it came time for the fourth group to draft its new members, Taylor thought about what he'd heard of La*chaim's behind-the-scenes debate. At its inception, the co-ed group sang mostly Hebrew-language liturgical songs and frequently sang at local synagogues. In recent years, however, there was a push from within the group to perform more on-campus gigs, using American pop songs written by Jewish songwriters, which were more accessible to the everyday college audience. This latter route still gave La*chaim plenty of musical options, but the older members worried about the implications for their group identity. Were they selling out to become more mainstream?

La*chaim's president Rachel Stein read the names of the four students they were drafting. "Yael O'Connor, Elizabeth Schwartz, Antonio Schiffman, Ryan Berg."

After Rachel's turn at the podium, Greg himself came to the stage. He was already smiling.

"For this first round, the Dinos take Arthur Fiegen-schube, henceforth the *Bambiraptor*." There was chuckling in the audience. Taylor remembered Arthur as being a particularly gentle-voiced tenor, and thought the new dinosaur name fit perfectly.

"Also, William Lund, henceforth *Colymbosathon eclpecticos*." Tall, Viking-esque William Lund swam butterfly on the University's swimming team. The prehistoric creature name came from the Latin meaning "amazing swimmer with extra long penis."

Greg stepped back into line and called for the next group. "And *now* the Gobfellas . . . I said, the Gobfellas!"

Derek was drooping his head down, pretending like he'd fallen asleep while standing up. When Greg yelled for him, the Fellas' president started, shook off his drowsiness, and stumbled front and center.

Everyone knew what was about to happen, even the sophomores, who'd been informed by the upperclassmen. As much as Taylor's fellow a cappella veterans were trying to *appear* disinterested, they were nevertheless waiting expectantly, wondering if this might be the year the Gobfellas would be forced to act more humbly.

But when Derek arrived at the podium, he was all bravado. "Chaz Johnson, Russell Sterling, Lawrence Norman, Dustin Crawford." He pounded the podium with his fist. "BOOM! Fellas out!" With that, his fellow members got up to leave, noisily joking and laughing amongst themselves.

No one asked if the Gobfellas would be interested in any candidates that might be "passed" to them from higher ranked groups. Everyone knew the Fellas didn't take people who ranked them less than first. For them, there was never a round two.

The Gobfellas were just as cocky as ever, but they hadn't drafted Akash! Taylor made eye-contact with Sid in the audience. The music director nodded: The Chorderoys should claim the friendly baritone in the second round.

There was significantly less action in subsequent cycles of the Draft, with newly available singers being "passed" or "claimed" one name at a time. After Taylor drafted Akash, Guillermo started another unruly chorus of "CHOR-DER-ROYS! CHOR-DER-ROYS!" until Sid calmed him down again.

The Notabelles inducted some new alto "sisters" when auditionees were passed down from the Harmoniums. La*chaim claimed the soprano they'd been wanting. The Dinos nabbed a pale blonde bass who, in keeping with their paleontological theme, they promptly pronounced *Dracorex Hogwartsia*

Gradually, certain singers' names were dropped as no group decided to take them. As Taylor listened, he felt a twinge of sadness for the auditionees who slipped through the cracks near the end. Since these singers would have the exact same result as those ruled out before the Draft, they'd never know how close they'd come.

When the last decision was made, Greg shared the much anticipated good news: "That's it, everybody! Congratulations on your new singers!" Wild cheering and applause filled the B-school auditorium. This was the one time each year when Brighton's a cappella community was most unified: Auditions were finally over!

Taylor had just started walking towards the other Chorderoys when someone grabbed his arm.

"Hold up. I need to speak to you," Dani hissed. Her fingers dug into his upper arm. "*Privately.*"

Taylor went ghost-white and very nearly fainted.

Nearby, Greg gathered his things and slung his heavy black bag over his shoulder. "I'll keep these preference cards for a few months, just in case we need a permanent paper trail," he told the other presidents.

Meanwhile, the Chorderoys were filing towards the exit. "Go—go ahead and warm up," Taylor called to them, his voice shaking. "I'll—I'll be outside in a minute."

Sid nodded and shepherded the rest of the Chorderoys out.

The excited chatter diminished as the chamber slowly emptied. At last, the door was closed behind them, and suddenly it was just the two group presidents at the front of the indoor amphitheater, alone.

Bright fluorescent lights cast their two elongated shadows against the auditorium's giant projection screen. Whatever business Dani had in mind for their private conversation, Taylor was dreading it.

Dani leaned forward so that she was within inches of his face. "Taylor Ashley Stuart: I need you to stop worrying about our agreement."

Taylor squeezed the flaps of his cargo shorts. He hated being called by his full name. "But . . . but I haven't said anything," he muttered defensively.

"It makes no difference what you have or haven't said! Appearances are always more important, anyway. All night, you've been looking like a guy who just killed a Care Bear in cold blood. You're acting guilty, Taylor. And if you keep it up, people are going to get suspicious!"

Taylor couldn't help doing it: Without thinking, his hand rose to pull his eyebrow.

In a flash, Dani snatched his wrist and pushed it firmly to his side. "That's exactly what I mean!" she chided. "I need you to control your trichotillomania!"

Taylor's jaw dropped; horror filled his hazel eyes.

Dani smiled as she defined the condition: "*Trichotillomania*: An anxiety disorder characterized by compulsive pulling of facial hair. The tic worsens with high-stress situations. Oftentimes, the person doesn't consciously realize what he or she is doing."

Taylor stared at the floor. His nervous tic was something he kept entirely private, yet his self-declared enemy had diagnosed it on her own. "But . . . but how did you know?"

Dani chuckled lightly. "Just because you and I aren't BFF anymore doesn't mean I don't still *see* you!" she scoffed, as if it were the most foolish of questions. "You kept pulling whenever I was around, so I searched Google."

The Harmoniums' president smoothed the fabric of her red dress against her hips. "Now, I personally believe that what we did was entirely legitimate—nowhere in the ACUAC charter does it specifically say it's against the rules."

"At the same time, I know you," added Dani, with a new note of condescension. "And I know that if you don't get it through your head that what we did was morally acceptable, then you'll go on acting neurotic for the rest of the year. And then *everyone* will know you're hiding something! So here's what we're going to do—"

Suddenly, Dani grabbed Taylor's offending hand, clutching his fingers in her own. As their skin touched, Taylor felt the nerves tingle up his arm. He was shocked as Dani began *massaging* the inside of his palm!

Dani's voice was unusually calm and even. "Whenever you start to worry about what we did, I want you to relax and try to regain some perspective. Remember this story:

"There were two a cappella group presidents. One of them wanted a new alto soloist. His strongest female performer was graduating the next year, and he wanted someone to fill her spot." Taylor knew she meant Olivia.

"The other president wanted a strong soprano," continued Dani, "Her group was bottom-heavy and she needed someone who could consistently hit those critical high notes.

"The problem for the two group presidents was the rankings: The two freshmen at issue ranked the groups in the exact *opposite* way from what the groups really needed." She was referring, of course, to Caroline and Nicole.

Dani worked her fingers to the inside of Taylor's wrist, attempting to massage the stress away. "Now, if the groups were smart," said Dani, with additional condescension, "They would have agreed to pass the singers to each other. That way they could both get the type of talent they needed. But the two presidents knew that wouldn't happen. The other members weren't so forward -thinking.

"So the two presidents did what any good leaders would do in their situation," said Dani, proud and firm. "They traded."

When Taylor spoke, his own voice sounded distant to him. "But what if they—" He caught himself. "I mean what if *we*—get caught?" Regardless of its technical legality, Taylor knew the trade felt shady.

"Shh now," chided Dani softly. "How would that happen? The computer records reflect the new rankings, and the singers themselves won't know how they were sorted. There's no danger unless one of the two presidents gives it away, and that's not going to happen."

Dani worked her fingers back to the tiny joints at the top of Taylor's palm. Her sing-song voice was quiet and entrancing. "There were two people who saw what needed to be done, so they did it. There is absolutely nothing wrong with that."

Taylor stared in silence at his fingers, remembering aca-events much older than tonight's deal.

Dani beamed. "See, you're more relaxed already," she said. She lowered his hand gently to his side. "Perhaps therapy is my true calling."

The alto gave him an approving pat on the head and stepped back. "Remember that story, and I guarantee you'll have fewer worries." Dani gathered her red purse and walked to the door. She called over her shoulder, "You're *welcome*, Taylor."

Taylor stared up at his tall shadow on the projector screen as he replayed the day's events in his mind. "Wait!" he called.

Dani turned and gave her warmest smile. "Yes?"

He spoke softly. "That story isn't true."

"Pardon me?" said Dani. Her tone remained polite, but her green eyes had become piercing.

Taylor cleared his throat. "You've twisted it," he said, suddenly more assertive. "In your version, we were *both* acting in the best interests of our group. But if what the Harmoniums really needed was a soprano, then why did you start by asking for Ben Jensen?"

The mere utterance of Ben's name made Dani bristle.

"You started by offering Nicole in exchange for Ben," said Taylor, remembering out loud. "It was only *after* I kept refusing that trade that you offered Caroline instead." Taylor took a small step towards her. "Why were you so insistent?"

Dani maintained her perfect eye contact. "Like I said, we needed a soprano."

"Was that all?" Taylor leaned his head forward. The gel-covered tips of his shiny black hair stuck out in short, spiky points. "Here's another story: As soon as you heard Nicole sing, you felt threatened. Big alto voice, big personality—you knew she was direct competition. If Nicole were in the group, you might have to share your spotlight. You were *desperate* to pass her off. But, much to your chagrin, the rest of your group wanted her. If you were going to get your way, you'd have to act preemptively, before the other Harmoniums had an opportunity to vote on it."

Taylor pointed an accusatory finger. "Admit it! This wasn't about what was best for your group. This was about what was best for Dani!"

The Harmoniums' president shook her head, admitting nothing.

Taylor took a deep breath and sighed. His voice was low. "Danielle Rosemarie Behlman: I know you, too."

There was silence in the auditorium, with no Violet around to interrupt with peculiar niceties.

Finally, Dani rolled her eyes. She was all business now, without any hint of her earlier nurturing charade. "If you really know me, Taylor, then you'll also know this: First, I don't view any a cappella singer's group affiliation as set in stone. Sure, the Chorderoys will have Ben Jensen for initiation tonight, but whether he *stays* with you . . . well, that remains to be seen.

"Second, although we 'collaborated' earlier this evening, nothing has changed between us," continued Dani, smoothing her skirt as she shifted subjects. "I have absolutely no problem with SG eliminating Brighton's inferior a cappella groups. In fact, I've made it something of a personal goal to ensure that the Chorderoys don't survive this budget slicing."

Taylor shook his head. "You don't really mean that. You'd rather outperform us than have my group disappear."

"Are you sure about that, Taylor?"

He wasn't, actually. A frown spread across Taylor's tan face. Besides personal recognition, what did Dani really want? As his confusion grew, so did his anger, which began to show in his eyes. "Your ambition . . . your grudges about our past—that's your own business," said the Chorderoys' president. "But I will simply not allow you to take away something that . . . something that I *love* so much."

Dani smirked. "Good luck with that." She turned and walked away abruptly, her red heels clicking with each step.

"And control your tic!" she called over her shoulder. She let the heavy door slam behind her.

Taylor stayed alone for a few minutes in the auditorium, silently mulling over secrets new and old . . . Finally, he gathered his strength. The night was not yet over; the Chorderoys had a "gig" this evening.

And even with the stress and tension of tonight, he knew it would still be, as always, his favorite performance of the year.

♫

When Ben heard the knocking on his door, he and Caroline were playing their guitars in his dorm room. They sat together on his lofted twin bed, feet dangling off the edge. Caroline was playing a classical acoustic version of "Stairway to Heaven," and Ben was following her lead.

Since it was so late at night, Ben was fully expecting to see his next door neighbors in his doorway, politely requesting that he keep down the volume. Or perhaps it would be his roommate, Wilson, who regularly forgot his key. He hopped down from the bed and opened the door.

What he saw instead was a crew of nine smiling faces, who proceeded to sing the Root, followed by the Third, followed by the Fifth—the three simple notes of a warm major chord:

Welcome . . . welcome . . . welcome to the Chorderoys!

Ben stood in the doorway in his gym shorts and t-shirt, stunned. A camera flashed. Suddenly, the whole crew charged into his room. Everyone was giving him congratulatory hugs, which were all somewhat awkward with the guitar still strapped across his shoulder.

"We love you, Ben Jensen!" Violet cried.

Taylor gulped uncomfortably when he saw the room's *other* inhabitant sitting on the twin bed. He faced a quick moral dilemma: Should he tell Caroline that the Harmoniums were on their way so that she'd be less worried? But his sense of propriety stopped him short; it wouldn't be fair to ruin the Harmoniums' surprise.

"Come on, Ben, we're kidnapping you!" Taylor said enthusiastically.

"Gotta leave the guitar here, though, man," said Dylan, pointing. "No instruments *allowed* anymore!"

As Ben walked toward the door, he turned to Caroline. Her face was flushed red with embarrassment, but she nonetheless mouthed 'Congratulations!' and forced a smile. Ben wanted to say something comforting, but his new group was already ushering him into the hallway, hurrying him along to the next dorm . . .

The second of the Chorderoys' newbies was currently watching old 90s cartoons in his dorm room, trying to cheer himself up.

An hour ago, Akash Sheffield-Patel had heard the commotion as the Gobfellas charged the stairs in their "Fellas formal," yelling and hooting wildly. Akash had watched as they'd run right past his door. It wasn't *him* the Fellas were initiating that night, but Chaz Johnson from the other end of the hall.

As the drunken group stormed off, it had begun to sink in: The singing fraternity had rejected him. He would never swap "Fella stories" with his Uncle John during

Thanksgiving. Akash feared the worst. Maybe he actually had a terrible singing voice, and no one had ever had the heart to tell him the truth.

Depressed, Akash had turned to one of his classic mood-boosters: Streaming old *Doug* and *Recess* cartoons online. (He might also have felt better had he known that the Gobfellas were at that very moment dragging Chaz to the quadrangle, where he would be formally initiated with a swift kick to the balls—Uncle John had never shared his group's strange hazing rituals during those family dinners.)

Then, all of a sudden, there was a pounding on his door. Akash stumbled across the room to answer it:

Welcome . . . welcome . . . welcome to the Chorderoys!

As the group snapped pictures, Ben thought the lanky Akash looked a lot like Scooby-Doo in "Rut-Ro!" mode. The group congratulated their new baritone with hugs and handshakes before dragging him along to "sing in" the next newbie.

The third new singer lived in Arthur C. Sheffield Hall, which was named, of course, after Akash's famous grandfather. When the alto opened the door, she was wearing a scarlet red dress and loads of theatrical makeup:

Welcome . . . welcome . . . welcome to the Chorderoys!

The gaudy dress dated back to the 1940s and was part of Nicole's psychological exercise for theater. Nicole was auditioning for the role Blanche DuBois in the Drama Department's production of *A Streetcar Named Desire*. By dressing the part of a grandiose southern belle, Nicole hoped to remove all barriers between her and the character.

Dylan gave Guillermo another of their communicating looks: Definitely a crazy.

Although Nicole was somewhat surprised to see that it was the blue and white group at her door, she handled it well, instantly tearing up with gratitude and insisting on another group hug.

As the crowd made their way to the final dorm, Nicole and Akash greeted each other. "You helped me pick my 'lovechild' parents!" remembered Nicole.

When they reached the last room, the twelve singers gathered in the hallway. Guillermo pounded on the door, but there was no response. Apparently the last newbie and her roommates were all remarkably sound sleepers.

But Violet wasn't about to give up on the chance to welcome her new soprano baby into the group. She tested the door handle and found it was unlocked.

The Chorderoys crept into the room. Taylor picked out Renee's tiny form lying on one of the three twin beds. When they were in position, Sid flipped on the lights and blew his music director's pitch pipe.

Welcome . . . welcome . . . welcome to the Chorderoys!

Renee shot up from her pillow just as the camera flashed. She squinted as her eyes recovered and the smiling people surrounding her bed came into focus—the figures of a dozen singers, who'd just "sung in" their thirteenth member.

"Oh my God!" Renee wasn't inclined to grand displays of emotion, but she heard herself shouting. "Oh my God! Oh my God! I made it!" Someone thought she was actually good at something besides school and splash-less swan dives!

From the way she was hyperventilating, Ben wouldn't have pegged her for an athlete.

"I'm in an a cappella group!" Renee cried. "A singing group!"

Violet thought Renee's reaction could not be any cuter. She flung her arms around her new soprano baby and gave her an enormous hug. "Newbie shot!" cried the maternal soprano.

Considering how shocking it must have been to wake from such an obviously deep slumber, Renee's two room-mates were gracious in offering to take a group picture. Though the line-up of the four newbies was spontaneous, it would become photographic tradition: Akash Sheffield-Patel, the tallest, his lips curled back into a shy grin; his arm around Nicole McLain, flashing a big stage smile, her cheeks rose-pink with blush; next to her, the petite Renee Murphy, wisps of chestnut hair sticking up where her head had been lying on the pillow; and Ben Jensen, smiling wide, but peering to the right, in the direction of Caroline's dorm.

Finally whole, the Chorderoys trekked together to the other side of campus, enjoying the warm summer night air. As they walked, the newbies greeted each other. "My rescuer!" cried the theatrical alto.

"Purse girl!" returned Renee, who hadn't stopped smiling.

Ben received Caroline's text message while they were walking. She'd kept it brief: HARMONIUMS! ☺

Ben sighed. At least he and Caroline would be singing *nearby* each other. He quickly texted back his congratu-lations. He was relieved, naturally, but then a distressing thought occurred to him: What if Caroline hadn't actually ranked the groups as they'd decided? What if she'd changed her mind?

Fortunately, Ben was too distracted to dwell on this. Like the rest of the newbies tonight, Ben was in the process of being "kidnapped" by his new group, and it was the strangely happy sort of kidnapping that would temporarily wash such worries away.

♫

The Chorderoys' tradition was to take the new members to a crude 24-hour-diner which served surprisingly delicious Chili Mac and chocolate malts for super-cheap. The restaurant was selected years ago on the sole basis of its name, Roy's Diner. At the end of their celebratory night each year, the troupe was lucky enough to take a picture with "Roy" himself. Old Roy ate a good deal at his establishment; he was just as fat, jolly, and wonderful as would be imagined.

While Ben was enjoying his milkshake and fries, Caroline was eating an especially delectable crêpe. Dani loved hosting the Harmoniums' annual midnight welcome breakfast. The warm aroma of pancakes, pastries, biscuits, and espresso melded together and filled her studio apartment. Dani resolved to invite more guests over to her place this year so that she could cook for them.

Meanwhile, two singing groups were enjoying their traditional films. Each year the Dinos watched the ultimate sci-fi B movie, *Dinosaur Attacks 3: Raptors in Manhattan*. Veteran group members had memorized the many glitches in the plot, including the complete misuse of actual scientific terms like "Faraday's cage" and "chaos theory." At the same moment, the women in the

Notabelles were mixing chocolates and boxed wine during their annual screening of *Dirty Dancing*. By the last number, the ladies were all twirling and belting along to "(I've Had) The Time of My Life."

Initiation Night was Game Night for La*chaim and yes, somebody always brought a dreidel as a joke. The traditional Manischewitz, however, was quite intentional. The Jewish group freely enjoyed the sweet concord wine as they played get-acquainted-quickly games like "Never Have I Ever" and "Five Fingers."

Even the new members of the Gobfellas were relatively happy, although still in pain from the kicks they'd just received in the quadrangle. After their "initiation ritual," the upperclassmen took them over to the "Fellas House" for the official initiation barbecue. The pledges gobbled down burgers and bratwursts as they listened to the senior Fellas share grossly exaggerated stories of their sexual conquests.

Brighton U's a cappella newbies would forget some of the particulars—exactly how much personal information they had confessed over a bottle of Jewish wine; which freshman spotted the cameraman in *Raptors in Manhattan*; the unique queasiness that comes after overindulging at Roy's Diner. What remained from that night was the feeling: the very real sense that something special had just begun.

Chapter 10

Songbuilding

The semester was underway, and the newbies were hard at work with their new singing groups. During that Tuesday evening's practice, Ben felt like an especially slow learner.

"Let's try to make that *ahh* sound warmer," coached Sid, the music director. "Darken your tone; make it nice and round." This particular *ahh* came midway through the song, when the tenor part supported the solo with a wide vowel sound. Sid sang an example: first the wrong way, a harsh, bright *ahh*; then the correct, rounded *ahh* he was seeking.

Ben tried to imitate.

"That's better," said Sid, always encouraging. "It's what we call a padding note, so sing it with lots of space, as if your mouth were filled with an enormous warm marshmallow."

The Chorderoys' tenors were in one of the glass-walled practice rooms on the top floor of the music school, rehearsing their part separately. In the group's arrangement of "Your Song," the tenor part resembled the delicate acoustic guitar in Elton John's original recording. As Ben followed Sid's example, he remembered how he and Caroline had played guitar in these practice rooms earlier in the semester. Back when they were just jamming, there'd been refreshingly little discussion of technique.

After Ben finished the line, Sid corrected him gently. "This is very small detail, but the guitar phrase is dim-

*n*im-*n*im, *d*im-dah-*n*ah. The difference between the d's and the n's is important to the texture."

"Yeah, sorry man, but if you mix up your *dim*'s from your *nim*'s again we're gonna have to cut you from the group," said Dylan sarcastically. The high tenor leaned lazily against the upright piano; like the rest of the returning members, he remembered his "Your Song" part from last year.

When the tenors finished, they walked downstairs to the large classroom where the Chorderoys rehearsed together. The sopranos and the altos were still off in their individual practice rooms for sectionals, but the basses had already returned. As a baritone, Akash had more of a middle voice, but he was singing low bass for this song, along with Gary

Meanwhile, Guillermo, the group's vocal percussionist, was rehearsing his beatboxing in the corner of the room.

When Guillermo took a break, Akash asked, "How do you do the bass and snare sound?"

"It's hard to explain with words," said Guillermo. (This was an understatement: It's actually *impossible* to explain with words.) "But when I do the kick drum it feels a little like I'm saying the word 'boot.' And my snare has a 'k' consonant. So if I were to connect the kick drum to the snare drum, it's sort of like I'm saying 'boots, skirts, boots, skirts.'"

Guillermo demonstrated the drum pattern:

BOOM sss KUTT sss / BOOM sss KUTT sss / Bootsss Skirtsss / BOOM sss KUTT sss.

At Guillermo's urging, Akash gave it a try. "*Boots, skirts / Boots, skirts . . .*"

The rest of the men in the room gathered around to listen to him. "*Bootsss skirtsss / Bootsss skirtsss.*" Akash took a deep breath. "I feel like I'm just saying the words with extra spit on them."

"Keep going," said Gary, gruffly.

All eyes were on Akash as he continued: "*Boots, skirts / Bootsss skirtsss / BOOT sss KIRT sss / BOOM sss Kut sss / BOOM sss KUTT sss.*"

Sid smiled. "That's already an excellent kick drum," said the music director. "And the snare is really starting to improve. You might be a natural!"

Akash grinned sheepishly.

The sopranos and altos returned all together, led by Joanna, the Chorderoys' assistant music director. "We've been working through our blend issues," said the diligent soprano.

Sid nodded and said with his calm tone, "Let's all gather in a tight circle. Newbies, please set your music on the floor." Looks of panic crossed the freshmen's faces, but Sid insisted, "I'll bet you've memorized more than you think."

The rehearsal room contained four tall, curtained windows. Sid proceeded to draw them closed, blocking all the light coming in from the street. The newbies looked at each other, confused as to what was happening.

Sid walked to the corner of the room. "Remember, keep it nice and slow and even," he advised. He blew the pitch pipe—a sort of miniature harmonica—and the sound of an E-flat filled the room. Then he turned off the lights.

The darkness was complete. In the pitch black, Ben heard the music director softly counting:

"One…Two…Three…Four…"

Dooo—

The Chorderoys' version of "Your Song" was Sid's arrangement, and it began with the original's instrumental

119

introduction. The sopranos sang gentle "piano" arpeggios, rolling up and down the chords. *Dim, dim, dim, Doh dim doh...*

While he waited for his entrance, Ben listened for Renee's voice on the high soprano line. He discovered something remarkable: In the darkness, he both heard and *felt* the diver's voice from the opposite side of the circle. As Ben listened, his lack of sight brought out new harmonies; he could feel the notes pulsing through the air.

Taylor came in with the solo, sweetly singing Elton's part. Already, Ben had noticed how much more relaxed and genuine the group president seemed when he was singing.

The rest of the men joined the background. The basses were the anchor, their low notes echoing throughout the circle. *Doom dah, Doom dah, Doom dah, Doom...* Meanwhile, Ben and Sid were on the second tenor line, singing "guitar" and adding texture with those pesky, but important, *dim*'s and *nim*'s.

The first chorus cued what Sid had called the "vocal orchestra," but Ben hadn't understood the description until now. The sopranos and altos sang as "violins" and "violas," respectively, adding sustained suspension beneath the melody line: *voo—, Voo—, Vooo—, voo—*

In verse two, Guillermo came in with vocal percussion, introducing a kick drum, cymbal, snare combination: *Boon dah Kut sss / Boon dah Kut ss / Boot ss Kiht sss / Boon dah Kut sss.* Ben listened closely for the hidden words in the pattern.

A few voices over in the circle, Ben heard Nicole singing the alto part. Her extra loud *VOOO* stuck out, and Ben understood why Sid and Joanna were so often reminding the freshman alto to focus on blending in with the other voices. It wasn't that Nicole was off-pitch; she was just singing her part as a diva rather than an instrument. Singing accompaniment would take more practice for her.

For the penultimate build, the chorus of voices all grew together in support of Taylor's solo. Their many interlocking harmonies streamed into each other and melded, nice and warm. They sang loudly together:

Ahhhh—

It was the heartfelt vowel that he and Sid had spent so much time practicing. When the entire group finally sang it in unison, blending together, Ben felt the nerves in his arms tingle with excitement.

Taylor sang the last lyric, and the block softened slowly, releasing their energy in a gradual *diminuendo* . . .

When they finished, there was silence in the circle.

Finally, there came a gentle speaking voice. "Well done," said Sid.

"Gorgeous!" cried Violet.

Taylor flipped on the lights. With practice nearly over, he quickly reminded them of their schedule for this week, especially the details for the charity concert at which they were performing on Friday night.

"Our first gig with the newbies!" cheered Guillermo, who was always celebrating such "landmarks."

As the four newbies walked back to the freshmen dorms after practice that night, Ben was still thinking about that last song—how surprisingly awe-inspiring it had been to sing in the dark. He knew that when he got back to his dorm room, he had plenty of course reading to do for Introductory Philosophy, but at the moment he felt too energized for homework.

"You guys want to go to Badger's?" Ben asked. Badger's Café was the on-campus coffee shop that served ice cream and snacks late into the night.

"Yes! Let's!" exclaimed Nicole, without hesitation. Akash agreed.

Renee resisted at first—she had an early morning practice the next day—but eventually she, too, gave in to the temptation of socializing. The group turned towards the café and walked off into the night air, which was just beginning to cool with the onset of fall.

♫

Caroline stood in line by the counter at Badger's, watching the four Chorderoys newbies sitting in the same booth, eating ice cream and chatting together.

It had been a long day for the new Harmoniums soprano. After class, she'd had yet another planning meeting for the Harmony Halls community action committee. Then she'd raced across campus to make it in time for a cappella rehearsal. Too busy to grab a bite earlier, she was only now having a late-night dinner.

As Caroline watched Ben and his new Chorderoys friends, she felt a pang of sadness. She and Ben hadn't talked much the past few weeks. Or, more accurately, they weren't conversing normally. When they walked back from class together, Caroline sensed him avoiding the subject of "music" altogether.

Considering how much music was on their minds lately, this was an extremely awkward topical sidestep. For her part, Caroline was enjoying her first weeks in the Harmoniums. She'd found it exhilarating to be surrounded by such talented vocalists, and they'd all made her feel welcome. While Caroline waited in line for her panini, she stared intermittently at the Chorderoys' booth, wondering why she and Ben were suddenly excluding each other from such an important part of their lives.

Suddenly, the soprano felt a hand on her shoulder: "Late-night dinner?"

Caroline turned to face Dani, who was wearing one of her many red blouses and her friendliest smile. The freshman nodded.

Dani raised her plastic cup. "I just ordered a chai to help me through studying, but I haven't eaten either, actually." The Harmoniums' president leaned in. "Interested in a home-cooked meal? I believe I have the ingredients for Chicken a'la Pampalini back at my apartment. You can bring your books over, we can eat and study for a few hours, and then I'll drive you back."

Caroline glanced at the Chorderoys' booth, at the sandwich line, and then at Dani's chai. "You know," she said finally, "If it's no trouble for you, that sounds fantastic."

Dani beamed and pushed back a strand of strawberry blonde hair. "No trouble at all."

They were just walking out the back door when a young woman caught Dani's arm. The stranger had short cropped hair and black framed glasses. She peered up at Dani with serious eyes, and spoke in abrupt little bursts: "Dani – Thanks for our conversation – I appreciate your being straight with me – I've taken your advice – The committee just approved my application – I'm officially on the Treasury Council – Our talk was very helpful."

Dani's face brightened. "That's delightful news, Candace! Congratulations! Don't give me too much credit, though. The Treasury Council, like me, simply saw you for the talented young woman that you are. I'm so pleased that someone with your gifts will be shaping this University's financial policies."

Candace was still smiling when they said goodbye.

As they walked to the parking lot, Caroline was curious. "Do you mind if I ask about Candace?"

"Of course not," said Dani. Candace Bauer, she explained, was one of the many auditionees who had e-mailed Dani after tryouts this year, asking why she hadn't been selected. Replying to such inquiries was difficult, but Dani tried to carefully personalize each response.

Candace wrote back that she insisted on discussing the matter in person. At their meeting, Candace's unique skills emerged: The former New Jersey state high school debate champion kept firing argument after argument for why the Harmoniums should have taken her. ("Next, I will discuss my potential contributions to the group in three categories: Vocal contributions – Technical contributions – Social contributions.")

When Dani finally had the opportunity for rebuttal, she didn't even address the issue of Candace's general lack of musical talent. Instead, she tailored her argument to her audience:

It was quite clear, said Dani, that Candace had a natural knack for debating policy matters. Why not put that talent to good use by debating and *creating* policy for Brighton's Student Government? Candace's gifts should be employed on a much larger scale than they would in a niche singing group. Furthermore, Dani knew for a fact that there were currently a few openings on SG's Treasury Council.

Dani's redirection had worked. "It always helps to listen," concluded Dani, smiling charitably at the young soprano. "If you listen, people tend to reveal their greater usefulness."

As Caroline listened to Dani's story, the freshman kept thinking back to the sight of Candace personally thanking Dani for her courtesy. Like the image of the Chorderoys sitting apart in their separate booth, the mental snapshot fixed itself within her mind.

They made their way to Dani's car—a blood-red Mazda Miata. Dani was chatting excitedly and seemed quite pleased that they were spending time together, and Caroline was quickly warming to the idea of Dani's proposed girl-to-girl talk.

"You'll have to tell me all about your friend Elliot tonight," she said, exceedingly bubbly, "But *first*, why don't you tell me about Ben Jensen . . . Is he always as nice as he seems, or is he just another of those tools who hides it well?"

And with that, Dani rolled out of the parking lot and they were off.

Chapter 11

Gigging

Wilson Doyle, Ben's randomly assigned roommate, was a quirky fellow. He liked to toss out a few favorite expressions even when they weren't at all applicable to the situation. When Ben asked him if he had dinner plans, Wilson would reply, "When in Rome." To an inquiry about whether or not a particular TV show was on that night, he'd say, "Touché, buddy. *Touché*."

There was also the *Mean Girls* issue. Both Ben and his roommate admired the film, but Wilson's interest bordered on obsessive. Ben would return from class and discover that Wilson was once again watching Lindsay Lohan and Rachel McAdams duke it out. As he watched, Wilson would eat his favorite snack: crackers topped with swiss cheese and frozen gummy bears.

Wilson was weird, there was no doubt, but it was hard to tease someone with such specific oddities outside of those particular situations. By contrast, Wilson always found ways to poke fun at Ben's a cappella involvement, no matter the context. When an attractive girl from the floor complained about the lack of real dancing at fraternity parties, Wilson said, "You should bring Ben. He's really good at jazz hands." Leaning in, he would explain to the girl in a low insinuating voice, "A cappella."

The last week in September, Wilson came back to their room with a flier. He dropped it on Ben's desk. "*Tunes for Transformation?*" he read, with a mix of incredulity and delight. "Are they serious?"

Actually, Tunes for Transformation was a rather serious event, despite its cheesy alliterative name.

("Typical a cappella," Wilson would say.) It was Brighton U. a cappella tradition to hold a major charity benefit concert in the fall. All six of the University groups would perform a short set of songs. The funds from ticket sales would support inner-city education programs and urban renewal projects—the singing, therefore, being the catalyst for a bit of "transformation."

"I'm going to this. We're *all* going," Wilson proudly announced, speaking for all of their mutual friends on the floor. Wilson ran out of their room into the hallway. "Everyone's going to see Big Ben perform his first a cappella show on Friday," he told their next door neighbors.

"It's for the cause!" added Wilson, with a devilish grin.

If Wilson had been at the Chorderoys' last practice, he would have found even more reason to make fun of Ben's new a cappella habit. Taylor had spent a substantial portion of the rehearsal lecturing the group about something he called the "acabop."

"We don't just sing with our voices," stressed the Chorderoys' president. "We sing with our whole bodies. And if our bodies look disconnected from the music, it's going to be boring for the audience."

Unfortunately, Taylor's lecture target was just about as subtle as one of Wilson's a cappella digs at Ben. Applying his experience as a teaching assistant, Taylor unsubtly punctuated each of his recommendations with a big-eyed glance at Renee Murphy. The serious diver seemed incapable of grooving comfortably with the music.

Ben watched as Taylor's "how to bop" tips failed disastrously on his fellow freshman. Rather than let her hands hang straight, Taylor suggested that Renee keep her arms above her hips as she sang. He also advised keeping some bend in her knees, so that she wouldn't look so rigid. After following his instructions, Renee looked like a crouched quarterback, arms extended at 45 degree angles, ready to receive the hike.

Taylor sighed. "Scratch that. Just try to imitate Violet and Olivia. And don't forget to *smile*." By now, the group had politely informed Renee that she often had a very serious expression, especially when she was concentrating on her singing part (the infamous "Look That Could Kill Puppies").

Tunes for Transformation would take place in Blair Chapel, an elegant space with marble floors and stained glass windows. In the past century, Blair Chapel had hosted thousands of religious services, weddings, speakers, and educational events. Politicians and academics had inspired audiences from its dais. More recently, it had become the University's primary entertainment center, a venue for rock concerts, comedians, film screenings, and—the relative newcomer—a cappella shows.

When Ben arrived at Blair Chapel before the concert Friday night, he and his fellow freshmen Chorderoys were dressed in their group formal wear for the first time. Like many college groups, they wore variations on a theme. For Ben, the outfit was relatively simple, a white button-down shirt, a skinny blue tie, and navy suspenders. Sid wore the opposite color combo and a special Chorderoys tradition: the music director's all-white fedora.

The ladies wore a solid blue or white dress paired with a singular piece of "flair." Olivia, for example, wore a low-cut white sundress and a long navy necklace that hung almost to her waistline.

As the Chorderoys waited to warm up their voices, Violet encouraged her "soprano baby" to be more creative with her flair. "I bought this just for you, Renee!" The maternal soprano held up a white belt with a comically oversized buckle. "It'll look cute because you're so itty-bitty!"

Renee politely declined; her simple silver bracelet was flair enough for her.

Meanwhile, Ben watched Taylor pacing nervously up and down the chapel hallway, holding his cell phone to his ear. The group president was leaving frantic voice messages for two late singers. "It's seven fifteen, we perform first, and we need you here immediately!" he barked at Guillermo's answering machine, tugging at his eyebrow with his non-phone hand.

It was hard for Ben to determine what caused Taylor's constant state of anxiety: his general temperament, the responsibility of being 'in charge,' the new threat of Student Government cutting back a cappella groups, or something else entirely. Whatever the cause, Ben was always a little worried for his TA.

Taylor had just sent off another round of desperate text messages when Guillermo ran in, his cheeks reddened, the tail of his blue corduroy blazer flopping wildly behind him. "There's been a disaster!" he cried. "As of right now, there's no afterparty!"

The half of the Chordcroys that were just as appalled as Guillermo by this development gasped, while the other half sighed in relief that this was all that was the matter.

"Why not?" cried Dylan.

Guillermo shook his head somberly. "Apparently the Tunes for Transformation planning committee was more concerned with the logistics of fundraising than with our post-show entertainment."

"Some people . . ." Dylan muttered.

"I'm trying to throw something last-minute together with Greg," explained Guillermo. "But it's still just tentative."

Sid nodded. "Well, keep us informed," said the music director. "In the meantime, 'I am a Cow.'"

This would have been quite the personal revelation if it weren't one of the Chorderoys' standard vocal warm-ups. The group gathered in a circle, Sid blew his pitch pipe, and altogether they stretched their high ranges, singing out on a major arpeggio: *I am a cow, Mooooooooooooo.*

As they climbed the musical scale, Sid substituted various other animals. Ben heard Guillermo's bellowing voice beside him. *I am a duck, Quaaaaaaaaaack.*

The Chorderoys had moved on to a vocal diction exercise called "Red Leather, Yellow Leather" when Nicole finally walked up to the group. Her cheeks and eyes were red, and despite her efforts, the tears were still streaming down her face.

"Oh darling, what's wrong?" asked Violet.

"I—just—saw—the cast list," Nicole managed between sniffles. "I got—Blanche—DuBois."

There was a chorus of sad aw's from the group; it seemed the appropriate response to Nicole's tears.

"Wait, in *A Streetcar Named Desire?*" asked Taylor. The Chorderoys' president knew his Tennessee Williams. "But that's the lead!"

Nicole nodded. "It's—my—dream—role," stammered the drama student. "I'm—so——*happy.*" There were suddenly many, many more tears.

As they realized the actual situation, the group began to congratulate her. Sid told Nicole that getting a lead part was remarkable for a freshman. Violet took the alto's hand and offered to help her reapply her makeup.

Once the two women had left the group for the restroom, Dylan asked, "Just to clarify, that was her reacting to getting the part she wanted, right?" He muttered quietly to Guillermo, "I *said* she'd be a crazy."

Nicole returned a few minutes later, her makeup repaired and her eyes still glistening. Around her neck, she wore a string of giant stage pearls as flair against her bright blue dress.

The Chorderoys followed Taylor through the back hallway of the chapel. As they walked, they passed the other singing groups, traveling through the overlapping circles of sounds: The Notabelles shook out their joints while counting "crazy eights"; the Dinos warmed their lower registers, descending the scale with *Down the elevator, down the elevator, down the elevator*; La*chaim sang the Three Stooges' classic tongue twister, *Bi-by-biki-biki-by, biki-bo, biki-by-bo-bi…*; the Harmoniums practiced perfect enunciation by repeating the line, "Lips, Teeth, Tip of the Tongue!"; and the Gobfellas "warmed up" by re-watching raunchy YouTube videos on their smartphones.

Since they'd drawn the closing act for August's Recruitment Concert, the Chorderoys were *opening* the show tonight. The white-and-blue clad group gathered in the tiny waiting room backstage.

Guillermo motioned for everyone to come close to him. Out of his jacket pocket, he suddenly produced an individually wrapped slice of yellow cheese. "For you newbies, we have this tradition before we go on stage."

Sid chuckled. "It's hardly tradition," said the senior. "Guillermo started it just last year."

"Time does not tradition make!" scoffed the paunchy percussionist. "It's traditional because it's awesome. Before gigs, we always slap the cheese."

Ben stared blankly at the golden slice, completely bewildered. Slap the cheese?

Dylan explained, "Basically, when Mo was a kid, he decided that he really liked the feeling of sliced cheese in its packaging. One day, out of the blue, he tried slapping it."

"It was completely spontaneous!" cried Guillermo, excited by the memory. "Cheese had never done anything wrong by me!"

"Anyway, child Mo thought this was a revelation," continued Dylan, "And last year, he decided to share the joy with us."

Guillermo held the cheese out and straightened his spine deliberately, as if the slap to come were a very serious matter, indeed. "Now I know there might be some metaphor to be made—"

"Or *innuendo*," inserted Olivia.

"—But the fact is, we don't need a reason. Slapping the cheese is fun, and I'm certain it makes us sing better."

"Well, I don't know about that," muttered Sid.

"Scientifically proven!" said Guillermo, as if his confidence alone could make it true. "Now everyone circle up. We're gonna slap and pass along."

Taylor suddenly noticed the outline of a square in Guillermo's jacket pocket. "Hey, is that a whole *package* of cheese?" he asked. "Did you run by the store for this? Is that why you were late?"

"Less talking, more SLAPPING!" With this brusque proclamation, the vocal percussionist gave the cheese a forceful hit. After so much anticipation, the only sound was a small crackle of the plastic wrap. Guillermo's face lit up and the whole group laughed, including Taylor.

Guillermo passed the cheese slice along to an extremely hesitant Renee.

"Just SLAP IT, sillyface!"

Renee's slap was a quick little thump with her middle finger—swift and sharp. A smile stretched across her face.

"Fun, right?" Guillermo asked.

Renee nodded fervently. "Oh yeah."

As the singers passed the cheese slice around, no two Chorderoys hit it the same way. For Olivia, the slap was a definite spank. By contrast, Violet's was an affectionate pat.

"No, no," chastised Guillermo. "You've got to *slap* the cheese."

After staring at the cheese for some time, channeling some hidden component of her personality, Violet finally gave the cheese a real disciplinary hit. The group laughed so loud that Taylor had to calm them. "They'll hear us out in the auditorium!"

Meanwhile, the audience was watching a photographic slideshow of the underprivileged children they were helping, completely oblivious to the cheese slappage occurring backstage.

The Chorderoys moved the cheese around the circle, slapping and giggling, making comments like "*Nice* slap" and "Ooh, that was a good one," when they suddenly heard the emcee's voice over the speakers. They filed in line beside the door to the stage. Ben heard a muffled voice mention "the Chorderoys" and suddenly they were filing onstage, facing those overpoweringly bright and hot spotlights.

The Chorderoys formed their two lines and curved into an arc. Ben, shorter than most of the men in the group, was in the front row with most of the girls. "Woohoo! Go Big Ben!" he heard a familiar voice shout from the balcony. The ironic nickname only reinforced his front-row placement.

Sid blew the pitch pipe and counted off the starting tempo . . .

It was only about halfway through "Ain't No Mountain High Enough/She Will Be Loved" that Ben realized consciously that he was singing before hundreds of people. His brain registered his surroundings in flashes: Violet's smiling to his left, Sid's discreet conducting to his right, and out in front, Olivia's shimmying and Taylor's rhythmic bopping.

Between songs, Ben spotted Wilson and his floor-mates in the front-row center of the balcony. Wilson was grinning from ear to ear, either exceptionally proud of his charitable contribution, or—more likely—excited for the opportunity to make more a cappella jokes.

As the group began "Your Song," Ben tried to remember Sid's tips for tone and musicality. The voices surrounding him were familiar, but with subtle acoustic differences. Now with his own bass mic, Gary's low notes were louder and more resonant than in the practice room. And sandwiched between Violet and Renee, Ben heard their choral *voo*'s immediately in his ears and a split-second later in the echo of the sound system.

But the biggest surprise was the pause before the end of "Your Song." Ben knew to expect a moment of silence following their group *Ahhh*, when their thirteen voices cut off in unison before continuing again. What he didn't expect was such a *loud* silence. The quiet itself seemed to reverberate throughout the vast interior of the chapel.

In spite of the blazing spotlights, Ben got chills.

On Sid's cue, the block of singers came back in, ending the sweet love song with a gradual *decrescendo*.

There was another extended, though less pronounced, silence, then more clapping. The Chorderoys bunched together for a group bow.

A moment later, they were all back in the offstage waiting room, where the Notabelles were preparing to

135

sing next. The all-female group's president stared suspiciously at the yellow slice of cheese that had re-emerged from Guillermo's pocket.

Dylan patted his friend's back. "Hungry boy."

The Chorderoys snuck through the back hall and down into the chapel basement, where they could talk more loudly, for smiles and congratulatory hugs. "I love you all!" Nicole cried.

Guillermo promised to keep everyone informed about the afterparty he was organizing. "I'll try my hardest," he said gravely, as if party-planning were the most important responsibility of this event.

So as not to disturb the concert, the Chorderoys waited until the Notabelles had finished their set to claim seats in the back of the chapel. As Ben watched the remaining groups sing, he realized that in little less than a month, he'd already started to view a cappella differently. Before, it had just been impressions and attitudes; now, he was singling out specific attributes—movement, blend, tone, dynamics.

To Ben's relief, it was still fun to watch, despite the technical development of his musical ear. The Dinos' *High School Musical* medley made him happier than he'd care to admit to someone like Wilson, and he laughed throughout La*chaim's parody, "Jewish Paradise," a re-imagining of "Gangster's Paradise." (*Spun a dreidel once or twice / Always take my mom's advice / I'm nice and circumcised, livin' in a Jewish Paradise.*) The Gobfellas once again sang their striptease version of "Let's Get It Started," which was still sort of funny, even on its thousandth rendition.

When the Harmoniums took the stage, Dani's alto voice still wowed Ben. But unlike the Recruitment Con-cert, she no longer had his full attention during "I Can't Make You Love Me." Ben kept peering *behind* the soloist

136

at the slim soprano in the corner of the block. Caroline looked especially elegant in her black dress and Harmonium-red sash, her dark hair shimmering in the spotlight, smiling as she sang the high harmony part. She seemed happy with her new group.

As the concert ended, the song "We Are The World" came over the loudspeakers, as if to underscore the well-meaning grandiosity of the event organizers.

Wilson rushed over to greet his roommate. "Dude, I'm busting this move out at parties from now on," he said, demonstrating his hyperactive take on the acabop, bouncing up and down, shadowboxing to an imagined beat. "Gonna get me all the ladies."

But Ben's other friends surprised him; instead of poking fun, they seemed genuinely interested in the details—how the Chorderoys picked their songs, who arranged their music, how they memorized their parts. "Can you do the mouth drum thing?" asked Ben's floor-mate.

"What? Oh, you mean V.P.!" He remembered Guillermo's *boots, skirts* lesson and shook his head. "No. Not yet, at least."

"V.P. is an abbreviation for 'vocal percussion,'" Wilson explained, although Ben wasn't sure how he knew this. "Acatypes are always abrev'ing."

Their conversation was interrupted by a familiar voice. "Hey, Ben!" Caroline motioned him over to where she was standing. "I want you to meet *Elliot*!"

As Ben walked over, he sized up his competition: Elliot's long brown bangs fell ever-so-casually to one side. Trimmed masculine whiskers shadowed his face. A single poof of chest hair spilled over his faded gray button-up. His kneecap poked through what seemed to be a delib-erate hole in his skinny, skinny jeans.

He stood *over* Ben, slim, slender, and with a permanent slouch, like a condescending crane.

The boys shook hands.

"Elliot just flew in from Berkeley . . ." said Caroline, beginning what was, for Ben at least, a very uncomfortable introduction:

He was her boyfriend of two—count 'em—two years. Now in school in California, Elliot was designing his own major in Music Journalism. Apparently, the University's music quarterly was too "jejune," so he'd sought "real" work in journalism, freelancing for an area magazine.

Elliot proceeded to list all the band names he'd been covering on the west coast. When the tenor recognized a band name, he felt a pang of jealousy; when he didn't, he felt fierce annoyance—how pretentious!

Worst of all, meeting Elliot confirmed Ben's most terrible suspicion: His favorite soprano was long-distance-dating a *hipster*.

Ben played guitar, ragged on Top 40 radio, read *McSweeney's*, and generally prided himself on avoiding musical clichés. That is to say, Ben wasn't the least pretentious guy at Brighton. But he was an old-fashioned, awkward nerd at heart, not the kind whose knowledge made him feel superior to others. He was no hipster.

Ben stared at the black canvas shoes of the opposition, trying to think of possible weaknesses. Perhaps he could emphasize their different interests. "You got a huge dose of a cappella music tonight," Ben muttered. "How'd it compare to all those 'real' bands?"

A wry grin stretched across Elliot's face. He raised his thick eyebrows. "Actually, I love this stuff."

Caroline smiled and grabbed her boyfriend's lanky arm. "Elliot and I *met* in high school show choir," she explained.

Suddenly, Greg Hollis wrapped his arm collegially around Elliot's shoulder. The Dinos' president was always popping in—a cheerful gopher, always right on cue. "Don't be deceived by the avant-garde persona. This kid's singing voice sounds like *butter*. He's a natural crooner." Greg turned and gave Elliot his standard handshake-turned-hug.

Ben stared in disbelief. The too-cool hipster saw all the best bands, but appreciated a cappella. He went way back with Greg, one of the nicest guys Ben knew. And he could sing. It appeared, Ben thought, that the universe truly was aligned against him.

Greg, Elliot, and Caroline proceeded to reminisce about their old show choir days, and when Ben couldn't take the mushiness anymore, he excused himself.

The other Chorderoys freshmen were chatting in the upstairs balcony. When Ben walked up, Akash said, "I think we might grab a bite at the cafeteria while we wait to see if this afterparty materializes. You interested?"

Ben nodded, eager to further remove himself from the hipsteria.

Renee shook her head sadly. "Wish I could, but there's a dive meet early tomorrow," she explained. "I shouldn't stay out."

Akash's face lit up. "Oh really? Is the meet here at Brighton?"

"No, across town, sort of a long drive." Renee hesitated, then added, "But there'll be other meets on campus."

"Great! Well, I'll have to come and cheer you on," said Akash. He caught himself, and corrected, "Err . . . *we'll* have to cheer you on . . . me and the other Chorderoys, I mean." He smiled sheepishly. "Dive good tomorrow err . . . dive well. Score high and stuff!"

139

Renee grinned and said goodnight.

Before Ben could ask Akash about that curious interaction, Wilson interrupted them. "I heard something about food!" he said. "I'm in— if you'll accept a non-singer in your company, that is."

They were, of course, perfectly willing to accept a non-singer, but Ben was a little surprised that Wilson wanted to hang out with them instead of going to the party that was in full swing on Frat Row. Nonetheless, the three remaining Chorderoys freshmen proceeded with Wilson to the central campus cafeteria.

Ben and Akash had gotten their food and were waiting in the cafeteria booth when Nicole walked over with a bowl of pasta primavera. The theatrical alto wore the strangest expression, smiling and furrowing her brow at once. "Your friend just asked me if I wanted to get coffee sometime." All of a sudden, Wilson's request to join them made sense.

"Wilson?!" Ben exclaimed. "Did you say yes?!?"

Nicole shrugged and nodded. "He seems . . . intriguing." Suddenly thoughtful, she said, "I'll be right back," and scurried off to the bathroom.

Wilson strolled over with a bowl of linguine and meat sauce and two cheesy breadsticks for dipping.

"You asked out Nicole in the *pasta line*?"

Wilson shrugged. "When in Rome," he quipped.

Akash laughed. Ben shook his head.

The group had nearly finished their late-night dinner when Ben, Akash, and Nicole's cell phones buzzed in rapid succession. Ben read Guillermo's text message aloud: "'Acaparty is ON. Hollis and I are combining forces.'"

"'Bring your A game,'" read Nicole. "What does that even mean?"

140

There was a sudden gleam in Wilson's eye. "Wait, can non-a cappella people attend these parties?"

"Probably," said Ben cautiously. "Why? Are you interested?"

Wilson looked at Nicole, then back at his roommate. He shrugged. "Sure. Something to do."

But Ben wasn't about to let him off so easily. "You've been making fun of a cappella people for weeks—what could possibly persuade you to choose an acaparty over Frat Row?"

Wilson rolled his eyes. "Just think how much fun it will be for me to see all you acatypes together in the same place. What a spectacle! There'll be dancing and cheering. Singing. Everyone will be harmonizing."

"Just because it's an a cappella party doesn't mean people will be singing," said Ben, though as soon as the words were out, he doubted them.

"How would you know? You haven't been to one yet!" cried Wilson. "I'm expecting real-life musical theater. Everyone's gonna break into spontaneous song and magically know all the dance moves."

Nicole's face lit up, as if the most sublime vision had just passed before her eyes. "That'd be amazing!"

Ben just shook his head.

"Or maybe they'll have a bunch of instruments there and you'll have to smash them in protest with baseball bats!" offered Wilson. He raised an angry fist and demonstrated. "Screw you, REAL drum set. I've got my V.P.!"

"Maybe the playlist will consist entirely of Disney songs and show tunes and boy bands," said Nicole wistfully.

"Maybe there'll be a bouncer, and before you can enter, he'll make you sing those 'Carol of the Bells' and

'Shenandoah' arrangements we all learned in high school choir," suggested Akash.

"Hey, I remember those!" said Wilson.

"Without changing keys midway through," clarified Ben.

"Crap. I'm screwed!"

Everyone laughed, and they continued joking about hyperbolic a cappella afterparties, secretly wondering which ideas were completely ridiculous and which contained the tiniest grains of truth.

♬ |

Chapter 12

Afterparty

As the four freshmen walked to the a cappella after-party, Wilson kept listing his ridiculous expectations for the event: "Spontaneous outbursts of song, fully choreographed show tunes, fistfights over the superiority of *Aladdin* versus *The Lion King* . . ."

But when they arrived at Guillermo's off-campus apartment, the four freshmen encountered nothing quite so grand. Guillermo and Dylan were playing Beer Pong on a narrow table in the living room. Eight or nine people from various singing groups were scattered throughout the room, conversing in little clumps with others from their ensemble. An indiscernible hip-hop song played over portable iPod speakers; with each bass pulse, the tiny speakers rattled like crinkly aluminum foil.

"We have Greg's apartment, too, for when there's overflow," called out Guillermo as the freshmen approached. He motioned to his apartment's side entrance off the kitchen.

Wilson turned to his fellow freshmen. "What overflow?" He sighed, thoroughly disappointed. "This party's a bust. Ten minutes and I'm heading to Frat Row."

Greg seemed to have heard him, which was either proof of his extraordinary hearing or, more likely, proof that the party was, indeed, pretty lame. In any case, he walked over and put his hand on Ben's shoulder. "Stick around. It'll heat up soon."

Laughing to himself, Greg said, "Taylor's coming, and I know you're dying to party with your super-cool TA.

Caroline will be here, too. With Elliot, of course." He gave the freshman a sympathetic look. "Although, I get the sense you'd prefer she come solo."

Ben's jaw dropped. How did Greg know? But before he had time to ask, one of the Dinos called Greg over. "Gotta run!" said the co-host. "Help yourself to drinks!"

On the way to the kitchen, Nicole asked Akash to hold her purse while she went to the bathroom. "Just for a minute," she said sweetly.

Wilson took a long time exploring the selection of beverages in the refrigerator, taking special delight in suggesting all of the most stereotypically girly options for his singing roommate. "Coconut rum? Peach schnapps? Cherry appletini?" He pulled a beer out of the fridge and leaned against the kitchen counter. "You know, Akash, buddy, I like you. You're actually pretty cool, for one of these acatypes."

Ben groaned.

"And as your friend, I was wondering," continued Wilson, "Have you noticed Nicole asking you for many *favors* this week?"

Akash stared down at the purse he was holding. "What do you mean?"

"Little things here and there," said Wilson casually, "Like getting her silverware. Refilling her soda. Sharing your fries. Things like that."

Ben thought back, and remembered that Akash had, in fact, performed these tasks for Nicole back at the cafeteria. But what was Wilson getting at? These were all neutral gestures.

"Interesting that she's been asking you, specifically," observed Wilson, wearing his most devilish grin. "Very interesting."

Suddenly, Ben understood his roommate's implication, and he was simultaneously amused and appalled. "Oh, come on! That's ridiculous!"

"Why?" asked Wilson indignantly. "She's in our same lecture!"

Akash stared back and forth, confused. "What're you talking about?"

"The Self-Perception Theory, or SPT," explained Ben. "It's something we learned in Psych 100."

"Wait!" interrupted Akash. He turned to Ben. "You're in Psychology? Psych, politics, philosophy, music, finance . . . what's your major, Ben?"

"He's undecided," sighed Wilson, acting the beleaguered parent. "Hopelessly undecided." Unlike Ben, Wilson was 100% sold on his Psychology major. He'd heard it was the best route for law school.

"Anyway," continued Ben, "The SPT is an explanation for how our attitudes change. The traditional approach said that attitudes come before behaviors: We feel this way about this, therefore we act accordingly."

"Okay . . ."

"But the SPT turns everything around!" interjected Wilson, thrilled by the reversal. "It says attitudes are the *result* of people's actions. People act a certain way, and afterwards they try to rationalize it by adjusting their attitudes to fit those behaviors."

"I guess so," muttered Akash. Currently, Akash was in the pre-med program, planning to become a physician like his father and grandfather. Ben got the impression that Akash might have inherited the MD's traditional skepticism of psychology as a "science."

"Hang on. This has a point," said Ben, hurrying to explain before Nicole returned from the bathroom. "Last week, our professor was talking about how the SPT operates in relationships. The theory infers that having someone do favors for you could strengthen the bond between those two people. The person performing the favor subconsciously thinks, 'Hey, I'm helping this person: I must like her a lot.' The attitude would then conform to fit the behavior."

"Soon enough, a full-blown romance is born!" said Wilson, wide-eyed.

Akash hesitated. "So . . . you think Nicole is asking me favors in order to—"

"Seduce you, yes," finished Wilson. He smiled and nodded. "She might have said yes to me in the coffee line, but it's *your* bod she wants, man."

When Nicole returned, she took back her purse and thanked Akash. After rummaging through the refrigerator for a Diet Coke, she handed Akash the bottle. "Could you open it? I'm terrible at these things."

Wilson smirked as Akash twisted the cap, which came off easily.

People continued to stroll into the party gradually, forming more separate clumps of conversation as they arrived. They stuck mostly to their own small circles, with minimal group-to-group interaction.

Slowly, though, the atmosphere improved, aided by enhancements to the background music. Someone found a bigger speaker in the adjoining apartment and switched out the mp3 player. The first song on the new playlist was a classic—"Jessie's Girl" by Rick Springfield.

Akash wasn't consciously aware when he started singing the bass line: *Doom-ba, Doom-ba, Doom-ba* / *Doom-ba, Doom-ba, Doom-ba.*

Ben looked around and saw someone like Akash in every circle: a guy moving his lips, singing 'bass,' acting as if nothing were out of the ordinary. The a cappella-cizing was instinctual.

"Here it comes," groaned Wilson.

The song "Super Bass" brought actual dancing, albeit within each small social clump. Wilson teased Ben's attempt at rapping. "Take it easy, Nicki Minaj!"

Violet walked over with a wine cooler. Her cheeks were flush. "Where's Rey-rey?" she cried. Violet's nickname for her "soprano baby" was a drunken innovation; fortunately, she would soon forget it.

Akash told her about the dive meet.

"Oh, no! But she's my favorite!" Suddenly worried, she added, "But I love you all, too." The maternal soprano gave each of them a sloppy hug, even Wilson.

As Violet walked off, the freshmen laughed amongst themselves. (There's something intrinsically funny about seeing one's elders tipsy, even if the age difference is relatively small.)

By "Party in the USA," the beginnings of a dance circle had formed in the living room, although it was still rather amorphous, an amoeba of smaller circles poised to bud off again if awkwardness struck. All around him, Ben heard voices singing Miley Cyrus's *harmony* line! Dozens of girls, and more than a few adventurous guys, were singing up the third!

"At this rate, I'm going to need another," Wilson groaned, rolling his eyes. When he came back with his drink, the dance mob was singing "Since You've Been Gone."

For a short while, Ben found himself dancing with Caroline, who'd apparently lost Elliot for the moment. Just for fun, Ben jumped up to Kelly Clarkson's octave, singing in his highest falsetto. Caroline laughed and grinned.

147

But then, at the start of the next song, a new crowd joined their portion of the dance blob. Caroline was pushed inward – Ben outward – and suddenly the tenor was separated back into his original Chorderoys cluster.

During the techno beat of DJ Sammy's "Heaven," Ben noticed a group of three dancers at the fringe of the circle: Taylor, Olivia, and Greg. The tall alto was in the middle, while the two guys danced on either side. Ben thought it was an unusual coupling, but wasn't sure what to make of it. It was clear from Taylor's cheeks—bright red shining through his fading summer tan—that the group president had a few drinks in him, too.

The songs flowed into each other. During Flo Rida's "Club Can't Handle Me," some Dinos demonstrated "the worm" move. La*chaim's Rachel Stein started the line dancing during "Cotton-Eyed Joe." T-Pain's "Low" evolved into an impromptu "booty drop" competition. Guillermo was the clear winner, slapping the ground and coming up slow for sustained "booty drop" action.

When Aerosmith's "I Don't Want to Miss A Thing" came on, Wilson gave his first indication that he might be overindulging himself. Ben corrected his roommate's lyrical error. "Surrender! Not Suspenders!" Ben yelled.

But Wilson couldn't hear Ben's corrections, just like he could never hear when he was sharp or flat. He was simply singing at the top of his lungs, and with increasingly fewer inhibitions.

From the corner of his eye, Ben could see Caroline and Elliot. They were swing dancing, swinging in and out, touching arm to chest. Caroline even did a little "spin-around" with the hipster, which Ben found both completely inappropriate for Aersosmith, and disgustingly cute.

Meanwhile, Gobfellas president Derek Ross was shrieking painfully during the bridge, arrogantly behaving as if he could out-sing Steven Tyler. During one of his excessive riffs, he stumbled drunkenly back into Akash. "Watch where you're going, asswipe!" snapped Derek.

Ben had never seen Akash glare at anybody, much less so angrily.

Nicole came up to them. "I'm thirsty!" she yelled above the music, directing her comment at Akash. "Want to get some water with me?"

Nearby, Wilson broke into hysterical laughter, and accidentally spilt some of his beer on Kara from the Notabelles. Disgusted, she danced away from their side of the circle.

Wilson was oblivious. "SPT! SPT!" he chanted.

"What's he talking about?" asked Nicole, confused.

"Nothing," Ben lied. He stared over at Elliot and Caroline. They'd clasped their hands and were singing the final lines to each other. Although Ben obviously couldn't hear him through the dance mob, he imagined hipster Elliot's perfect crooner voice singing, as Greg described, "like butter." He felt nauseous.

Ben turned to his fellow newbies. "Stay here. I'll bring you that water."

As Ben fought his way back through the crowd, Bon Jovi came on. Even in the presence of so many big voices, Ben could hear Wilson belting out "You Give Love a Bad Name." He looked back to see his roommate aiming an imaginary rifle at his heart.

Once Ben had edged his way out of the circle, he walked through the living room, out into the hall, and into the other apartment, where there was indeed an "overflow" of guests, exactly as Greg had predicted.

149

Dani was standing in the kitchen, drinking her freshly mixed martini, leaning against the counter, alone.

"Hello, Ben Jensen," she said. "How's the party?"

"Um . . . it's pretty good," said Ben, eyeing her drink suspiciously. A green cloud surrounded the olive at the base of her glass.

Dani pointed to a clear handle of gin, a jar of olives, and a mini bottle of vermouth. "Always my contribution to the party," explained the Harmoniums' president. She lifted her cocktail; it shimmered in the light. "Want one?"

Ben shook his head. "I was just getting some water." He scooted past her and filled a plastic cup. Ben wanted to bring it to Nicole immediately, but felt guilty leaving Dani there without having a real conversation—it seemed immature. He went with the first topic that came to mind: The party itself. "It was really quiet here when I first arrived."

Dani smiled. "Fascinating how it heats up, isn't it? There's always that initial inter-group aloofness at the beginning of the year. It's a hangover from auditions, you see."

Ben tilted his head. "What do you mean?"

"Well, auditions are quite competitive, Ben, you've no doubt picked up on that," she said, swirling the wide-brimmed glass in her fingertips. "Everyone wants the same talented people, so there's a natural tendency to cling to one's own group. A primitive 'Us' versus 'Them' mentality."

Dani pushed back a strand of strawberry blonde hair and took another sip of martini. "That's the mode we're in at the beginning of the year, at least. It takes some time before we warm up and get reacquainted." She sighed. "Assuming we were ever really acquainted to begin with. The real tragedy, in my opinion, is that so many a cappella singers apply the so-called 'Limited Contact' rule against each other."

The Harmoniums' president eyed him closely. "There really shouldn't be so much distance between us. Not when we're all so much alike."

The word "alike" reminded Ben of the crowd on the dance floor. He wondered whether there might be some truth to Wilson's notion of an "acatype."

"Do you think that a cappella people have similar personalities?" Ben asked.

Dani beamed at the question. "In some ways, certainly. We're bound together by a serious love for music."

The Harmoniums president expounded upon her views of Brighton's a cappella culture, and as she spoke, she once again commanded Ben's full attention. Maybe it was her speaking style, nonchalant and confident, with perfect pitch inflections. There was also her frankness, speaking openly of tensions and rivalries. For whatever reason, Ben was enthralled. He sat on the kitchen counter and, having forgotten his original purpose, drank from Nicole's cup of water.

After reflecting on Dani's words, Ben said, "Auditions competition explains why the older members distance themselves from the other groups. But what about the newbies? Why aren't they out meeting everyone in Brighton's a cappella scene?"

Dani smiled softly. "Well, the newbies have an auditions hangover, too, don't they?" She leaned forward. "Don't tell me you haven't felt it."

Ben thought of Caroline and the nagging feeling he had that she'd changed their agreed-upon group rankings. They still hadn't discussed their final choices.

"A little," he admitted.

151

"Of course you have," said Dani quickly. "We all have questions. For instance, I ask things like 'What did they think of us?' and 'What factors went into their decision?'"

Her eyes locked onto his. "And 'Why didn't they rank us *first?*'"

The tenor knew that he'd been targeted. His heart pounded in his chest. Thinking fast, he redirected. "Well, what's your solution?"

Dani wasn't expecting the volley. "Pardon?"

Ben cleared his throat. "You say these unresolved questions are bad, that they prevent solid intergroup friendships. If they're such a problem, what's your proposed solution?"

Dani thought for a moment. "*Dialogue,*" she finally answered. "Mutually initiated conversation. Only talking will put our minds at ease."

"Mutually initiated conversation," repeated Ben, softly. He liked the phrase.

"Exactly," said Dani, straightening her spine. "And who knows what may evolve from our conversations. Internalizing our feelings leads to nowhere; we simply must keep talking."

With sadness, Ben thought back to the image of Elliot and Caroline in each other's arms, and the very particular emotions he'd been keeping inside.

The ringing cell phone interrupted his contemplating. "One moment," he told Dani. "Wilson? WHAT!?! Wait —where are you? Right. Okay. Yes. Yes. I'll be right there."

Ben hung up the phone and pushed himself off the counter. "I've got to go. My friend . . . Well, it's a weird situation, but he needs me."

Dani nodded. She took another sip of martini. "I'd like to keep conversing, Ben Jensen. For potential's sake."

She smiled. He smiled back.

"Good night, Dani," he said, and left to find Akash on the dance floor.

As he and Akash walked up the street away from the apartment, Ben explained the situation: They were going to rescue Wilson, who had been instructed to call friends to escort him home.

The cop car was a few blocks away. Wilson and the officer were standing outside on the sidewalk, talking. Ben's roommate shifted his feet uneasily from foot to foot.

The police officer was a stocky man with ruddy cheeks, bushy brows, and a smooth bald head that shone yellow in the spotlight. He looked tired and cranky. "You two friends with this guy?"

Ben nodded. Clearing his throat, he asked, "What's the problem, Officer?"

"Noise violation," said the cop. "Disturbing the peace. Seems this guy was *singing* as he walked. Only thing is, the neighbors didn't appreciate his serenade."

The officer pulled out a notepad and read from it. "2:13 A.M. Neighbor phones in. Reports drunken boy singing. Off-key. Repeating words 'I'll make a man out of you!' Please make him stop.

"2:17 A.M. Different neighbor. Identifies song as 'Circle of Life' from *The Lion King*. Rendition is 'painful,' 'offensive.'

"2:22 A.M. First neighbor, again. Boy still singing. Direct quote - 'If you don't shut him up, I'm going to go out there and . . .'" The officer glanced up without finishing. "You see the problem?"

Wilson, having been forced to sober up quickly, kept his voice low and stared humbly at the sidewalk. "I'm sorry, Officer. I was walking back from . . . a friend's house and . . . I just wasn't thinking."

"Of course you weren't," said the officer, shaking his shiny head. "You three freshmen?"

They nodded.

"Of course you are," huffed the policeman. He paused for what felt like a very long time. "I'll tell you what I'm going to do: I'm not going to issue a citation. I'm not going to take you in. But this is a one-time deal. If this happens again, I'm going to book you with everything I can charge, *including* underage drinking. Understand?"

"Yes, Officer," said the boys in unison.

The policeman turned to Ben and Akash. "And *you* two, when you're at a party and you've got a friend who's so sloshed he's gonna walk back belting show tunes, be a buddy and walk him home. Keep each other from making fools of yourselves, alright?"

"It won't happen again," said Akash seriously.

"Good. Now I suggest you three walk home together. Quietly. And be safe." The officer wore the faintest hint of a smile on his face. "No more singing."

There was a chorus of "Yes, Officer" and "Thank you, Officer." The policeman nodded a curt goodbye, got back into the patrol car, and drove away.

For a while, the three freshman just stared quietly at the curb.

Finally, Ben broke the silence. "*The Lion King?*"

"*Mulan?*" said Akash.

"Your stupid a cappella party rubbed off on me!" cried Wilson, his voice still trembling. But as the minutes passed and they began walking, he relaxed enough to smile at his own absurdity. "Touché, fellas. *Touché.*"

Akash's phone beeped. He read the message. "Nicole's wondering where we went. She wants to walk home with us."

"Only you got a text?" said Wilson. "Wow, this chick is really working the Self-Perception Theory!"

"Shh! Keep your voice down," said Ben. The neighborhood surrounding campus was virtually crime-free—except for the occasional noise violation—but Ben nevertheless felt a duty to walk Nicole home. He also felt a little guilty for never bringing her that water. "We should go back and get her."

So the three walked back to the apartment, where the afterparty was finally losing steam. All that remained was a dedicated, but increasingly fatigued, chorus of partiers swaying in a circle, belting the lyrics to Mika's "Happy Ending."

The boys found Nicole, and the four freshmen trekked back to campus together, talking quietly, with Ben and Wilson walking out in front. "Minus your run-in with the law, would you say the acaparty was a success?"

"Err, it was decent," said Wilson. No longer happily uninhibited, he was back to his usual anti-a cappella teasing. "I hope I didn't lose too much masculinity back there."

In response, Ben quietly hummed the tune of *Mulan*'s "I'll Make a Man Out Of You." They both laughed.

Sometime later, Ben looked back and saw Akash with his arm around Nicole's shoulder.

"She's tired," Akash explained.

Ben nodded. When he turned back, his almost-criminal roommate had that mischievous gleam in his eye.

"SPT!" he whispered.

♫ |

Chapter 13

Solos

"UGH!" groaned Guillermo. "I need a breakfast burrito to settle my stomach!"

It was the Sunday afternoon on the day following the Tunes for Transformation afterparty, and the Chorderoys were all in pretty poor shape. The past hour of singing had been under pitch *and* lacking in energy, the worst combination for producing decent-sounding a cappella.

Dylan was even too tired to crack a joke. "Me too," he grumbled.

Ben watched as Sid gently attempted to salvage the practice. Since most people had damaged their voices by singing loudly and shouting during the festivities, the music director had the group speak, rather than sing, the rhythms of the new songs they were learning. After that, he worked on the blocking of the songs, identifying where singers of each part should stand within the double arc and physically rearranging their positions accordingly.

Ultimately, the music director simply had to resign. "We'll end a little early today," he said, after a lackluster attempt at speaking through their latest ballad. "But next practice, we're going to be auditioning the solo for 'Use Somebody.' Every guy should learn the solo part and be prepared to try out."

When practice ended, the sophomore men rushed straight to the campus taquería.

Solo auditions were something Ben hadn't really considered before he'd been drafted into the Chorderoys, but they had nonetheless been a big part of the year so far. For each new song, singers with a given voice type

157

auditioned for the leading part; afterwards, the rest of the group would vote on their top choices for the solo.

Thus far, Ben thought the group's solo choices had been reasonable and, for the most part, predictable. Nicole McLain waltzed into the solo for Adele's "Chasing Pavements." Her treatment of the song as a heartbreaking musical monologue was actually very close to the original. Olivia, unsurprisingly, nailed the sensuality of Lady Gaga's "Pokerface." And Taylor was the clear choice for "The Show Must Go On" by Queen. What he lacked in Freddie Mercury's stage presence, he compensated for with his sheer (vocal) angst.

But when Ben arrived at the Chorderoys' next practice, he was less certain about who would take that evening's solo. "Use Somebody" by Kings of Leon was a loud power ballad with an earnest, alternative feel. In describing his arrangement of the song, Sid had repeatedly emphasized the background echoing the soloist's "cry for direction." Since the solo had a fairly accessible range, the music director encouraged all of the men in the group to try out, creating a wider-than-normal playing field.

Before the individual solo auditions that Tuesday, the Chorderoy men sang a few verses in unison to ensure they knew the basic melody. As they sang together in a circle, Ben could *feel* the differences between each of the other male voices: Taylor's was brighter; Sid's smoother; Akash's breathier; Guillermo's louder; Dylan's lighter; Gary's barely audible. Unlike singing in the block, there was no single "correct" interpretation of the solo line.

Then came the actual tryouts. Ben's hands shook as Sid called him up. It now occurred to him that he cared very much what the rest of the group thought of his voice, even more so than in his initial audition: Now, he knew his judges personally.

The freshman tenor sang through the first verse and chorus two times, and before he could think much about it, it was time for all of the men in the group to leave the room so that the ladies could deliberate on what they had just heard.

For about fifteen minutes, the banished men sat on the floor in the hallway outside the rehearsal room, chatting amongst themselves, with Dylan and Guillermo continuing to rave about how the taco shop had miraculously cured their Sunday hangovers. When the door opened, the guys stood up to go back inside.

"Not all of you," said Joanna. "We've got a tie, so we're going to invite all but the top two to come in and help us vote."

The tall athletic junior seemed to be taking her role as assistant music director even more seriously than normal. "Ben and Sid, please stay outside. The rest of you, we'd like you to come help with our decision."

As the men walked in, Ben felt the stares on him. Akash gave him a surreptitious thumbs-up.

Taylor was less subtle. As he walked by, he patted Sid on the shoulder. "It would be a good first, buddy."

The rest of the men walked back into the classroom, leaving Sid and Ben on the floor of the Music School hallway, alone.

Ben cleared his throat. "Sid, have you not had a solo before?"

The philosophically inclined music director shook his head, and answered in his always calming tone of voice, "A solo? No, not yet."

Ben couldn't believe it! Four years in the Chorderoys, and Sid hadn't gotten a solo? What could possibly be the

159

explanation? He thought of Sid's creative musical arrange-ments, his perfect pitch, the way he memorized all four parts for each song. The music director was clearly very talented. And while Sid's voice was perhaps softer than most, Ben knew it was good.

It seemed the music director could hear his thoughts. "I don't take it personally. The Chorderoys haven't really sung a song that fits my voice yet, at least not during my time. And, trust me, it never works to force it. Something as delicate as music cannot be rigged. It's about picking the best singer for the song, not seniority."

Ben nodded, although he wasn't sure he fully agreed with Sid's point. After putting so much effort into the group as music director, he thought Sid simply *deserved* the opportunity to be showcased, whether or not that opportunity was rigged.

At that moment, the door creaked open, and Joanna invited them both inside.

Both men waited silently at the front of the room.

Joanna made the formal announcement:

"Congratulations, Mr. Jensen."

Ben felt his jaw drop and hang loose. His eyes glazed over. He looked like a child who'd just forgotten he could breathe through his nose.

There was a chorus of congratulations.

When Ben looked back, the music director nodded his way. "Congratulations," he said. "We're out of time for now, but we'll run through it first thing next practice." With that, Sid ducked his head and quickly exited the rehearsal room

The group stared out the door after him.

Guillermo broke the silence. "I think he has GRE class tonight."

Ben frowned, not so sure. He knew Sid was in the process of studying for the entrance exam and preparing applications for graduate schools, but it wasn't at all like him to dart out right after practice.

Nicole flung her arms around Ben for a hug, temporarily interrupting his worrying. "ANOTHER freshman soloist! Go US! Congratulations! You *totally* fit the part!"

As Nicole went on about how excited she was for him, Ben felt his cell phone vibrate. He glanced at the message: MEET ME IN PRACTICE ROOM 12 WHEN YOU GET OUT. LET'S CONTINUE OUR CONVERSATION.

Ben knew that if he stuck around much longer, he would probably be invited to celebrate with his fellow newbies at Badger's Café. Normally, this would be great, but this was a message he didn't want to ignore.

He politely excused himself, and walked quickly down the hall and up to the top floor of the Music School, to the row of soundproof piano practice rooms.

As Ben walked in, Dani was playing "Für Elise." She leaned in and out of the keys with her shoulders, milking each melancholy chord and lush arpeggio.

When she came to the final passage, her fingers floated off the keys. The notes hung gently in the air. She could be so graceful when she wanted to be.

"I didn't know you played piano."

Dani turned and shrugged. "*Everyone* knows 'Für Elise.' But yes, I took lessons for ten years."

"Impressive," said Ben. He'd been saying that word a lot the past few days. Since the Tunes for Transformation afterparty, he and Dani had indeed been "continuing their conversation." Ben was really enjoying their talks—Dani seemed to know something about all his favorite topics: pop culture, politics, indie music . . . even random things, like herbal teas and SNL trivia. After two months of

161

oddly stiff conversations with Caroline, it felt good to speak so freely!

Ben wondered, of course, whether these talks with Dani were leading to something more. And yet, Dani kept underscoring the practical utility of their friendship, how they were "setting the example" for others in the a cappella community. Oddly, Ben knew this professional distance made her seem even more attractive.

Dani smiled up at him. "How was practice?"

"Great," said Ben. He hesitated, not wanting to brag too much, and still feeling a little uncomfortable because of Sid. "Actually, I got my first solo. 'Use Somebody' by Kings of Leon."

"Congratulations, Ben Jensen!" She stood and gave him an enormous hug. "Of course, you're the shining star of the Chorderoys these days, so this is extremely predictable news!"

Ben wasn't sure how to interpret this, so he mumbled a "thank you."

"So, give me the play-by-play," said the Harmoniums' president, with wide, excited eyes. "Who were you up against? Was there a top two—top three? Who do you think voted for you? Better yet, who voted *against* you? That's juicier."

Ben tilted his head, stammering, "Um . . . I don't know err . . . not sure I should—"

"You're right. I'm so sorry." Dani nodded solemnly. "You're very right not to share. Gossip is one of my vices. But I know it, and I'm honest about it." She looked deep into his eyes. "Points for honesty, right?"

Ben relaxed, shrugged and smiled. "Sure."

She pushed back a loose strand of hair behind her ear. "Anyway, the solo is absolutely well deserved, but I'm *still* more interested in hearing about you as a person. So let's please continue our conversation! I want to hear more about the real Ben Jensen." By now, Ben had noticed the frequency with which she called him by his full name. The formality underscored her comparative air of sophistication.

Ben frowned, suddenly thoughtful.

"What's wrong?"

"It's just that, I feel like I've told you a lot about myself. I told you about my parents, my hometown, what I want to do with my life—"

"Something 'cool' that 'helps people,' if I remember correctly."

"Fine, it's vague, but at least it's honest!" Ben retorted. "And it's personal," he added defensively. He sighed. "But what have I learned about the real Dani Behlman? What's one of her secrets?"

Dani frowned. "Well, let me think . . ."

After only a few seconds' hesitation, she replied, "Okay, truthfully, I only played piano for *seven* years, not ten. I round up. I actually quit taking lessons in ninth grade and I've always been somewhat ashamed that— Hey! What's that face for? This is me being completely honest!"

Ben shook his head. "I know, I know. But going from 'really impressive' to 'slightly less impressive' isn't the kind of secret I had in mind."

"Fine," Dani huffed. "I'll think of something else."

The Harmoniums' president stared at the piano keys for a long while, as if she were drawing from them for inspiration. Suddenly, she grabbed Ben by the hand, and gave it a little squeeze. "Come with me. I'll *show* you my secret."

The sun was just beginning to dip as Ben and Dani walked across campus. It floated down slowly, its

163

brightness muted by an increasingly overcast sky. All around, there were the earliest traces of winter: less of fall's brilliant colors, more crispy brownness in the trees.

Dani led Ben to the massive student activities center, the headquarters for the many extracurricular groups on campus. In the foyer, students were playing ping-pong and pool while watching the game on big screen TVs.

The elder songstress led him up two flights of stairs and down a hallway Ben hadn't known existed. He passed signs for the KBUR campus radio station, and the official "weapons depository" for Garthnor, the University's medieval battle reenactment society. Ben sidestepped a plastic broadsword and spikey foam mace that had been left in their path.

When they came to an unmarked door at the end of the hall, Dani punched a numerical pass code into the keypad, and ushered him quickly inside.

"What is this place?"

Dani beamed. "The one, the only: Brighton A cappella Storage Room."

Ben's eyes widened as he absorbed his surroundings. The room was filled with boxes upon boxes of old a cappella group memorabilia—old concert programs, ancient group banners, mountains of unsold CDs. He picked up a raggedy box of Gobfellas cassette tapes that were cheesily titled "Gob Gob Gob, Gob Gobra Ann." He smiled at the excess candy from long-ago auditions seasons, the leftover enticements once used to lure singers into trying out.

While Ben explored, Dani rummaged through one particular box, looking for something specific. Finally, she held up a book with light blue binding. "The Chorderoys' old scrapbook," she explained.

Ben skimmed through the pages, spotting familiar settings like Roy's Diner and Blair Chapel. "Look at Sid's hair!" he cried. Three years ago, the future music director had sported an unruly 'fro. Now that he'd shaved it close, he looked far more distinguished, like the philosophy professor he hoped to become.

Dani interrupted by handing him another book, this one in red casing with gold string sewn into the binding. "The Harmoniums have one, too."

As Ben looked through the Harmoniums' scrapbook, he noticed one recurring picture: A shot of the new members on Draft Night each year, eating bacon and eggs, enjoying the Midnight Welcome Breakfast which Caroline had described. When he came to the photo of the Harmoniums' newbies from three years ago, Ben stopped to inspect it carefully.

"Notice anything?"

In fact, Ben had, but the thought was still working its way through the back of his mind—a twinge of discomfort, a sense that the pictures themselves were incomplete. He couldn't exactly put his finger on it.

Finally, it came to him: "You're not with them."

Ben looked up into Dani's eyes, bright and green, with the slightest hint of witness. He flipped through the other pages from that year, searching for evidence to the contrary, as if the picture from three years ago had to be a mistake.

"I'm not in there," said Dani. "I'm not with the Chorderoys, La*chaim, or the Notabelles, either."

Softly, she explained, "I didn't make *any* of the singing groups as a freshman. I tried out, of course, but I just didn't make it."

Ben stared at the floor, suddenly very uncomfortable. He thought back to the first time he heard Dani sing "I

Can't Make You Love Me." In his mind's ear, he heard Dani's powerful belt, her strong, crisp tone, her perfect dynamic control. There was no doubt in Ben's mind that Dani had an amazing voice—had always had an amazing voice—the kind of pure vocal talent with which a person can only be born.

"I don't get it," Ben muttered.

Dani shrugged. She sat down on one of the more stable-looking stacks of boxes and crossed her legs. "Why I didn't make it? Any number of reasons. Maybe I didn't blend well with the other singers during callbacks. I admit: Conforming to someone else's tone used to be quite difficult for me.

"Or, perhaps it was my personality. I'm not a laid-back person. When I want something, I make my wishes known. Sometimes genuine passion scares people off." Dani paused, inspecting Ben closely. "At least, that's what I'm told."

Ben shook his head, still confused. It seemed to him that the validity of the entire auditions method was now up for debate. What did it mean if good singers were never offered solos—weren't even invited into groups?

Dani caught Ben's eye, and held it. "And to be *especially* honest with you, Ben Jensen, I wasn't always so confident. In fact, I used to question whether or not I was actually a good singer." She straightened in her seat and continued stoically, "I've since trained myself not to have such doubts."

Ben stared down at the old Harmoniums photo, thinking carefully about how to phrase his question: "Were you . . . *okay* that year?"

Dani shook her head. "I was devastated. You see, I'm not like you, Ben Jensen. You play guitar, you make friends easily, you've got your various other interests. If singing a cappella didn't work for you, you'd be bummed, but you'd work it out."

She leaned forward and stared deep into his eyes, as if to urge understanding into them. "For me, it's very different. Without this talent, I'm just another motivated smart girl—a dime a dozen. Singing is all that makes me more. I need it."

"So yes, the year was rough," continued Dani, relaxing a little, "But I got by. I did amateur theater productions, sang in the concert choir. I went to as many a cappella concerts as I could. It was painful seeing other freshmen on stage without me, but I had to go anyway. I had to keep breaking my heart so I could remind myself how much I wanted this.

"Even as a freshman, I made friends in the aca-community, mostly by crashing their afterparties. But they were strange relationships: One part envy, two parts hopeful. Of all my singing friends, I was probably closest to Taylor . . ." Her voice trailed off suddenly.

After a few seconds, Ben broke the silence, "Dani?"

The Harmoniums' president frowned and shook her head, shirking an unpleasant memory. "Long story short, I tried out the next year and my result was much better. I was thrilled, of course." She smiled softly. "Thrilled and relieved."

Ben's mind raced. He wondered what effect Dani's delayed start had had on her drive for power. Her Harmoniums' leadership position was even more impressive now—group president after only one year!

"When I finally got in, it meant so much more to me," she finished, her voice trembling. "That's why I love my group so much. That's why I will always, always be loyal to the Harmoniums." She sniffled.

Ben walked over and put a comforting hand on Dani's back; it seemed the appropriate thing to do.

Dani looked up at Ben with those gleaming green eyes. "There you go. That was my attempt at total honesty."

"I appreciate it." After a moment's reflection, he continued, "And I know you just said you had no other talents besides singing, but I really don't think that's true."

Dani laughed a little. "Well, I know I'm good at a *few* other things. I'm obviously good at—" She paused, "Wait, what did you have in mind?"

"My sources tell me you're an excellent chef."

A wide grin stretched across her face. "See? Not all gossip is bad." The Harmoniums' president stood up and held out her hand. "How about we continue this conversation over a homemade dinner?"

Ben hesitated. Dinner, he knew, was a step. "Um, well, I've still got some homework to finish for tomorrow."

"Bring it with you. Come on, Ben Jensen. You owe me a secret now."

After some thought, Ben finally relented. He took the hand she had extended. "I suppose sharing a little more about myself isn't a huge price for a gourmet meal."

"It'd better be a juicy secret, too," teased Dani, as they walked back through the student center's hidden hallways.

At least in Ben's book, that's the night it became official: He and Dani Behlman were dating.

♫ |

Chapter 14

Pressure

Hmm— Luuuu— sang Renee. The petite soprano's background syllables at the beginning of "Chasing Pavements" supported Nicole's solo. When Nicole came to the chorus of the Adele cover, the sopranos transitioned to the more open-voiced *Ahhhh*. From Renee's position in the block of singers, she saw only the shadowy back of Nicole's head and the glow of stage lights around her frame. All the same, she felt annoyed.

As the Chorderoys sang on stage, Renee tried to pinpoint her problems with her female classmate. It wasn't a vocal issue; the diver was objective enough to admit that Nicole had the superior pipes, especially for an Adele solo. It was more a matter of emotion, the way Nicole conjured such soulful passion on a whim. During her most recent solo audition, Nicole had actually teared up. What kind of person could *feel* so much on demand?

Renee had another, more specific complaint: The gestures. For Nicole, a poignant lyric required a movement—a balled fist, a hand thrust, a stomp. And when she *really* got into it, Nicole would actually karate chop the air. As Nicole began the refrain, any invisible people in front of her were due for a beating.

Not that this particular audience would ever seriously complain about a surplus of motion, or emotion. With few exceptions, they were the most tolerant and encouraging audience imaginable: The parents and siblings of Brighton's many a cappella singers.

It was Brighton University's Parents Weekend, a time which provided those moms and dads who simply could not wait until Winter Break with the opportunity to "get a feel for" (read: investigate) their children's new environment. The University also sponsored several demonstrations of student talent during the weekend, such as the "Singing Spectacular," in order to remind parents why they were sending in such hefty tuition checks.

Renee knew that some students could screw up a hokey rendition of "You Are My Sunshine" and still receive wild adulation from their parents. Renee also knew that this was *not* her situation. In fact, she was shocked her parents had flown in at all—there wasn't even a diving meet this weekend. It was so uncharacteristic of them that it made her nervous.

From the corner of her eye, Renee noticed Violet giving her an extremely wide stage smile. Renee got the hint and tried to look more energetic as she sang, hoping she hadn't been displaying "the stare that could kill puppies" because she was thinking about her parents.

When Sid cut off the group at the end of the song, there was enthusiastic, but formal, applause. Catcalls were apparently not as popular with the over-forty crowd.

After the show, Renee met up with her mom and dad. Mr. Murphy gave his daughter a hug. "Good job," he said, in a tired voice. Her father was a technical writer for a science publishing company and an introvert in the classic sense: Public spaces exhausted him.

By contrast, Renee's mother was downright fidgety. As the crowd slowly filed out the double-doors, Mrs. Murphy tapped her toe against the chapel's marble floors. "If we don't make our dinner reservation . . ." she muttered. Renee was fairly confident her mother had never sat through a concert of this length in her life; non-competitive events made her uncomfortable.

Once outside the auditorium, they drove to a steakhouse, one of the finest in the area. Mrs. Murphy waited only until the salad course before dropping her conversational bombshell: "Honey, your father and I are concerned you might be *overextended*."

Renee rested her salad fork. "What do you mean?"

Mrs. Murphy took a lot of medication for shoulder pain. As she spoke, she rolled her upper arm in quick little circles like a baseball pitcher doing warm-up exercises. "Honey, you've simply got too much on your plate right now," said Renee's mother. "You can't do everything, you know."

Renee frowned. "I'm not trying to do *everything*. It's really just three things: diving, school, and a cappella."

"Too much, honey. Too, too much." Mrs. Murphy repeated. Her voice was calm but critical. "I don't know why you put so much pressure on yourself."

"I'm coping fine, Mom." Renee focused on spearing a grape tomato, hoping she could end discussion on this topic by simply refusing to look up. Meanwhile, her father was vigorously cutting slices of his wedge salad. He, too, was hoping for a conversational reprieve.

But Mrs. Murphy had other plans. "An opportunity has presented itself, Honey. An extremely unique and important opportunity."

"Oh, Patricia . . . I don't know if right now is—"

"No, Aaron, we can't be complacent," said Mrs. Murphy, cutting him off. She pushed forward her salad, which she had hardly touched, and smiled widely. "Your father and I spoke to Coach Perdiro a few weeks ago. We asked him about all the opportunities still available to you, given your progress since last fall."

The fall of Renee's senior year of high school had been the critical period when coaches offered D1 athletic scholarships to incoming students. Renee's swim club coach had been disappointed Renee hadn't been recruited by schools with larger diving programs. He had always told her parents she was an Olympic contender.

"Coach P. thinks the best option available to you is to submit a transfer application to Stanford. They still offer full athletic scholarships to sophomore transfers *if* they have excellent grades."

Renee stared fiercely at the breadbasket.

Mrs. Murphy went on, trying to sound tender. "Honey, since you've been a little girl, the family dream has been to get you to the Olympics. You've always been so driven, and you just might have the talent, too. Stanford has the resources you need. The coaches are superb; the program is at the very top of the country. They can get you there. But the longer you wait, the faster your window of opportunity is closing."

Mr. Murphy added in his light, gentle voice, "And even if the Olympics don't pan out, Stanford is an amazing university. That degree will carry you far."

"But Brighton—"

"Brighton is a *fine* school," Mrs. Murphy interrupted. "Stanford is spectacular."

The waiter came to clear their salad plates and comb the breadcrumbs off the table. There was silence while he worked.

With the server gone, Mrs. Murphy jumped back in. "Honey, your father and I are afraid that if you have too many distractions, the transfer application will be unsuccessful. We'd hate for you to squander your only shot because of your obsessive involvement in a college glee club."

Renee's cheeks burned as her suspicions were confirmed: This all boiled down to her singing. She

172

looked at her father, who had privately stressed to her the importance of trying new things her freshman year; her father, who used to *sing* B-E-P standards with her on every drive home from practice.

But her father said nothing. His eyes were fixed on a melting square of butter.

Mrs. Murphy leaned forward. "How much time do you spend with that singing group every week?"

Renee shrugged. "Six, eight, sometimes ten hours. It depends on our gig schedule. But I enjoy it, Mom! It's not work for me. I really enjoy the singing."

There was a new note of derision in her mother's voice. "I'm sorry to say it, Honey, but it's not *really* singing. I suppose it's actually singing for the soloist— that Nicole girl, for instance, I thought she was very good. But for the rest of the group, it's just nonsense words. 'Jimmer-jammer' and 'mai-tai-na' and 'jin-jamba-jam.'" Suddenly, she burst out laughing. She held up her Bloody Mary. "Ha! I just realized those background words would make great names for cocktails!"

Renee gave her mother the stare that could murder puppies, but this time, it was entirely intentional. Unfortunately, Mrs. Murphy had grown accustomed to that look since the onset of her daughter's adolescence; now, she hardly noticed it.

"Honey, I've been watching you for years," said Renee's mom. "When you're diving off the block, flipping and piking, twirling in the air like a beautiful acrobat—that's who you are! But this new singing thing? It's a *phase*. It's fun, it's very trendy, but it's just not you."

Renee wished their steaks would arrive. When her cell phone beeped, she checked the message immediately, knowing full well it would annoy her mother to use it in a fancy restaurant.

Akash had forwarded her an event invitation:

THE GOBFELLAS PRESENT, "DON'T BRING YOUR PARENTS"

PARENTS WEEKEND = LAME SAUCE. WASN'T THE WHOLE POINT OF COLLEGE GETTING AWAY FROM THEM? AND SO THE GOBFELLAS HAVE GRACIOUSLY INVITED THE REST OF THE A CAPPELLA COMMUNITY OVER FOR A GUARANTEED NIGHT OF PARENTAL DETOXIFICATION AND DEBAUCHERY. WHATEVER HAPPENS, WE GUARANTEE IT WILL NOT MEET WITH MOM AND DAD'S APPROVAL. ALL WE ASK IS THAT YOU DON'T BRING YOUR [EXPLETIVE] PARENTS WITH YOU. SERIOUSLY.

Below the description, Akash had written:
INTERESTED?

Renee remembered all of the other times Akash had invited her to a cappella afterparties. She'd always said no because of morning diving practices.

There was practice tomorrow morning, too, but this time things were different. Renee wanted nothing more than to let loose and be irresponsible.

"Honey, please put that away."

Just as the sizzling steaks arrived, Renee shot off her response:
HELL YES.

♪

Akash watched from the sidelines as Renee utterly dominated in yet another round of Beer Pong, even though he was confident that this was her first night ever playing the drinking game.

"She's a laser!" cried Derek, president of the Gobfellas and her most recently defeated Beer Pong opponent. "How many is that?"

"Seven," said Wilson. He gave his tiny teammate another congratulatory high-five. "Seven games in a row."

As far as Akash could tell, the theme of the Gobfellas' first afterparty was simply competitive drinking. The Beer Pong table was a gift from a rich alumnus, custom built with LED lights, a "moat" of churning water for cleaning off ping-pong balls that fell on the floor, and the Gobfellas' maroon *GOB* insignia painted in the center. There were also specially designed tables for Quarters and Flip Cup. All around, Fellas were dueling each other in spontaneous matches of Chug the Beer.

Between rounds, the winning pair came over to chat with Ben and Akash.

"Throwwwing lllittle balls into cups of beeeer," slurred Renee. The petite soprano laughed hysterically. "It's so STUPID. It's AWWWESOME."

Ben was busy texting on his phone. "I've got to head out," he quickly announced to his groupmates. "See you guys at practice tomorrow."

When Ben was gone, Wilson shook his head. "Still sleeping with the enemy, eh?"

"Just to be clear, I don't think he and Dani are 'sleeping' yet," said Akash. "But good for you for using an expression correctly. It *is* a little weird, though."

"What, Ben dating a cougar?" asked Wilson.

Akash laughed. "No, just how quickly it happened. It's pretty suspicious, but none of the Chorderoys are sure how to bring it up with him."

Renee gave Akash a little punch in the arm. "Here's an idea: WHY DON'T WE JUST LEEEAVE PEOPLE ALONE AND LET THEM DO WHATEVERRR THEYYY WANT?" As Renee yelled, she stumbled off balance and back into the Beer Pong table, knocking down cups and spilling beer all over her pants, the table, and floor.

"Party Foul!" cried half-a-dozen Gobfellas, in unison. Not that it was the first mess of the evening. The floor of the "Gobhouse" was perpetually sticky from spilt drinks.

While Wilson cleaned up, Akash tried to convince his groupmate to retire from the game. At first Renee resisted, but Akash appealed directly to her competitive spirit: "The cups that just fell are going to count for them, so it's better to leave now with your record still intact."

"Oh, ALLLL RIGHT."

Akash walked her to a nearby couch and went to look for some towels to help dry her off. When he returned, one of the Gobfellas already had his hand on her knee, creepily holding her in place while he flirted.

"A diver, eh?" said the Fella, a junior named Trent. He inspected her figure. "You must be in good shape. Have you seen the movie *Swimfan*? You'd like it. I've got the DVD upstairs." He reached for her hand.

Akash's sudden rush of adrenaline boosted his protective instincts, if not his creativity. "Nope! Nuh-uh! She hates movies!" he cut in.

"But I—"

"No movies!" Akash reached out to Renee.

Renee looked back and forth at the two men. Slowly, she took Akash's hand.

"Come on! Everyone wants to fuck a Fella!" yelled Trent, as the two of them walked off.

Outside the apartment, in the brisk November air, Akash was reminded that Renee was still not quite herself. For one, she kept stumbling over the little cracks in the sidewalk as they walked back to campus. For another, the petite soprano, usually so economical with her words, was ranting in a completely disjointed fashion:

"When you find something new, you know, and you think it will be kind of fun, just because it's so new, but then you do it and you start to really love it, and that's weird, because it's very, very new, but that's what made it awesome to begin with. But it all comes down to this, really. You see, parents *suck*. Parents really, really, really suck . . ."

As Akash listened, he thought back to an awkward exchange he'd had with his parents earlier that evening. During dinner, they'd raved on and on about the Chorderoys' performance—they were *those* kind of parents. But just as they were finishing their cheesecake, Akash's father mentioned that Uncle John would be willing to put in a good word for him with the Gobfellas. "If you're interested, you could switch next semester," said his dad.

Akash had answered truthfully: He was extremely happy in his group and couldn't imagine transferring. He realized now that the Chorderoys were where he actually belonged. Akash's parents dropped the subject immediately. He could tell they were embarrassed for bringing it up at all.

"Parents suck," continued Renee. "Maybe it's just part of the job description, but they totally suck."

"They mean well," said Akash, sighing.

Renee looked up at the baritone. Without any sensible impetus or transition, she blurted out, "I'd like to sing something. I'd like to sing something right now."

Akask furrowed his brow. "I'm not sure that's such a great idea. Remember what happened to Wilson?"

The little soprano reached up and put her finger over Akash's mouth. "Don't worry. I've got a place."

Renee led them on a detour around the freshmen dormitories, veering towards Brighton's Athletic Complex. The AC was an imposing stone building that stood tall and blackish-gray in the night sky. When they arrived, Renee pulled out her student ID card and slid it through a scanner. The door unlocked with a metallic *clunk*.

"Athlete's privilege," explained Renee, holding the door open for him. "The divers get extra access so we can train outside of practice."

The halls were lit only by those few flickering fluorescents which were programmed to stay on at all hours. Renee swiped her card at another door and motioned Akash inside.

It was a huge room with thick concrete walls, silent but for the hum of the filtration system. There was a long sheet of cool still water. A dive platform towered in the distance over the Olympic-regulation pool.

They were alone in Brighton University's Natatorium.

"Are you sure 'athlete's privilege' extends to visiting the pool at—" Akash checked his watch, "2:45 in the morning?"

But Renee wasn't listening. Instead, she climbed atop a dive block near Akash, the slightly elevated perch from which sprint swimmers began their races. "Guess who I am?" She held up her hands and flailed her fingers as she began "Chasing Pavements."

At first, it was pure parody, and it was dead on. Renee nailed Nicole's karate chop, slicing the notes in all the right places. She growled her *r*'s in just the same way,

178

belting *therrre* and *nowherrre*. She even remembered Nicole's little stomp before the refrain.

And then, just as suddenly, Renee dropped the Nicole act. She looked over at the diving platform, then at the ceiling. When she started singing again, Akash recognized her second ballad, too: "Against All Odds (Take a Look At Me Now)," by Phil Collins.

A new, pleading voice echoed throughout the chamber and across the water.

Akash listened closely, and though it was Renee's usual high timbre, it was sung with such conviction that she sounded altogether different. As he listened to her sing of lost love and hopeless reconciliation, he was transfixed.

Her final sad note echoed throughout the pool room, bouncing up and down the concrete walls and ringing in the baritone's ears.

As they walked back to the dorms, they hardly spoke at all. Akash sensed Renee sobering; she seemed even more thoughtful than during her second song.

At last, she reached out to grab his hand, and their fingers interlocked naturally.

Chapter 15

Poaching

One rehearsal near the end of the semester, Dylan sang the solo, facing the block as they sang subdued background chords:

> *O Holy Night, the stars are brightly shining*
> *(oooh)*
> *It is the night of our dear savior's birth . . .*
> *(Nahh, dah, nah, ohhh—)*

As Ben watched from his position in the group arc, he marveled at the irony: The most mischievous person he knew sang with absolute innocence. Dylan's tenor voice was clear and boyish; the notes floated in the air like little bubbles.

Each year, the Chorderoys fundraised by singing holiday songs at a few paid gigs. Taylor was most excited about the Hunters Bank Christmas party. An employee of the bank, Rosemary Cooper, had personally contacted the group. They were to sing two songs from her list of ten suggestions.

Dylan's voice gently hovered on the high notes. *Noel, noel— O night— / O night Divine.*

When the song was over, Taylor asked Dylan for feedback. "Since you were facing us, could you comment on the group's overall 'look?'"

The group president had emphasized that Hunters Bank was a lucrative gig—several hundred dollars for just two songs. He wanted them to perform well so that they would be invited back next year. Based on Rosemary's highly traditional song suggestions, he thought their appearance should cater to a more old-fashioned audience.

"How was our visual cohesiveness?" asked Taylor. "Were our movements appropriate? Any comments on our professionalism? How about our blocking?"

Ben smirked, sensing the group president was ticking items off a memorized list. Although there were still a few months until Brighton's regional elimination round of the World A cappella Championships, Taylor was already starting to drill them on visual performance criteria. Terms like "appropriateness of movement," "visual cohesiveness," and "overall professionalism" probably came straight from the WAC judges' ballot categories.

Dylan's eyes widened, excited for the rare chance to criticize without consequences. "Olivia, we might be interpreting the song title differently, but I'm not sure rubbing your hips qualifies as an appropriate movement."

"My bad," the alto responded.

He turned to the group's shortest member. "Renee, a brief comment on professionalism: I'm getting a professional vibe from you, but it's more 'professional serial killer' than 'professional Christmas caroler.'"

Renee frowned. "I was trying to look sincere!"

"Right, sincerely interested in killing puppies," Dylan replied. "An eensy bit of Christmas joy, please. Finally, Mo, you know how you like to grab your gut when you sing?"

Beatboxing clashed with the old French carol, so the Chorderoys' vocal percussionist was singing along with the rest of the block.

Guillermo nodded. "I like the acabelly move."

Dylan smirked. "Well, you're missing the mark today, buddy. It's more of an acahernia."

Guillermo tested the maneuver, checking his hand positioning. "Oh, crap! It *is* an acahernia. All this time, I've had my hand on my—"

"Okay, thanks for all the constructive feedback, Dylan," interrupted the music director. Sid was in efficiency mode and eager to keep moving. "Let's sing 'Baby, It's Cold Outside.'"

This particular "guy-courts-gal" duet dated back to the 1940s. Together, the Chorderoys had selected Guillermo and Violet for the solo parts. Ben found it hilarious to imagine a real-life romance between the two: Fart-joking, maturity-of-a-seventh-grader Guillermo together with the overly sensitive, awkwardly complimentary Violet. As a couple, they would never work, but the musical reality was different. The singers had just the right vocal chemistry for the old "cat and mouse" routine.

When the song was over, the Chorderoys were in a generally happy mood.

"Anyone want to go to Badger's before the show tonight?" asked Akash.

Violet's face lit up. "Coffee and ice cream! Yes please!"

"As long as Mo and I can mix some *special* coffee," said Dylan. "We'll be needing extra help to get through this."

"There will be no drinking before the show tonight!" huffed Taylor.

"Wait—what show?"

Suddenly, all eyes were on Ben, as if it was an especially dumb question.

"Nicole's show," Akash explained, breaking the silence. "It's the opening night of *A Streetcar Named Desire*. We're all going together."

Ben's cheeks went red. He remembered Violet collecting ticket money weeks ago, but he'd completely forgotten in the interim. "Oh no, um, I've got other plans."

Akash gave him an especially pointed look. "Plans with Dani?"

Ben gulped and nodded. "But I'll—I'll go some other time this weekend. I definitely want to see it!" As Ben tried to excuse himself, he felt worse and worse. He knew it wouldn't be the same going to see the show without the rest of the group. Nicole had been talking about opening night for months.

As the Chorderoys filed out of the rehearsal room to Badger's Café, Taylor caught Ben's arm. "Could we talk for a few minutes?"

When it was just the two of them, Taylor said, "Listen, I know it's not really any of my business, but I feel like I should warn you about Dani."

Ben sighed. Dani had asked him if he'd had this sort of discussion with Taylor. ("You will," she'd said, with her usual air of confidence.) It seemed the elder songstress was right once again.

"It's not that she's in a rival group, *per se*. Sometimes intergroup relationships work just fine. But with Dani, she's . . ." Taylor struggled for words. "Well, I've known her for a long time . . ."

Ben thought back to Dani's revelation in the A cappella Storage Room: How disappointed she'd been about not making a group as a freshman, how determined she was when she finally joined the Harmoniums. But Dani had also alluded to something about her friendship with Taylor turning sour at the beginning of their sophomore year. Did Taylor really think Ben knew nothing of his girlfriend's history?

"A cappella success means a good deal to her, as I'm sure you've noticed," continued Taylor. "She's also extremely competitive. So please, proceed with caution. Be careful what you reveal about our group."

Ben didn't like being treated like an ignorant freshman. "Do you really think Dani's using me to *spy* on the Chorderoys?"

"Well . . . err . . . she could be." Instinctively, Taylor's left hand reached up to pull at his eyebrow; he forced it back into his pocket. "Maybe she'd like to know our plan for fighting SG's budget cuts. Honestly, I can't always tell what she wants. She's hard to predict." Taylor shifted his weight uneasily from foot to foot. "But given her history, I think it would be very hard for her not to see you as a competitive asset. She might not want to treat you that way, but Dani Behlman always thinks strategically."

As Ben walked out of the Music School and across campus, the words kept echoing through his mind: *Dani Behlman always thinks strategically.* Did Taylor have no faith in the authenticity of Ben's relationship?

When Ben arrived at Dani's apartment, the table was already spread: A bright red tablecloth, glasses for the dry merlot, rosemary seasoned potatoes, warm biscuits, caramelized chestnuts. Bing Crosby's classic version of "O Holy Night" was playing in the background.

"The Chorderoys are learning this right now, actually."

"That's interesting," said Dani, with little interest. She was preoccupied with examining the color of the tenderloin. Ella Fitzgerald's "The Christmas Song" came on, her husky alto filling the apartment. "Baby, would you mind uncorking the wine so it can breathe?"

At last, Dani pronounced everything finished. They made their plates and sat down. Ben tried the beef first. "Delicious!" he said.

Dani beamed.

"These are delicious, too," said Ben, pointing to the potatoes. "Delicious."

As he listened, Ben found himself in a sudden verbal rut. He said the same thing about the cranberry salad, the biscuits, and even the wine. Everything, all of it, was "delicious."

Dani frowned, clearly annoyed by the repetition. "Is everything okay?"

"Um . . . yeah, it's fine. Everything's fine."

She leaned in. "Really?"

Ben sighed and set down his fork. "It's nothing important. Taylor insinuated something after practice today." He stared deeply at his bowl of trifle. "It's not really a big deal, it's just . . . irksome."

Dani seemed unusually excited by this development. After a moment's thought, she asked, "This is good, right?" She motioned to the space between them. "Us, I mean. We aren't moving too fast?"

"Sure." Ben sipped the red wine. "This is fun."

Dani beamed. "What if we could make it better simply by doing something we both love?" She pointed up: Judy Garland's "Have Yourself a Merry Little Christmas" was playing in the air.

"Ben, what if we *sang* together?"

Ben looked out at all the food in front of him. Tentatively, he asked, "Can't we sing together whenever we want to?"

"A cappella, silly. In the *same* a cappella group." She looked straight into his eyes. "Ben Jensen, I'm talking about you joining the Harmoniums!"

For such a bombshell, Ben thought he should have a more immediate emotional response. Instead, he felt only a dull queasiness, as if the cranberry salad he'd just pronounced "delicious" so many times had not agreed with him after all.

"I know you've been hurt by the attitude some of the Chorderoys have had towards our relationship," said Dani, with grave sincerity. "To be honest, I hate to see you so uncomfortable."

She leaned over the small table, her eyes glowing green and gold in the candlelight. "Besides, there would be so many benefits if you were in the Harmoniums. With your tenor voice, it'd be—perfection!"

Her smile was soft. "And, of course, it'd give *us* much more time together."

As Dani spoke, thoughts flew throughout Ben's mind—fast, emotionally charged thoughts without any semblance of order. Oddly, the first question he blurted was strictly technical: "Is it even *legal* to change groups like that?"

Dani straightened in her chair. "I tend to support individual freedoms, Ben Jensen. But if it's any relief, changing groups is also perfectly acceptable according to the ACUAC rules. Here, let me show you."

When she came back to the table, Dani held a familiar piece of cardstock in her hand. Ben skimmed the text:

RANK GROUPS IN ORDER OF PREFERENCE WITH "1" BEING YOUR FIRST CHOICE . . . DO NOT RANK A GROUP UNLESS YOU WOULD BE INTERESTED IN JOINING THEM.

Ben recognized it as the A cappella Group Preference Card, the same version that he'd used to rank his favorite Brighton groups before the Draft.

With her pinky, Dani indicated the fine print at the bottom of the card:

MARKING A GROUP ON THIS PREFERENCE CARD REPRESENTS A COMMITMENT TO SING WITH THAT GROUP FOR <u>AT LEAST ONE SEMESTER</u>.

"At least one semester," Dani read sweetly. "That means after finals, you can do whatever you want." She smiled. "You'll be a free agent again."

Ben's queasiness was getting worse. "Can you excuse me for a moment?"

As he stared into the mirror above the bathroom sink, Ben tried to calm himself and think in terms of pros and cons.

Dani was right that there would be some conveniences to being a Harmonium. It would certainly be easier for Dani to make time for them if they had the same rehearsal schedule. And he and Caroline could sing together again, like they used to in the days before auditions.

But the mere idea of not being a Chorderoy filled Ben with an overpowering sense of loss. No longer going to Badger's Café with his newbie class . . . Missing out on Dylan's sarcasm, Guillermo's antics, Erin's hippie-isms, Sid's wisdom . . . Even thinking of Taylor's trichotillomania made Ben wistful.

Despite splashing them with water multiple times, Ben's cheeks hadn't stopped burning. Something was unsettling him, something besides the fear of aca-separation. The whole subject of transferring a cappella groups felt *unnatural*. He couldn't put his finger on it, but there was something entirely wrong about the way it had come up in their conversation.

Ben washed his hands with Dani's cherry blossom hand soap and returned to the table.

"Of course, I'd have to discuss the matter with the group to make it official," continued an enthusiastic Dani, as if there'd been no interruption. "But I know they loved your voice. They'll adopt you immediately, just like I have. It'll be like you've been with us since Draft night—as if you've *always* been a Harmonium!"

Dani stopped, finally taking note of his silence. "What's on your mind, baby?"

Ben's eyes focused on the group preference card lying on the table. That, he realized suddenly, was the problem. By now, he'd grown accustomed to Dani's tendency to plan ahead, but her ability to produce the letter of the a cappella "law" so quickly represented a whole new level of choreographing.

He felt a penetrating pang of fear: What if this conversation wasn't spontaneous at all?

Ben forced himself to look straight into those bright eyes. "Tell me, did you think much about this before tonight?"

"No!" cried Dani. "No, no, no. I mean, I've obviously imagined what it'd be like if we were singing together . . . but it was all very hypothetical."

Ben's mind reeled in spite of her response. Had Dani's purpose for their time together been simply to personalize her second pitch for the Harmoniums? Was her big revelation in the storage room just a tactic to get Ben to sympathize with her—to *trust* her?

Meanwhile, Taylor's words echoed through Ben's mind: *Dani Behlman always thinks strategically . . .*

"I need you be completely honest with me," said Ben quietly. "When you talked to me at that first afterparty, were you hoping you could persuade me to join the Harmoniums?"

Dani paused. Her eyes began to glisten. Finally, she said, "The thought had occurred to me, yes."

In that moment, all Ben knew was that he had to leave. Not argue, not accuse—just get out of the apartment.

"I'm sorry," he said, standing up and pushing down his napkin.

"Wait—Ben—stay!" cried Dani. "I got excited, and I butchered this! Forget I mentioned it. We can discuss it later. But please stay. I've made Bûche de Noël— Christmas cake—Delicious—French! Wait. Where are you going? At least let me drive you!"

Ben opened the door, and cold air seeped inside. "I'll walk."

(Perhaps the only thing that can overrule these sudden passions are the lessons learned from mothers, and Mrs. Jensen had instilled eighteen years' worth of courtesy education.) Abruptly, Ben turned and said, "Dinner was delicious. Thank you."

And then he left.

♫

When Ben arrived at the campus theater, he found a bench in the lobby and sat there, alone. Memories were flooding back to him now: Dani constantly disparaging the Chorderoys; all those complaints about conflicting practice schedules. He felt so stupid for never detecting any ulterior motive.

He, Ben Jensen, was the victim of a complete sham. He'd been just as naïve as everyone had expected him to be.

190

After sitting on the bench for a while, Ben somehow managed to consolidate his feelings of hurt and betrayal into two short sentences on his cell phone. Even then, he knew it wasn't a good idea to text angry.

He sent them anyway.

After some time, the doors opened and the audience spilled into the lobby for intermission. The Chorderoys gathered around Ben's bench, where he was still hunched over.

"Have you just been waiting?" asked Akash.

Ben cleared his throat. "I got here late," he explained. "But I thought I'd catch the second half."

"Cool," said Akash. The baritone eyed him carefully, trying to determine what was wrong. "Well, it's been a good show. Nicole's acting has been incredible."

"She's actually very believable," said Renee. Ben knew this was high praise coming from the small soprano.

Akash smiled his thin smile. "Glad you could make it, buddy."

The rest of the Chorderoys, all there to support Nicole, chatted around Ben's bench. Sid and Joanna discussed the playwright's literary influences while Violet tried hopelessly to arrange a shopping trip that weekend with her "soprano baby." Guillermo and Dylan plotted out a pornographic film entitled *A Streetcar Named Desire*.

And Ben felt that he was safe, and with family once again.

♫

When Dani received Ben's text, she was eating the Christmas cake by herself. She'd made her Franco-Génoise recipe from scratch; under no circumstances

191

would she be letting it go to waste. She hardly took a break from eating to check her phone. The message read:

SORRY, BUT I WILL NEVER LEAVE THE CHORDEROYS. I THINK WE WENT TOO FAST.

Dani speared another bite of chocolate sponge cake and dipped it into the raspberry sauce, making it even more delectable and moist.

So, Ben Jensen didn't feel like changing groups. So what? She'd asked him too soon, perhaps. She'd simply have to wait and try again. Next time, she would be even sweeter and more tactical in her approach.

The problem was the doubtful voice in the back of her head, which kept telling her that Ben Jensen was too loyal to make the switch, no matter how long she waited.

Dani frowned at all the leftover cake. Her decorating had been exquisite. Frosted in chocolate buttercream and sprinkled with powdered sugar, the cake resembled a snow-dusted Yule log. She'd even clipped a genuine spruce twig for the garnish.

Damn it, Ben Jensen! Why couldn't he just cooperate? She had no idea where she'd gone wrong. Had she really gone too fast, or had she simply failed to capitalize quickly enough on Ben's interest in her?

On the one hand, Dani knew that reclaiming Ben Jensen had always been a matter of pride—winning "back" the best new tenor of the year for the Harmoniums. At the same time, Dani wanted *him*, too. It was never strictly professional. And he was so cute when he'd first described them as "dating" . . .

Why hadn't she lied when he'd asked her how long she'd been planning to recruit him? What was it about this freshman that made her suddenly so frank and idiotic?

Dani felt food on her face. When she looked down, she noticed the white patch of sugar on her black blouse, a culinary snowblast that would require serious scrubbing. Damn it, Ben Jensen!

This didn't make her a bad person, did it? Sure, seducing a freshman to recruit him for her a cappella group sounded sketchy, but it was far more complicated than that. Could anyone else fathom her attraction to talent? Could a mere "civilian" truly comprehend the force that is an acacrush?

Of course she wasn't a bad person. She was the one who required her group to show the utmost courtesy to every singer who auditioned, even the awful ones. She was the only group president who had the courage to e-mail every disappointed auditionee and tell them what they needed to hear:

YES. YOU SHOULD TRY OUT FOR A CAPPELLA AGAIN. MEANWHILE, WORK ON THIS . . .

NO. YOU SHOULD FOCUS YOUR ENERGIES ELSE-WHERE. HAVE YOU CONSIDERED THIS . . .

She was the sole life coach for the aca-afflicted, and yet she still felt guilty. Damn it, Ben Jensen!

It was time to move on. She would refuse to distract herself with this little freshman anymore. She was Dani Behlman, and she needed to act herself again. She never should have wasted so much time organizing these cutesy dates. What she needed was to focus on her goals: Lead a phenomenal group; sing sensationally and be discovered as an artist; make big things happen.

Dani needed a way to push forward, to brush aside the annoyance that was Ben Jensen, to reinvigorate herself and her Harmoniums.

She was scrubbing a particularly stubborn chocolate stain when the solution occurred to her.

♫

For Ben, the next few weeks were already going to be difficult. His three-hour Psychology and Introduction to Business exams crept ever closer. A twenty-page term paper in Philosophy only drew out the intense period of trauma. None of this was conducive to the holiday spirit, and the fact that he hadn't spoken lately with Dani hadn't made things easier.

Brighton University administered certain large exams in the early evening. Ben was walking to his first such final when he spotted them walking across campus.

Caroline had winterized, wearing a dark woolen coat, red mittens, earmuffs, and a tightly wrapped scarf. Elliot's clothing was still black—black jacket, black leather shoes, gratuitous black shades. (Despite the lack of sun or snow.) They were holding hands.

Caroline called out. "Ben! Hey!"

Ben thought there were few things worse than trudging to a Calculus exam in frigid weather, but this was among them. As he walked over, Ben muttered, "Oh, hey . . . Elliot's visiting again . . . great . . ."

He shook the hipster's hand. "Must have been rough transitioning from Cali to this Midwestern arctic."

Elliot hung his arm over his girlfriend's shoulder, casual and possessive all at once. "The change of pace is good for me."

"We're on our way to the La*chaim concert," explained Caroline, pulling out a ticket for Ben's inspection. The ticket showed the single syllable "Fa," circumscribed by a Star of David with "La's" on each point.

It took Ben a moment to sing the melody in his head: *Fa La La La La, La La La*chaim*. "Oh, clever. But isn't that more of a Christmas reference?"

Elliot smirked. "Christmas. Hannukkah. Chrismukkah. Who knows? I applaud them for recognizing the essential hybridism of our times."

"Oh, I think it's just a joke," said Caroline cheerfully. "What are you up to, Ben? You should join us!"

Ben frowned. The opportunity to play third wheel was not the least appealing, especially in the company of a classic pseudo-intellectual. Ben explained that he had his Calculus exam soon, and held up his graphic calculator as tangible evidence.

Caroline stared up at her lanky boyfriend. "Elli, can I speak with Ben alone for a few minutes? There's some acadrama going on."

Elliot gave Ben a serious look before, at last, relenting. "Sure, I'll go grab us some seats and latkes."

When he was gone, Caroline looked around nervously to make sure no one else was in earshot. "Okay, Dani was really upset last rehearsal. She brought in all this cake and shared the sad news." Her voice was trembling. "Oh boy. I'm not sure how to phrase this exactly. Can I ask you something personal?"

Ben nodded, bracing himself.

"Did you break up with Dani via text?"

Ben didn't know how to answer. Of course, he wanted to say no. Using a text message to break up with someone was an instant qualifier for the Tool Hall of Shame. But wasn't that, in fact, what he'd done?

Or had he and Dani really been dating at all? Ben had always thought so, but it felt different now that he knew she was just hoping to recruit him. How could he explain to Caroline that Dani wanted him to transfer to the Harmoniums? *Sure, Ben, everyone wants you*, he imagined her saying sarcastically. But this wasn't egotism; it was a crucial part of the story!

And if they had been dating, was I THINK WE WENT TOO FAST enough to end it entirely? Was Dani seriously upset, or was she once again thinking strategically?

With so many questions flying through his mind, Ben couldn't speak coherently. "No . . . I mean . . . I don't think . . . well . . . it wasn't officially . . . done . . . It's . . . It's complicated." He stumbled into the cliché with great personal distress.

Caroline took a deep breath. "Well, try not to worry," she said, in a faint attempt at reassurance. "Group relations between the Harmoniums and Chorderoys have definitely been better, but hopefully we can avoid World War III."

The soprano glanced at Ben's calculator, then back at his wide brown eyes. "But I would like to talk in more detail when you have a chance. Can we plan on coffee?"

Ben nodded. For a few minutes, they tried to work out an acceptable time, but between their two sets of final exams and respective holiday gigs, it seemed they were both completely busy until the end of the semester.

Finally, Caroline said, "Well, maybe it'd be easier if we waited until after break. But we *will* have coffee sometime. Keep pestering me about it, okay?"

She smiled her goodbye, wished him good luck on his exam, and they went their separate ways.

♫

When the Chorderoys arrived at Hunters Bank, their first thought was that they must have stumbled into the wrong party. Based on the party planner's song requests, Taylor had told the group to expect something old-fashioned, subdued.

He'd guessed wrong. Hunters Bank put on a *raging* Christmas party.

Party guests surrounded the open bar. A cover band played Pitbull's "Give Me Everything." An enormous ice sculpture of a snowflake doubled as a champagne luge. Waiters delivered piping hot servings of Bananas Foster and Baked Alaska. Most of the guests were young professionals, ready to let loose on the company's tab. Everyone was dressed to the nines.

"I'm going to order a plateful of sugar cookies and something with peppermint schnapps," said Guillermo.

"You're such a girl!" teased Dylan, grabbing hold of a passing waiter. "Excuse me, could I have a Gingersnap Cocktail, please?"

The apologetic waiter said he couldn't serve them alcohol without company approval.

Just then, Taylor spotted Brenna Noboks, Student Government's treasurer, chatting in a huddle with a few other Brighton students. Taylor's stomach wrenched—why would the Chairwoman of the Treasury Council attend a holiday party out here in the "real" world?

And then it hit him. Brenna, like many of the Treasury Reps, was a finance major! What better place for finance majors to do their internships than a major local bank?

"We have to rock it tonight," Taylor whispered to Sid, all the while smiling in Brenna's direction. With the

Treasury Chair evaluating their performance, it might be their best chance to make a strong impression.

When Taylor met up with Rosemary from the bank, her highly traditional song requests at last made sense. The short, arthritic woman was an oldies fan. Although she'd been demoted to the largely honorific position of Party *Co*-Director, she was fighting to keep the golden days alive.

"I'm so looking forward to songs where I actually understand the lyrics!" cried Rosemary. With her veiny hand, she ushered them to follow her down the hallway. "I'm sorry, but we couldn't get you folks your own warm-up room, so I'm afraid we're going to have to do a little sharing."

"That'll be just fine," Taylor said through his stage grin.

But the group president couldn't even *fake* a smile when they arrived at the practice room. Fourteen Harmoniums stood in a circle, wearing green stocking caps along with their usual red and black motif.

They were rehearsing "O Holy Night," with Dani on the solo.

Silently, the Chorderoys followed Rosemary to the other side of the room, where a separate spread of cookies and sparkling water lay waiting.

"Now, your group will perform after this group," said the old lady, gesturing in the direction of the Harmoniums. "Let me know if you need any more goodies!" she said cheerfully as she made her way out of the "practice room."

When the aging party planner left, the panicked discussion began. Dylan was, for once, his group's most serious member. "She's singing my solo. What are we going to do?"

Taylor gulped and looked to Sid for guidance.

"We'll have to be flexible," said the music director, with calm determination. "In the meantime, let's warm up the other song."

Sid blew the pitch, and the Chorderoys began singing "Baby, It's Cold Outside," with Violet and Guillermo on the duet.

Just as Taylor's urge to rip out his eyebrows began to fade, he heard a strange phenomenon: Every time the Chorderoys' duet pair sang a line, he'd hear an echo of that same line a few bars later from across the room.

Finally, enough Chorderoys realized what was going on. The other circle was singing "Baby, It's Cold Ouside," too!

Sid cut off his group mid-chorus.

With a gulp, Taylor walked slowly over to face the other group president. They met in the middle of the makeshift practice room. "We seem to have chosen the same two songs," said Taylor, with more than a hint of suspicion in his voice.

Dani pushed back a strand of strawberry blonde hair. "It was a rather limited selection."

Taylor shoved his hands into his pockets. "Well, why don't we split the songs? That way we can both do songs from the list, and the audience won't hear duplicates."

The Chorderoys' president knew it was obvious to everyone in the room why his group needed some sort of arrangement. If the 'Roys ditched the songs they had prepared and sang modern pop-rock so as not to repeat the Harmoniums' set, they'd be going against instructions, and might not be invited back. By contrast, if they sang the exact same songs as the Harmoniums, they'd look unoriginal and bore the audience.

And that audience happened to include the treasurer who was overseeing the a cappella budget cuts!

"How about you take 'O Holy Night' and we'll take 'Baby, It's Cold Outside?'" Taylor offered, hoping that she would be more likely to show mercy if he conceded her solo.

Dani waited just a moment. Her eyes narrowed as she stared down her rival president.

"No, we won't be dividing the songs," she said quickly.

"WHAT?!?"

Dani adopted an infuriatingly soft tone of professionalism. "Taylor, these are the songs my group has selected in advance. We made our independent plans. Accordingly, your group retains the right to sing whatever you choose."

"You know that Student Government is watching tonight, don't you?"

Dani stared straight ahead, admitting nothing.

Behind him, Ben stepped forward. "Come on, Dani," pleaded the freshman. "Don't you think we can *compromise* a little? Please."

But there was to be no compromise. Dani didn't even acknowledge him. She turned her back and spoke only to her group. "As we walk towards stage, remember to gauge our audience. It's incredibly important to take the temperature of the crowd."

The Harmoniums had been especially deferential to their leader that week. They followed her out of the room, an orderly block of red, green, and black.

When they were gone, Taylor felt Olivia's hand on his shoulder, urging him not to pluck his brow.

Guillermo and Dylan quickly devised a backup plan. The twosome would do a short stand-up bit about it being the season for "sharing." Inadvertently, the groups were "sharing" the same songs. "Corny, but it's the best I've got," said the paunchy percussionist.

After a few minutes, the Chorderoys returned to the action of the party. Taylor waited by an ominously big-bellied Santa Claus ice sculpture while he waited for the Harmoniums to finish their set.

Dani walked confidently to the mic stand, wearing a long red gown and sparkling silver heels. She was the only Harmoniums member with no stocking cap. "We're going to slow things down a little," she said, in an especially cooing alto. "This song goes out to Rosemary, the sweetheart who personally invited us tonight and is a true beacon of the Holiday Spirit."

The Harmoniums' music director blew the pitch pipe.

Dani started slow and quiet. Over the years, Taylor had seen her master the talent of restraint.

O Holy Night, the stars are brightly shining . . .

Taylor watched her interact with the audience, marveling at the control she had over them as she sang, her delicate balance of intimacy and power—such a contrast to the timid freshman he'd met three years ago.

During the chorus, she thrust her arm forward and moved into her chest voice. Every financier was gawking.

Fall on your knees! Oh hear, the angel voices!

The tone was tender, warm but bold. She sang forth the proclamation, the music bursting from her frame:

Noel, Noel! O night, O night Divine!

For Dani Behlman, singing was always a test of endurance; to hold the high note was to triumph.

Noel! NOEL————

She not only sustained it, but crescendoed as it reverberated all around her.

And then, she shifted once more into the soft, careful voice of control.

O night . . .
O night . . . Divine.

The ancient carol finished to raucous and well-deserved applause. Taylor looked around. Sure enough, Brenna Noboks was cheering wildly.

For a long time, Dani stood there, soaking it in, smiling at her sweet victory.

When the Chorderoys at last took the stage, Taylor watched Guillermo and Dylan proceed with their forced comedy routine, which received a few polite laughs. Even still, the group president wasn't expecting the most rousing musical performance from his fellow singers.

First semester was ending, but Taylor didn't feel joyful at all.

♫ ‖

Chapter 16

Choreography

Violet stood facing the group. "Show me the final triangle!" she squeaked assertively.

From the back of the block, Guillermo bellowed, "Form...THE TRIANGLE OF THE APOCALYPSE!"

Renee smirked. Learning choreography was one of the diver's absolute least favorite activities. She did, however, enjoy when Guillermo gave the block formations more epic-sounding names.

"Okay, now the last square."

"Assemble...THE SQUARE OF ULTIMATE VICTORY!"

It was a few weeks into the spring semester, and the group's annual concert, "Chorderoy Soup," was rapidly approaching. Violet was busily teaching the movements for "The Show Must Go On," one of the choreographed songs the group would sing for their concert. It would also be part of their performance set for WAC later on in the semester.

After blocking the Queen song, the Chorderoys rehearsed the movements for Lady Gaga's "Poker Face." In this case, the soloist and choreographer were one in the same: Olivia. The alto had a knack for spotting all of Renee's errors and then making her corrections sound risqué.

Renee hated the song's starting pose, which consisted of crouching like a cat along with the rest of the singers in the front row.

"Renee, dear, less rigid. More *feline*!"

The short soprano bent her knee an additional half-inch and hoped it would do the trick.

"Five-six-seven-eight!"

For the first verse, the guys and girls broke from their cat formation into two groups at separate ends of the "stage" that had been taped onto the carpet. The ladies were supposed to sway their hips in time with the music.

"Renee, dear, you're supposed to thrust and *swoop!*" chastised Olivia. "Don't just move it—*sell* it!"

Renee sighed. Diving had given her a sense of rhythm, but the theatricality of choreography was beyond her grasp. What was the technical objective of this swoop? If the goal was to move the hip from one side to the other, why not get it there via the shortest possible means, moving it directly across?

But the worst was still to come. In the second chorus, the Chorderoys split into co-ed dance partners.

"Renee, cutie, you've got to *grab* Akash!" yelled Olivia. "No, no. Pull his collar like you mean it! Now shake it! Pretend that you actually like him! *Seduce* him!"

Renee's cheeks burned, and not just because Olivia kept embarrassing her.

There was an elephant in the rehearsal room: Akash had never once mentioned her singing to him that night in the Natatorium. Had he totally forgotten about their holding hands as they walked back? Or did he think she'd come on too strong, and was hoping to avoid the subject altogether?

Renee struggled enough with choreography without worrying about the awkward dynamic between herself and her dance partner.

When the song/torture was finally over, Sid ended practice. Renee's a cappella commitments for the day were not yet over, though: She and Nicole were off to Tabling Duty.

"Tabling" was a tool used by all sorts of extra-curricular groups to promote their causes in a high-visibility space, usually the central campus cafeteria. In the weeks leading up to the concert, the Chorderoys took turns "manning the table," publicizing and selling advance tickets for their major annual concert.

Renee sensed that selling lots of tickets had greater significance this year. With Student Government pledging to scale back a cappella, all of the groups were trying to prove just how popular they were with the student body.

As the freshmen girls set up shop at the cafeteria entrance, Nicole babbled excitedly. "Guess what? The Theater Department just officially set the date for Drama Prom in April! They've rented this gorgeous converted opera house downtown. But there's one problem—well, it's kind of the story of my life, honestly . . ."

At this point, Renee tuned Nicole out completely, focusing her energy on counting the money in the group cash box. Why would she care about a social event that was more than three months away, least of all one called Drama Prom, a name composed entirely of words she disliked?

As she counted through the dollar bills, Renee considered all of the legitimately dramatic events in her own life: The Midwestern Regional Dive Competition next week. The Chorderoy Soup concert the week after that. Her complete floundering in Organic Chemistry.

On top of all this, her mother had been calling her daily, pressuring her to complete her transfer application to Stanford. "Your window of opportunity is closing," harped Mrs. Murphy. "Day by day you're missing out! Don't squander your only shot!"

Nicole may have starred in *A Streetcar Named Desire*, but Renee was confident she understood drama, too.

"So what do you think?"

"What?" Renee blinked, startled back to the present.

Nicole smiled sweetly. "I said I was considering asking Akash to Drama Prom. You're allowed to bring someone from outside the Theater Department." Softly, she said, "But would *you* be okay if I brought him?"

Renee's eyes widened. She felt a sharp, sudden sense of alarm. "Why wouldn't I be?"

"Well . . . I heard that . . . I didn't know if you felt . . . you know . . ."

"I'm not sure what you mean," said Renee quickly. She closed the cash box; the change clanked around inside. "It's totally fine with me."

The alto leaned in. "You're sure?"

With great effort, Renee looked straight into her eyes, determined to seem stoic. "Go for it."

A giant smile stretched across the alto's face.

Abruptly, Renee reached for her backpack and pulled out her laptop. "If it's all right with you, I think I'm just going to do homework for a few minutes—I'm pretty behind. Can you handle ticket sales? If a massive crowd appears, I'll be here to pitch in." The petite soprano highly doubted this possibility. Usually, prospective ticket buyers came up in manageable groups of two to three people. (Despite all efforts, the Chorderoys were not exactly triple-platinum.)

"Of course!" said Nicole. "Do your homework! I'll handle everything!"

Using her computer, Renee created a new document and typed WHY STANFORD at the top. In her sour mood, she felt that it was time. She was finally going to draft the transfer admissions essay. As she typed, Renee discreetly angled her computer screen away from Nicole for more privacy.

Before long, Nicole had found a new conversation partner. Greg Hollis, tabling for the Dinos, had arrived and set up next to the Chorderoys.

Although Renee tried to focus on drafting her admissions essay, she couldn't help overhearing the two thespians chattering. She quickly gathered that the Dinos' president and Nicole were both taking "Musical Theater Interpretation" that semester.

"How're the singing telegrams selling?" Nicole asked.

"Well, we've only sold a few dozen," said Greg, in his always-effervescent tenor. "But the deliveries so far have been hilarious! We customize them, of course. Just yesterday this freshman ordered one for his roommate: A specially-timed performance of 'Beat It.' So cruel, and yet, so genius!"

"GROSS!"

Greg laughed. "Good times."

Cynically, Renee wondered if the Dinos might actually be selling the singing telegrams to prove how much they were involved on campus, thus scoring more points with Student Government, and not just for ordinary fundraising. Renee stared silently at her still-blank computer screen, feeling generally depressed with the world.

"Of course," continued Greg, "We sometimes deliver love songs, too. The surprised look on the other partner's face—it's adorable!"

His voice quickly turned bitter. "Then again, the people who buy love songs are operating under the assumption that their significant other *wouldn't* have a complete nervous breakdown if we came to their door. I imagine this makes the gesture more romantic."

"What do you mean?" asked a concerned Nicole.

"Never mind," said Greg abruptly.

Renee, still silent, thought hard. What had so upset the leader of the Dinos?

After some time, the diver realized: The two chit-chatters to her right were silent, too. Even before she knew for certain, she *felt* it—the scary realization that someone was looking over her shoulder.

Renee turned and saw the glow of the laptop screen reflecting in her onlooker's wide blue eyes.

Nicole gulped. "Are you transferring to Stanford?"

The irony made Renee's skin burn. Of all the people to catch her, it had to be the Chorderoys' most overdramatic, gossipy member. Renee mumbled to the Universe, "Seriously?"

"Are you really going? Would you be gone next fall? What about the Chorderoys? Do you mind if I ask *why* you want to leave? Are you not happy here at Brighton?" Throughout Nicole's interrogation, Greg remained completely silent, staying out of the co-ed group's drama.

"No!" cried Renee. "It's the athletics—it's the academics—it's . . ." She stopped, lest she mention her parents and have to explain a whole host of additional issues. Renee took a deep breath. "It's a practical rather than an emotional matter. I'm not sure you'd completely understand."

Nicole's voice began to falter. "Well, are you going to tell the rest of the group? It'd be terrible if you just didn't show up next fall."

The mere insinuation made her livid—as if she'd ever put the Chorderoys in such a bind, leaving without notice! The diver leapt up, shoved her laptop back into her book bag, and grabbed a stack of concert fliers to post independently. She hurried off without a word, leaving Nicole staring after her.

♫

Dani Behlman stood before a Chorderoys' concert poster hanging in the Music School hallway, disgusted.

CHORDEROY SOUP—what an annoyingly plebian name for a concert! Dani had always thought "soup" was a nasty word, anyway. A standard cafeteria food.

From the photo, it appeared the 'Roys' were using a generic "mystery" theme that year—how cliché! She glared as she recognized each "character" in their group picture:

Sid Davis was a Holmes-like detective, with an enormous spyglass and a long overcoat. For some reason, Dani had always found Sid's easygoing nature off-putting. Not ever having sung a solo for his group, not even in his senior year. How could he not be resentful?

Guillermo was Inspector Gadget, digitally altered so that he was "flying" through the air using a helicopter hat. Look at that cheesy Photoshop editing—classic Taylor!

Dani's alto rival was dressed as a *femme fatale* maid, with a tight black corset. Typical Olivia, zero concern for class.

Her eyes froze on Ben Jensen. He and that Akash kid were dressed in 1950s sweaters, red and blue, respectively. The tenor's golden hair was parted perfectly to one side. It appeared they were supposed to be the Hardy Boys. She assumed it was some stupid joke, since they didn't look at all like brothers.

It was the sight of Ben that made her do it. She reached up and ripped down the Chorderoys' poster, crumpling up the paper and stuffing it into her purse. Dani then proceeded to tear down all of the Chorderoys' posters hanging in that hallway. Her fury had taken over; she never once checked to see if she was being watched.

In part, of course, it was a strategic move: The less people knew about the 'Roys' concert, the less people would show up, the less impressed SG would be with them, and the likelier Treasury Council would be to abolish the Harmoniums' competition.

But junking the Chorderoys' posters was mostly a symbolic gesture, and even as Dani tossed them into the garbage bin, she sensed that it was primarily a message to herself: Spring was here; the big concerts and WAC were just around the corner. Literally and figuratively, she was about to go on stage.

Dani Behlman was stepping up her game.

Chapter 17

Harmony

Nicole McLain had put on the album which had never failed to energize her: *All the Way*, the Greatest Hits of Céline Dion. After all these years, Nicole still loved every track, even "My Heart Will Go On." Her admiration for Céline could not be understated—all that beauty and passion, wrapped into one big voice.

It was late afternoon on the day of the Chorderoys' annual concert, and Nicole was getting ready in her dorm room. She struggled to fasten the tiny clasp of her pearl necklace, unable to keep her shoulders stationary—who could stay still with Céline in the air?

The butterflies in her stomach surprised her. She hadn't been especially nervous before *A Streetcar Named Desire*, even playing the part of Blanche Dubois. But tonight, her role was different. Flat or sharp, she'd be Nicole McLain, freshman alto in the Chorderoys. She'd be singing as herself.

As she fastened her high heels, Nicole skipped ahead to "Love Can Move Mountains." The warm gospel melody continued ringing in her head as she walked across campus, carrying three blue gift bags.

Nicole had asked the freshmen to arrive a little early to Blair Chapel so she could present each of them with a good luck gift. The others were waiting outside the chapel doors when she arrived.

"Very handsome, boys," said Nicole, grinning widely. The alto thought Akash in particular looked especially snappy. He wore a royal blue shirt, a white silk tie, and shiny tuxedo shoes with fake alligator skin around the toes.

"And you look gorgeous, Renee."

The short soprano muttered a toneless "thank you." Since Renee had abandoned Nicole while they were tabling at the cafeteria, the two had barely spoken.

Nicole cheerfully handed out her bags. "Open them!"

Akash went first, pulling out a blue-and-white varsity letterman jacket. The alto had found it in a thrift store, and affixed a blue "C" patch onto the chest. Nicole admired her handiwork as Akash flipped the jacket around to see his name printed on the back.

Next, Ben pulled out his book—*501 Hipster Jokes*. He laughed. "I'll definitely use these!"

Finally, Renee opened her gift bag, pulling out a CD in a bright blue jewel case. She stared at it, confused.

"It's just a compilation of songs I thought you might like," said Nicole tentatively. "I'm sort of old-fashioned in that I still enjoy making tangible CDs for people instead of online playlists."

Renee muttered another barely-audible "thank you." As the quartet walked inside, however, Nicole thought she caught her smiling.

♫

An hour later, Violet was hovering over Renee. "You're going to need much more blush than you think," the motherly soprano insisted.

The Chorderoys had finished their soundcheck and were waiting in the prep room backstage. The ladies busily applied make-up in front of the wide mirror, with Violet offering Renee much-needed assistance.

"Apply the mascara *liberally*," suggested Olivia. "She'll look smoking hot on stage with darker lashes."

Renee flinched as the brush came close to her eyes, and her neck twitched involuntarily as she tried to sit still. "I'm not very good at this," she admitted.

"It's okay, it's okay," cooed Violet. "Three more years of aca, and you're bound to improve."

"And you can always ask around for assistance," added Olivia.

It was then that Renee realized something: The older girls spoke of her future in the Chorderoys with casual certainty. They didn't act as if they had any idea that she might be transferring to Stanford. Had Nicole actually kept quiet about what she'd seen on Renee's computer?

When the girls finished primping, the genders joined together in a circle, and Sid led the group through a final round of vocal warm-ups. As Renee sang, she listened to her groupmates stretch their voices:

I am a cow, Mooooooo—
I am a duck, Quaaaaack—
I am an elephant . . . Womp.

(Sid always called out elephant when they were reaching the very end of their high ranges.)

Next came the more technical Chord Exercise, Renee's favorite. Sid divided them into small groups and assigned them each a different note of the scale, then instructed specific singers to move up or down a note, finally leading them back to the warm major chord.

They finished up by practicing diction, repeatedly singing the lines, *Gilet, jupon, jamais, jaloux!* and *Poppy petunia, poppy petunia, gladioli.*

And then, with a nod from Sid, Guillermo proclaimed that it was time: He pulled the slice of yellow cheese from his coat pocket.

While the group took turns slapping, Renee noticed the hum of chatter in the audience as Blair Chapel began filling with students.

Soon, she heard the muffled voice of the emcee through the wall. The group quickly gathered in the hallway. Before she knew it, she was running onstage with the rest of the Chorderoys.

Renee stared into the bright onslaught of the spotlight, her fingers still tingling from slapping the cheese. There were cheers, including Wilson's distinctive, "WOOHOO! BIG BEN!" shouted from the balcony.

Renee looked out at the dark faces of the audience, her eyes still straining to adjust. She thought about how many small acts of faith were required to sing a cappella: Finding her first note from a single pitch, staring into an abyss of stage light and shadowy faces, trusting that her fellow singers would join her.

The metallic note reverberated from Sid's pitch pipe, echoing throughout the chapel.

Renee opened her mouth to sing.

♫

"I suddenly have a much greater appreciation for your 5 A.M. shower performances," said Lauren, a fellow diver and one of Renee's two roommates. "*Jang-in-a jang jang, zena jena jen joh* makes much more sense in context."

Cynthia, Renee's other roommate, chimed in, "Yeah, the two of us are going to write a book together: *Living With A Cappella: The Roommates Tell All.*"

Lauren laughed. "Seriously though, you were so great up there!"

Renee hadn't stopped smiling since the Chorderoys had taken their final bows. She couldn't believe so many of her teammates had shown up to support her. But when Renee saw Nicole walk by her cluster of diving friends, she quickly excused herself.

"Hey, Nicole, wait up! I just read the track list from the CD you made for me."

There was just a touch of suspicion in Renee's question: "How did you know I liked Billy Joel, Elton John, and Phil Collins so much?"

Renee had gone to great lengths to keep her pre-dive playlist a secret from the world. And yet, there was a total of *six* B-E-P tracks on Nicole's disc! How had Nicole guessed her favorite artists when no one else had? Had Nicole been looking at her computer *again*?

Nicole just laughed. "I can hear you, silly. You're always humming those songs when you walk, so I figured you must like them quite a bit."

Renee's eyes widened, impressed and a little alarmed by Nicole's astuteness.

"Oh, and I also added a few covers of those artists," continued the alto. "Mariah Carey's version of 'Against All Odds.' George Michael's take on 'Don't Let the Sun Go Down on Me.'"

Renee stared at the floor, deep in thought. Finally, she looked up at Nicole. "Hey, I know I sort of flipped out on you last week . . . Well, I'm really sorry about that. I hope we—"

But Nicole cut her off with a hug. "I'm sorry, too."

Taylor called everyone together for some Chorderoy group pictures. Renee added her digital camera to the pile.

As Renee walked back from the chapel to her dorm, she stared at the group picture glowing on her camera screen. The four Chorderoy freshmen were once again in the same row: lanky Akash, with that endearingly shy smile; Nicole, with wide sparkling eyes; Ben, with cheery red dimples; and Renee on the end. The diver looked so genuinely happy in the photo that she believed her expression might actually *revive* injured puppies.

After the concert, Lauren and Cynthia had gone out with the team, so when Renee got back to the dorm, she had her room to herself. She sat at the edge of her bed, still relishing her post-performance high. To have sung an entire show surrounded by friendly voices . . . To have felt the charged silence that comes just before applause . . .

Alone in her darkened dorm room, it occurred to her how much she liked how she was feeling.

Renee reached for her cell phone.

She spoke clearly into the answering machine. "Hello, Mom and Dad. I just got back from my Chorderoys concert. By the way, it was amazing. But that's not why I'm calling. I'm calling to let you know that I won't be transferring to Stanford.

"I'm old enough to recognize when I've been fortunate. Somehow I've stumbled into a very good life here at Brighton. I'm happy here. I enjoy my classes. I'm getting a world-class education. My friends are here. And I love the Chorderoys. Even if singing a cappella is something neither of you would have predicted for me, it's something that I love.

"As for diving, I think Brighton's team will give me many of the same opportunities as Stanford, especially if I work hard. I still enjoy diving, but I'm not going to let it dictate my entire life.

"I do love you both," Renee said more softly, "and I hope you respect my decision. Goodnight."

When Renee hung up, she realized how strangely *easy* her monologue had felt. It was as if, because she'd had those feelings pent up for so long, they'd had enough time to stitch together and burst out fully formed.

Renee leaned back on her twin bed, staring up at the ceiling. In a minute, she'd head over to Guillermo's wild afterparty, "Chorderbash!" But for now, she wanted to preserve this state a little longer: Calm, happy, and living fully in the present moment.

Chapter 18

Crises

Her message had said to arrive promptly at three P.M., but she'd given no indication as to the topic of their meeting. She had said only that she wished to "make him an offer."

By now, Taylor thought, he should be more used to Dani's methods, her deliberate withholding of information. In Dani Behlman's world, the rules of negotiation were the same as those for singing a solo: Never start in full voice.

The meeting place was familiar enough. Cecilia's Records was a vintage music store located on the loop of shops and restaurants just north of campus. When Taylor walked in, he was greeted by the strong aromas of lavender incense and hemp.

Dani was at the back of the store, leafing through the old records, admiring the classic album art. She carried with her a tiny cup of raspberry cream gelato from the shop next door.

"How'd you enjoy our concert?" asked Taylor. He'd spotted the Harmoniums' president chatting with someone in the audience while the Chorderoys were snapping group pictures after the show.

She didn't answer, still rifling through the albums.

Taylor cleared his throat. "Still a regular here, I take it."

Dani's eyes were fixed on her favorite Linda Ronstadt album. The cover art featured the big-voiced diva standing on a vast sandy beach, wearing a white night-

219

gown. Behind the rock matriarch, a shadowy cowboy rode his horse along the lapping waves.

"Every Sunday," replied Dani, without looking up.

Taylor sensed this might actually be an understatement. He knew Dani looked to the albums of her favorite female singers for inspiration. In these important weeks leading up to WAC, he felt sure she was visiting the store with increasing frequency.

Dani moved down the aisle, and hovered above the classic opera records of Maria Callas. She took another bite of gelato.

"Your message—"

"Taylor, I wish to propose a deal," Dani cut in. "But in order for you to understand my terms, I have to remind you of a fundamental difference between you and me. You see, while you were freaking about the possibility of Student Government cutting your a cappella group—"

Dani paused to inspect his brows for damage.

"While you were merely worrying," she continued, "I decided to take action. Treasury Council is just another democracy. A small, essentially ignorant, but potentially important democracy. And democracies are composed of people, of course. People who can be moved, inspired, persuaded . . ."

Dani beamed. "*Planted.*"

Taylor felt the color drain from his face. He didn't like where this was heading.

"First, there was Candace Bauer," began Dani. "The New Jersey state high school debate champion reached out to me after she failed to make the Harmoniums. I encouraged her to run for Student Government so that she could wield those same policy shaping skills over the student body."

"Candace assures me she hasn't forgotten my early campaign support," said Dani. "She'll do what she can to repay her oldest ally."

Dani looped back around to the front of the record store so that she could start at the A's once again. Taylor remembered this same ritual from two years ago: Walking alphabetically through the artists, winding up and down the aisles, Dani slowly savoring her gelato, drawing energy from the musical labyrinth.

"Josh Peters was even easier," continued Dani. "He lived across the hall from me freshman year and was quite the Mandy Moore fan. I was practicing for my second attempt at a cappella auditions and wanted to master controlling an audience. Josh was the perfect test subject. I could always make him tear up when I sang 'Cry.'

"Months ago, I happened to bump into him at Badger's Café, where I reminded him of our tender moments together." She adopted her most innocent, Mandy Moore-esque voice as she demonstrated, "Can you help me, Joshy?"

Dani stepped back, and her voice took on a tone of disgust. "Unfortunately, sensitive 'Joshy' reciprocated by sharing all his *feelings* with me, hours upon hours of personal issues. In retrospect, I should have emphasized that we were political allies, not bosom buddies. But I guess we can't all be Dr. Laura. It wasn't easy, but I got what I wanted. I secured vote number two."

She reached out to touch a Bonnie Raitt album, stroking the outline of the blues singer's red-auburn hair. "The challenge was securing the third vote. I didn't have any historic strings to pull. Fortunately, however—" Dani stopped in mid-sentence, transfixed by Cher's section of the aisle.

"Dani?..."

The Harmoniums' president started. "What? Oh yes. The third vote. Ronald Chang announced he would be spending spring semester abroad, and Student Government was worried. Last spring election, *Student Times* ran an article highlighting Brighton's 3% voter participation in SG elections. This time, the execs decided to skip the election altogether and open the position up to applications."

Seeing Taylor's stricken face, Dani grabbed his arm, feigning concern. "What, you didn't hear this? I'm afraid the opening was very poorly advertised. Just a few fliers hung around the business school."

Taylor forced himself to ask. "So you applied, and now *you* are the new treasury rep?"

"Please," Dani scoffed, rolling her eyes. "You know I don't do accounting—too banal. No, I found someone much better: Alexander Vandersall."

Taylor very nearly fainted. Alexander had been in the international politics course he TAed last semester. Whenever Alexander raised his hand, he reiterated his view that the United States should use the forces of capitalism to ensure its continued cultural hegemony. Alexander was also a finance intern at Hunters Bank, as Taylor had discovered on the night of the company Christmas party. He had fawned over Dani after "O Holy Night," and pleaded with his TA to put in a good word with her on his behalf.

Taylor knew Alexander would be perfect for Dani's purposes: young, entrepreneurial, assertive, and eager to perform favors for his favorite female Harmonium.

"Suddenly, I had three of the five members of Treasury Council on my side," explained Dani. "I might be a run-of-the-mill English major, but even I know that's a majority."

Taylor cleared his throat. "So that means—that is, if you're telling the truth—"

"Why bluff when you don't have to?" asked Dani, smiling.

"Well then, presuming you're right, and you have a majority of the Council behind you, that means the Harmoniums are definitely not getting cut this year." He took a deep breath. "Your group gets a free pass."

Dani crossed her arms. "We're safe, yes. I'd wager that we were always safe. Being exceptional still counts for something, you know. But I must admit, I like the added security of those three votes."

Taylor stared hopefully at a gaudy Dionne Warwick record, silently imploring her to say a little prayer for him and his Chorderoys.

"So, I'm guessing the offer you want to make involves your new political power."

Dani nodded. "Something like that. I've been watching the Chorderoys carefully. With your newbies, with your group's energy . . ." She inhaled deeply. "Well, it's very hard for me to admit this, Taylor, but I think the Chorderoys might *almost* be legitimate competition for us this year."

Taylor was too stunned to properly accept the compliment. Finally, he understood. When he spoke, he heard the complete lack of inflection in his own voice:

"You want us to withdraw from WAC."

"No, I want your group to be *mediocre* at WAC," replied Dani. "The effect is very different. If you guys are even slightly off your game, then the Harmoniums will sound that much better in comparison."

Taylor shook his head. "How exactly do you propose I tell my group that we should kinda-sorta suck during our biggest performance of the year?"

223

Dani grinned. "You don't have to tell them anything. There's an easier option. What if, instead of the whole group withdrawing, just *you* personally don't show up?"

The Harmoniums' president took a step closer; he could smell her sharp floral perfume. "I've been watching you sing the Queen solo, Taylor. It's—" She hesitated, "It's decent. My concern is that the judges will be less awed by my performance if another veteran soloist makes it look so easy. Why not remove the distraction? It'll be very simple. You'll fake sick or make some sort of excuse to miss WAC that night. The Chorderoys will either withdraw or have to perform with a last-minute substitute soloist. Either way, it won't be your group's best showing." She was beaming again. "After which, I'll perform my side of the bargain."

Dani stopped abruptly at the display for Dolly Parton, another of her favorites. "You see, my comrades in SG won't just protect me; they'll protect whoever I recommend! If you don't show up, then I will convince my fans on the Treasury Council to spare the Chorderoys the axe. I couldn't let my good friend Taylor's group fall to pieces simply because he happened to catch the flu at such a bad time."

Dani stared up at Taylor, her eyes bright and glimmering green. "Don't show up to WAC, and I will guarantee your group's safety. My only condition is your absence Saturday night. Are we in agreement?"

Taylor forced his hands into his pockets. "How do I know you'll follow through?"

The alto laughed lightly. "Such a *practical* question, Taylor. Being group president has improved you. But yes, I've considered this as well. If I breach, then you should bring up our trading scandal in your 'save-the-Roys' PR campaign with Student Government. Of course, it would be mutually assured destruction—damaging the reputations of both the Chorderoys *and* the Harmoniums—but avoiding that whole mess puts significant pressure on me to fulfill my end of the bargain."

Taylor was silent for a long time.

Dani stared at him and continued, more softly, "Why risk it, friend? It's just one show, one gig out of hundreds in your a cappella career. Don't be selfish. Why gamble the security of your group when all it takes is one night of staying in?"

Taylor jerked away from her. "This is too much, Dani. It's one thing to fight for a competitive edge, but asking me to abandon my group . . . That's just cruel."

Her green eyes blazed. "I don't need lectures in cruelty from *you*," she whispered fiercely. "Cruelty is the way you abandoned me last year."

"Dani, if you just let me explain, I think you might—"

She put her hand up to cut him off. (Taylor thought the gesture resembled Diana Ross in "Stop in the Name of Love" – the vinyl just beneath her elbow.)

"I'm not doing this to torture you, Taylor. I'm doing this for me. If I don't win an outstanding soloist award, if the Harmoniums don't advance to the WAC finals, then no one outside of this campus will ever hear my voice."

Dani motioned to the records all around her. "I'm doing this to be discovered. This is my moment, Taylor. It's my time to—"

"*Ma'am*, are you going to buy something today?"

The interrupting store clerk had walked over and was frowning at Dani. "I've seen you buy albums before, but technically you're loitering if you hang around for more than half an hour without purchasing, and my boss says I have to kick you out."

The Harmoniums' president straightened her spine with affronted dignity. "No, I'm not buying today. I have a big performance Saturday night." She glanced at Taylor. "I'll reward myself after that."

Dani gave her rival a curt nod, which Taylor took to mean that her offer was non-negotiable. She turned to leave.

"Wait!" Taylor called, jogging after her. "Suppose I do—I mean, suppose I *don't* show up. Then what happens? The Chorderoys would be safe, but wouldn't SG still cut one of the other groups?"

"SG has to make cuts," Dani agreed matter-of-factly. "I can guide their decision-making, but ultimately some-one has to go. The Gobfellas are an establishment, and hence non-touchable. But there's really no need to have *two* guys' groups on campus. I foresee the Dinos being axed."

Taylor gulped. The Dinos' mention contributed greatly to his impending sense of doom.

"Just be smart, Taylor."

With that, Dani turned on her heels. The bell rang as she exited the store and turned up the sidewalk, but her bright perfume lingered among the store's conflicting odors.

♫

Ben wasn't expecting Taylor's group text message that Friday morning: GUILLERMO AND OLIVIA HAVE MONO AND CAN'T PERFORM. Less than 36 hours before WAC, and two of the Chorderoys' thirteen voices were suddenly out of commission.

MEET AT MY APARTMENT AT 7 TO DISCUSS OPTIONS AND REHEARSE. The Music School was currently off

226

limits because of some event for glockenspiel players. Dozens of middle-aged musicians had lugged their mallets and metallophones halfway across the country for the event, which had temporarily banished the acas from their territory.

Ben found Taylor's apartment to be much as he'd expected: clean, modern, stylish, and not entirely comfortable. Having missed the Pre-Draft "talk" at the beginning of the year, he and the other freshmen were seeing it for the first time.

As he walked in the door, he spotted Renee standing in the corner spouting WebMD at their president. "The main symptoms are fever, sore throat, and fatigue—especially fatigue," she read to Taylor. "But even if they're completely wiped out, couldn't they at least get up and perform on stage for only twelve minutes?" Ben got the impression that the tough-minded diver believed in powering through. He guessed that she had never once used illness as an excuse.

Taylor shook his head. "The initial phase is acute. As of now, both doctors are insisting on bed rest."

Renee frowned. "But it's still a *possibility*, right?"

"Our operating assumption must be 'no,'" insisted Sid. Sitting in the lone recliner, legs crossed, hands gripping the arm rests, he sounded heavier-voiced than normal. "I feel sorriest for Olivia. We have tons of Senior Class events planned before graduation. It's a terrible time to be sick."

While they waited, Violet passed around two home-made "Get Well Soon" cards for everyone to sign. She would drop them off tomorrow, along with cupcakes.

Dylan arrived precisely at seven. He cleared his throat, folded his hands, and solemnly addressed the group: "Okay, I know this puts us in a real bind. But we mustn't forget our principles. Let us all take a moment to acknowledge that we owe . . .”

He paused.

“ . . . SERIOUS PROPS TO GUILLERMO!”

The words exploded from Dylan’s lips; his smile stretched from ear to ear.

“Honestly, I didn’t think he had it in him. Sure, he’s talked about his feelings for Olivia for months, but he kept making excuses—‘out of my league,’ ‘a cappella-cest is stupid,’ ‘gotta shed weight,’ et cetera. But he finally manned up! If he hadn’t caught this lame Kissing Disease, this would have been downright *awesome*! And to think, he was just going to keep the story of their epic hook-up to himself. Mo’s such a coy one. By the way, did anyone catch them together at the concert afterparty?”

“Um, maybe Guillermo and Olivia just shared a drink or something,” muttered Gary, in his grumbly bass. “Seems more likely.”

Dylan’s cheeks flushed red. “Shut up, skeptic!” His lip quivered as he spoke. “You think you’re always right, Mr. James Earl Jones?” Well, you’re not! Olivia drinks cocktails, Mo drinks whiskey and beer. Clearly, this was a tragedy of passion! Anyone who says otherwise is . . . is just *stupid*!”

Violet rushed to Dylan’s side to hand him the Get Well cards and to provide a much-needed, motherly pat on the back. “Now, now.”

Sid stood up, ready to take charge. His shaved head reflected the light flickering beneath the ceiling fan. “Taylor and I have been planning alternate arrangements. As we see it, we have three main options.”

Ben looked over at Taylor. The group president was sitting on his hands in his chair and looking extremely distressed.

228

The music director pulled off his silver glasses and held them as he paced back and forth. "One, we drop out."

There were disapproving headshakes. Everyone knew this would send a bad signal to Student Government right before they considered de-funding (and hence, terminating) one of the six a cappella groups.

Sid went on. "I know we're all thinking about the SG threat, but I don't think that should be the deciding factor. We've never sung, or not sung, because SG gave us permission." He inhaled deeply. "We've done it because it's what we *love* to do."

Although he'd heard it before, there was something about Sid saying he loved a cappella that filled Ben with a distinct sense of pride. If a cappella had captured the heart of the most thoughtful person he knew, Ben believed it could capture anybody.

"That's also why I think we should proceed with WAC," continued Sid. "We love to sing, and it's the biggest show of the year. Declining this gig doesn't feel right.

"Option two, we can re-audition Olivia's solo."

In the original set, Olivia was supposed to sing the solo on "Poker Face." When Sid mentioned the possibility of a new soloist, Ben saw every female's eyes widen with interest, except for Renee's.

"My view is this: Some solos are entirely about vocal communication; others are more influenced by stage presence. Olivia brought to 'Poker Face' a very particular charisma.

"If we're honest with ourselves," said Sid, slowly and carefully, "I think we'll realize that none of us can nail that song like she did."

Ben agreed with Sid's assessment. Olivia's persona was a perfect fit for Lady Gaga. He recalled the lusty way in which she made ordinary a cappella words like "pitch" and "tone" sound dirty.

"At least not with one day's notice!" added Violet.

"Right," said Sid. He replaced his glasses, looking more and more scholarly. "Which brings us to Option Three. Until 9 A.M. tomorrow, we can submit a new set list. After that, the WAC rules ban revisions."

The music director suddenly looked straight at Ben Jensen. "When you make a change like this, at the last moment, you're looking for a song with consistency. Consistently tight harmonies, consistently high energy, consistently strong solo work. The soloist's role especially important; the audience feeds so much from the emotional energy of that person's voice."

Sid took another deep breath. "That's why I firmly believe we should add 'Use Somebody' to our set."

The music director's words gave Ben a temporary arrhythmia. All year, Sid had drilled Ben's blend, tweaked his tone, and criticized him for breathing between measures. He was always polite, but he'd never once been highly complimentary. Now, Sid was arguing for Ben to sing one of the three main solos?

There were general murmurs of agreement with this suggestion.

"I think 'Use Somebody' would be great," Erin chimed in. "But there might be a problem. I was talking to Melanie after the Organic Foods Symposium—"

Dylan "coughed" into his hand, "*Hippie!*"

"—and she said that the Harmoniums have been learning 'Use Somebody' since mid-November. It's in their set list for WAC."

Ben felt his cheeks burn. Arranging "Use Somebody" was clearly Dani's idea. If Ben had agreed to Dani's plan and transferred groups second semester, she would have had his solo right there waiting for him. She had planned everything.

"Who's soloing in their version?" asked a frantic Taylor.

"Caroline Cooper."

There was a lengthy silence.

"So much for the Song-Staking Rule!" grumbled Joanna, furious about the injustice. According to the ACUAC charter, the first of the six groups to begin learning a song was supposed to have exclusive owner-ship of it for the year.

"I still believe our best choice is 'Use Somebody,'" Sid said resolutely. "The two versions won't be identical, especially with soloists of different genders. We've been working on our version for months—I'm confident it will be competitive."

Sid smirked. "And *damnit*, we had it first!"

Ben was quiet, trying to wrap his brain around this development. Two minutes ago, he didn't even know Caroline *had* a solo. (The coffee meeting they'd planned in December still hadn't materialized.) Now, they were going to sing that same solo head-to-head on the night of the biggest concert of the year!

As Ben struggled with the new scenario, though, the group was slowly reaching a consensus: "Use Somebody" was their best replacement song.

"All right, let's see how that set would sound," said Sid, once it had been officially decided. "Apparently we have permission from the neighbors to rehearse in here for a while."

231

The Chorderoys pushed Taylor's furniture aside, making his living room into their impromptu practice stage. As they sang the three songs, Sid timed their new set list with a stopwatch. "Eleven minutes, thirty-seven seconds," he announced, to everyone's relief. Still under WAC's twelve minute requirement.

"But that doesn't include applause between songs," cautioned the music director. "With that, we're cutting it very close."

Violet quickly devised a few extra elements of choreography for the block in "Use Somebody"—little things to make it more show-worthy, and which even Renee could pick up after just a few repetitions. The group sang short segments of the song, shared comments, and then repeated it, integrating and reinforcing the feedback as they went.

Sid ended the rehearsal after about an hour. "It's a solid song mix," he said, with his usual calm confidence. "Now let's rest our voices for the night."

As the rest of the singers filed out, Ben felt like he needed to talk to someone, but wasn't sure whether his question was more appropriate for Taylor or Sid.

He looked over to see Taylor leaning against his kitchen countertop, compulsively shuffling a deck of playing cards to keep his hands occupied. Ben remembered that, even before the Mono development, the Chorderoys' president had seemed extra-jittery during rehearsals this week.

Ben decided instead to speak with Sid, who was currently holding a hushed conversation with Nicole. Ben could hear only snippets:

". . . describe . . . strain?"

"It's dry . . . not sure . . . better"

". . . hydrated . . . rest . . . Be careful."

As Nicole walked by, she gave Ben an unusually muted smile.

"Ben Jensen!" exclaimed the music director, when she'd left. "You've just been promoted to our starting three!"

"I hadn't thought of it like that," said Ben, with nervous laughter. "I wasn't expecting it, that's for sure. But I was wondering: The Harmoniums most likely think we're still singing 'Poker Face.' Should we tell them we're singing 'Use Somebody' instead?"

Sid furrowed his brow, suddenly looking much older than his twenty-one years. After a few moments' reflection, he said, "Well, that's one of *those* kinds of questions, isn't it? Practical, emotional, and moral, all at once. On the one hand, technically, we've never had to say anything. Both groups are entitled to choose their own set lists, and attempt to keep them private."

Ben stared down at the well-polished tile, thinking aloud, "But wouldn't it be *nicer* to give them a heads up? Maybe not as strategic, but nicer, yes?"

"Was it very nice of a certain Harmoniums member to arrange 'Use Somebody' after they knew we'd already started learning it?" Sid returned. "For that matter, would it really seem nice of you to spring the news on them with only one day's notice?"

Ben frowned. Until that moment, he hadn't considered how awkward it would be to actually deliver the message. "So . . . you *don't* think I should tell them?"

"No, no, I'm just saying I don't have a clue, either," said Sid, with playful laughter. "If you want, I could send the Harmoniums an e-mail, but I honestly think it would be better for someone younger to make the call. It's your generation which will experience the repercussions, one way or the other."

Ben nodded gravely. "I'll think about it, and decide."

The music director grabbed his bookbag and walked slowly to Taylor's front door. Turning back, Sid asked, "Tell me, though. Do you think the decision would be equally difficult if your friend Caroline weren't on the solo?"

Ben's eyes widened. "Um . . . no. Probably not."

Sid smirked. "Something worth noting."

♫ |

Chapter 19

Soundcheck

My throat today is a dark, dried out tunnel of despair, Nicole had written.

It was the evening of WAC. Ben sat with his fellow Chorderoys in the pews of Blair Chapel, waiting for the official drawing to determine tonight's performance order. He continued to read silently from the handwritten note Nicole was circulating. The alto wasn't speaking.

The doctor this morning diagnosed it as acute laryngitis. She believed the hoarseness might be a symptom of overuse & prescribed an oral steroid to help strengthen the tissue. I can't tell if it's working yet.

Ben knew they wouldn't know for sure until the Chorderoys soundchecked with the audio equipment, and the theatrical alto attempted singing in full voice.

Around him, the Brighton University groups chatted excitedly in the pews. Ben watched Marianne LaRue, the regional WAC coordinator, shuffling her papers on stage. Marianne wore a shimmering gold-brown dress, flashy but professional. As she organized, she smiled with both rows of teeth, relishing her job's unusual combination of performance and protocol.

Finally, she stepped toward the microphone. "At this point, I need every ensemble to send forward its designated leader."

The Chorderoys looked at each other awkwardly. Their group president was missing.

That morning, Taylor had e-mailed his group a final reminder of when they were supposed to meet for WAC warm-ups, but he'd never shown up to the chapel. He wasn't answering anyone's texts or phone calls, either.

Ben was worried. He'd witnessed the compulsive card-shuffling last night, the group president's frantic attempt to control his tic; was Taylor *okay*?

Instead of their president, it was Sid who walked forward to draw the Chorderoys' number. Marianne took back the six slips of paper and announced the official order:

"(1) Gobfellas, (2) Notabelles, (3) Harmoniums, followed by a ten minute intermission. (4) Chorderoys, (5) La*chaim, (6) Dinos. Soundchecks will take place in the same order.

"Ladies and Gentlemen, please be advised that you must show up to your soundcheck on time. To ensure fairness, each group will have only fifteen minutes with the microphones—not a second more!"

Marianne smiled her enormous, two-rowed smile. "Now, let's have a fabulous WAC!"

The groups cheered, then quickly headed toward their various meeting places to discuss the outcome of the drawing. The Chorderoys followed Sid's lead to their usual alcove in the basement of the chapel.

It was Renee who asked the burning question. "What are we going to do without Taylor?"

There was silence. Without him, Ben believed the Chorderoys were very, very screwed.

"That's it!" cried Dylan. He pulled his car keys out from the pocket of his dress slacks. "I'm going over to his apartment to get him myself!"

Sid quickly grabbed Dylan by the shoulder. "You can't go," the music director said. "If Taylor doesn't show up to soundcheck, *you're* on his solo."

The usually-sarcastic tenor's eyes widened.

"Think about it," said Sid, in his determinedly calm baritone. "You're one of our few tenors who can consistently hit the Freddie Mercury high notes. Ben's already singing 'Use Somebody' and I'm preoccupied with Guillermo's vocal percussion. That leaves you, buddy."

For the next few minutes, Sid quickly verified that Dylan knew at least most of the lyrics for "The Show Must Go On," and the general musical arc of the solo. But the teaching moment was cut short. Soon, the Chorderoys had to trek back upstairs to the entry hall of the chapel so they would be ready to claim their limited time with the microphones as soon as it began.

At the prescribed minute, the tall wooden church doors burst open. Dani walked out of her soundcheck at a determined clip, her strawberry blonde hair bouncing with each step. Ben noticed her counting faces as she walked past, her green eyes quickly scanning her opponents. How much did she already know about their reduced numbers?

Caroline walked behind the Harmoniums' president, wearing her classy black shirtdress and red belt. Her cheeks were bright with blush. She looked straight ahead with an unfixed gaze, her mind elsewhere.

Seeing Caroline made Ben's stomach lurch. After some thought, he'd decided not to tell her about "Use Somebody." They never talked as much anymore; it seemed unfair that when they did he should have to be the bearer of the bad news. Despite his rationalization, he still felt like a giant chicken.

The Chorderoys hurried down the aisle to the front of the chapel. The heavy doors closed behind them with a loud *thud*. Marianne checked her watch. "Your sound-check time begins . . . Now."

Per Sid's instructions, they were soundchecking in the opposite order of their performance—third song, second song, first song. That meant Ben would soundcheck his solo in whatever minutes were left at the end. As they gathered on stage, Ben understood the scary rationale behind the music director's decision: Although "Use Somebody" was only added yesterday, it was suddenly the most stable song in their set list!

As the Chorderoys began Queen's "The Show Must Go On," Ben thought the basic melody sounded decent, but the overall feeling was off. The problem with Dylan's solo was its evenness. The sarcastic tenor's singing voice was naturally light and lyrical, lacking Taylor's wild dynamic contrasts. Ben remembered Sid's opinion that it was never good to "force" a solo, but what if they didn't have a choice?

The freshman also felt the hesitancy in his group's singing. With Dylan out in front, the members struggled to find their new positions in the choreographed "Triangle of the Apocalypse" and "Square of Ultimate Victory." The physical uncertainty came through in their voices.

Sid made the Chorderoys repeat the beginning, the finale, and the tricky part in the bridge. It was obvious that the music director wanted to rehearse their opening number several more times, but he knew their time constraints. He motioned for the next song.

Nicole walked out to the microphone. She flexed her fingers in and out of a fist as she waited for the starting pitch.

For about the first five notes of her solo, Ben thought the freshman alto was going to be just fine. Quieter than normal. A little croaky. But passable.

But when she came to the chorus of "Chasing Pavements," Nicole's voice simply collapsed. Adele's poignant lyrics came in husky, parched whispers, as if Nicole hadn't had water for days. Phrases that she usually belted to the heavens were completely unsupported.

Nicole tried to power through, clenching her fists and stomping for emphasis in all the usual places. With the steroids, the visual performance was probably more expressive and defiant than ever—just not the vocals.

Sid motioned the rest of the group into the *piano* dynamic, so that they didn't overpower their soloist. The command was unheard of; usually Nicole overpowered all of them!

By the second chorus, Nicole resigned herself to the fact that she couldn't sing anymore. She stepped back from the soloist microphone, hot tears welling in her eyes.

At this point, Sid began singing the solo from the block of singers. His voice was high and light, coming from the upper range of his baritone. He was only singing the melody so his group could track a leading voice as they continued to sing, but he nevertheless made the lyrics sound warm and expressive. Ben wondered if Sid had mastered the phrasing from his many solo rehearsals with Nicole, or if it had just come from a sort of music director's osmosis.

When the song finished, Sid didn't comment on the obvious problem of their utterly *broken* soloist—what could he say that would do anything more than eat up time? Instead, he motioned for the group to hurry on to their next song.

Ben grabbed the solo mic, felt the cool damp metal against his fingers. Sid counted off, and the block came in with its usual introductory chorus of *woah*'s.

The freshman took a breath, and sang the first line of the verse, jolted by the sudden amplification of his voice as it echoed around the chapel—

"STOP!" yelled Marianne. "You're out of time. Please exit immediately and invite in La*chaim."

Ben stared out into the vast, empty space, imagining the flesh-and-blood audience that was soon to be. So much for *his* soundcheck.

But he knew now what he had to do.

"I'll be right back," he told Akash. He walked quickly out the chapel doors, past La*chaim in their formal black and gold, and bounded down the stairs to the chapel basement.

Although Ben's solo soundcheck had lasted a matter of seconds, it was enough for him to know that Caroline deserved to be informed about the song duplication. She needed to know someone else was singing her solo, pour everything into her rendition, and never have any doubts that she had done otherwise. Ben's obligations as a friend and fellow musician outweighed the competitive advantage.

Flying down the stairs, Ben thought up his plan: He would search for the Harmoniums in every hallway of the chapel basement. He would politely separate Caroline from her group. Privately, he would tell her the entire situation.

But there was no need to search. Caroline was right there by the water fountain as he came off the last step.

"Caroline?" Ben was shocked. He'd been banking on more time.

The Harmoniums' soprano looked up, squinting a little. "Oh, hi Ben," she said, in an unusually cool tone of voice. "I'm waiting for—I'm waiting for someone."

Ben almost balked at her aloofness. "Um . . . yeah . . . here's the . . . okay . . ." He started and stopped half a dozen times more, struggling to put his moral dilemma into words.

Caroline crossed her arms as she waited. Her thin instrumentalist's fingers, painted with red nail polish, rested on each elbow.

He took a deep breath. "Yesterday morning, we found out that Guillermo and Olivia had mono and couldn't perform tonight, so we rearranged our set list and added 'Use Somebody.' I thought you should know that you and I are singing the same solo tonight."

Caroline's eyes fell to the floor. "Okay . . ."

Ben shuffled his feet, knowing the next part would be more difficult. "Actually, I really should have told you yesterday, as soon as I knew about the change. If it were my group, I know I would've appreciated the heads up. I guess I just thought telling you would be really awkward."

He shook his head and laughed a little, feeling like a complete loser. "And it *is* awkward. I'm sorry."

The graceful soprano reached out and put a comforting hand on his arm. "Don't be sorry. Trust me, there've been communication lapses on both ends. For a long time."

Ben stared at her hand. He'd long suspected her of changing her mind after callbacks and ranking the Harmoniums over the Chorderoys. Was she finally going to open up to him about her initial a cappella rankings?

Instead, it was Ben who started revealing his secrets. "You know, I wish we'd spent more time together this year. Yeah, we were in different groups—and I know

241

you're dating Elliot—but I remember us having . . . having *something* back in the fall. I mean, all those guitar jam sessions were fun, right?"

Caroline pointed upwards and smiled sadly. "Yes, but instruments aren't allowed in the a cappella world, remember?"

Ben shrugged. "Music is music. I don't think we'd be betraying a cappella with the occasional guitar duet."

"No, I'd think not."

As Ben gazed at her, he thought about how she had the kindest, prettiest brown eyes.

A familiar deep voice echoed down the hallway, the mere sound of which made Ben grimace. "You're kidding, right? You blow up at me for one understandable mistake. But here you are up close and personal with this guy right in front of me, talking about your 'jam sessions,' whatever that means." The voice laughed humorlessly. "What a hypocrite!"

Ben turned to face the dark-haired, black-jacketed hipster standing in the hallway. Apparently Elliot was visiting again. For an anti-corporate faux-bohemian, this guy was accumulating a ton of airline miles.

Caroline was quick to respond. "*I* would never cheat on you! Ben and I are friends." She shot Ben a sympathetic glance. "Friends who are honest with each other."

Elliot walked over to Caroline. He tried to put his arm around her shoulder, but she withdrew.

"It was all for artistic reasons!" said Elliot, his voice cracking. Ben had never heard him sound so *non*-nonplussed. "Don't you see, I was trying to become a professional journalist!"

But the career argument wasn't working with Caroline. She stared straight at the floor, refusing to look at him. "Elliot, if you actually care for me at all, then please go upstairs. I can't handle seeing you right now, not right before the show."

Elliot forced his body directly between the two singers, as if they couldn't possibly talk around his lanky frame. "Of course I care for you, Caroline. I love you. And I know you love me, too."

Caroline threw up her hands. "All I *know* is that you should go upstairs right now before you make a mistake you can't correct. I need some time to myself before we go on."

Reluctantly, Elliot trudged up the chapel steps, though not before glaring pointedly at Ben.

As soon as he left, Caroline was herself again. She explained in her usual bright soprano, "Dani actually told us about the song change. She's been close with Marianne since volunteering as a WAC usher her freshman year. Marianne e-mailed her the moment the Chorderoys sent in their revised set list."

Again, Caroline reached out, putting her hand on his shoulder. "But thanks for telling me anyway about the song change. It mattered hearing it from you."

They held their gaze for a long moment.

"You might need to head back to your group," said Caroline tentatively. "Dani mentioned that Taylor hadn't shown up tonight, and you guys were having to make a lot of last-minute adjustments."

"Gah—that girl knows everything!"

Caroline laughed. "Seemingly."

Unsure what else to do, the two singers gave each other a quick hug. Ben walked upstairs to rejoin the Chorderoys in their waiting room.

When Ben arrived, Sid was very patiently trying to re-explain the rules to his protesting group. "The set lists had to be finalized at 9 this morning. If we try to change any songs, Marianne will have us disqualified. We *can't* drop 'Chasing Pavements.'"

To Ben, the high pitch of Gary's voice highlighted the true anxiety of the situation. "Then maybe we should just withdraw!" In the excitement, the soft-spoken bass had leapt up into his tenor range.

At this point, Nicole lost it. Her face went red, tears poured down her cheeks, and she started hyperventilating, none of which were side effects of the steroids. "It's—my—fault," she blubber-croaked. "I'm so—sorry—It's my fault—I know it—I sang too much—too much—I wanted—so bad—the audience—the budget cuts—I'm sorry—it's all my fault—"

Renee was the first to comfort her, even before Violet. She put her hand on her back, a coach supporting a severely injured athlete. "Shh now. It's *not* your fault."

For a long time, no one spoke. There were no spontaneous compliments from Violet. No waxing philosophical from Sid. No cheerful, raunchy comments from Dylan. Just silent acknowledgment of a terrible situation.

Renee spotted him first, standing awkwardly in the doorway of the waiting room.

"TAYLOR!"

Ten Chorderoys whipped around in unison.

Taylor's eyes were bloodshot. His dress shoes were untied, his hair stuck up from lack of maintenance instead of gel. There were actually wrinkles in his button-up shirt. And half of his left eyebrow was gone, leaving a thick red welt where he'd uprooted the hairs. Never had the compulsively organized group president looked so disheveled.

"I'm so sorry. I—" But Taylor's apologies were muffled by the instant onslaught of hugs. First Renee, then Violet and Nicole, Erin and Joanna, Akash and Ben and Dylan and Gary, and finally Sid, who wrapped his long arms around the mass of singers.

Taylor was still apologizing when the group finally withdrew. "I'm sorry. There was just—someone was getting in my head. But I should have been here anyway. I should have been here for the group."

"You have such a gorgeous neck, Taylor!" said Violet, who'd just rediscovered her chipperness. "But come, let's do some touch-ups." Violet tapped her soprano baby to assist her, and together they took both Taylor and Nicole off with them to the ladies' restroom.

Sid turned to Dylan. "Would it be all right if—"

"Yes!" cried the tenor, assenting immediately to his solo's swift departure. "It's all Taylor's."

The girls and Taylor returned with remarkable speed. Although clearly still distraught, Nicole looked a lot less frightening without black mascara running down her cheeks.

Taylor, too, was much improved by the clean-up. His shirt was tucked so tight that the wrinkles were barely visible. His hair dripped from Violet's restyling in the sink. Most noticeably, where the red welt had been, Violet had drawn in an eyebrow with her make-up pencil. The color was all wrong, with two clashing shades of brown, but it was better than nothing.

Violet smiled at her work. "It'll look normal from stage distance."

"No, probably not," Renee admitted. "But it works. He looks a cappella-badass."

Everyone laughed at the petite soprano's tough talk.

Of course, Taylor's return meant only partial relief. The problem of replacing Nicole's voice remained. As the Chorderoys happily welcomed back their president, they considered their limited options. How could they replace Nicole's solo without damaging the group dynamic?

Ben's mind jumped all over as it attempted to process the schizophrenic developments of the past hour. Vivid snapshots danced behind his eyes: Taylor's entrance, complete with self-inflicted damage—Renee's friendly face as she comforted Nicole—the dark empty pews as he'd stared out into Blair Chapel—Caroline's smile as she thanked him for telling her the truth.

The electric bass of the walk-in music playing in the chapel faded, drowned out by the lively chatter of the growing audience. The competition was about to begin.

That's when it came to him. Ben pulled the music director aside and told him his idea.

Chapter 20

Dynamics

Technically speaking, it wasn't a last *minute* change.

"We have forty-six minutes if each group uses its full twelve minutes and intermission lasts the full ten," calculated Taylor. "Plus any time Marianne spends making introductions."

Forty-six minutes to revamp, again, the set they'd been preparing for months.

Time wasn't their only restriction, either. With the competition beginning, they couldn't risk singing at full volume and being heard on the other side of the chapel wall. Taylor recalled a specific WAC rule against competing groups creating "acoustical interference," a disqualifying offense.

The Chorderoys bunched together in a tight circle, softly singing their parts, with only the closed-circuit television beside them for an audience. The TV showed a live feed of the other groups' performances.

As Violet taught the group improvised choreography, Ben watched the Gobfellas perform Toto's "Africa." They played air congos and swung imaginary Tarzan vines as they sang—their interpretation of "African" chore-ography.

Sid seemed concerned that the changes might adversely affect the group's musicality. "Be conscious of your speed," he cautioned. "Don't forget what we worked on with dynamics: light and shade, loud and soft."

"And get peppy!" Violet encouraged them, with a less-than-subtle glance at Taylor's half eyebrow. "Like Olivia always says: Be *desirable*."

While Sid worked quickly with individual singers, Ben's eyes kept wandering toward the television screen. After Marianne introduced the Notabelles, the all-female group filed in from opposite sides, crisscrossing to form a perfect "V" formation, wearing shimmering purple dresses and matching black pearl necklaces.

For the rousing chorus of the Dixie Chicks' "Not Ready to Make Nice," the women stomped defiantly, with perfect synchronization. Next came "Alone" by Heart, complete with tight eight-part harmonies sung in a heart-shaped formation.

The Notabelles finished their set with Bonnie Tyler's "Holding Out for a Hero." During the last chorus, they lifted their two lightest girls over their heads like flying superheroes. The acrobats dismounted in unison, landing precisely on the downbeat.

The last of the three "girl power" songs earned the group thunderous applause.

"Notabelles for Outstanding Choreo award," Dylan predicted grumpily. "Why didn't we add more gymnastics to our routine?"

Violet's cheeks went red.

Sid called Joanna over to discuss how they should reconfigure the microphones between songs. While they powwowed privately, Ben couldn't help watching the next group's set.

Applause welcomed the black-and-red clad Harmoniums to the stage. Their first song, Estelle's "American Boy," was a Harmoniums' classic with fresh choreography. Ben noted Dani's artistic touch in the new dance moves, the strategically added spices of rumba and cha-cha-cha.

He quickly recognized the introductory chords of the second number, the familiar lyrics sounding high and clear. Caroline's interpretation of "Use Somebody" was graceful and tender, no echo effect required. Behind her, Ben heard delicate, middle-voiced harmonies. The chords in the arrangement never resolved predictably, but held their tension with spontaneity and mystery.

They were traits Ben recognized from their long-ago guitar improv sessions. He knew the truth intuitively: The Harmoniums' "Use Somebody" was not only Caroline's first solo, it was also her first arrangement. Her musical traces were all over it.

For the final line of the song, the block dropped out. Caroline sang, alone but unwavering.

The applause came a few seconds late, as if the audience members were coming out of a collective trance.

While the Harmoniums arranged themselves for their third and final song, Ben considered his situation. The Harmoniums' rendition of "Use Somebody" was, indeed, different, but they'd absolutely nailed it. The pressure to respond was on him.

Dani came forward to the microphone, her hips swaying with each step, fully confident in her role: the final soloist. The anchor.

Taylor, watching the TV alongside Ben, identified the song almost immediately. "Beyoncé's 'Best Thing I Never Had,'" said the Chorderoys' president, shaking his head at the screen. "Why does Dani always sing as the dejected lover?"

"Maybe—" ventured Violet.

"That was a rhetorical question," Joanna interrupted firmly.

As Ben watched, Dani seemed to stare straight into the camera lens, every bit the empowered girl done wrong. She belted her denunciation of her foolish exes.

Before the chorus, the cunning president flipped back her strawberry blonde hair and raised one hand to the ceiling. In the background, Ben heard Caroline's high soprano voice layered behind Dani's bold dismissals. The two women's voices blended uncannily, singing the refrain as soloist and back-up vocals.

For the finale, Dani pulled out all the stops, riffing through her highest passages. Raw emotion growled through every note; her brilliant voice ripped across the chapel.

When it was over, the applause came roaring. Dani stood still, soaking in the moment.

"And Dani for Outstanding Soloist," grumbled Dylan.

On the TV screen, the stage brightened. The Chorderoys heard loud chatter on the other side of the wall. Intermission had begun. They were next on deck.

Sid led them around the corner to the back hallway leading to the chapel's stage.

As they waited, Ben peered around at their faces: Dylan, who seemed lonesome and pessimistic without Guillermo; Nicole, who was still struggling to hold back croaky tears; Akash, who was shaking out his shoulders, trying to relax.

Much to everyone's surprise, however, Taylor was smiling.

The president held up a single, golden, plastic-wrapped slice of cheese.

"I grabbed it on the way out," he explained. "It's soy cheese, actually, but I think it'll still work."

The group stared in awe at the vegan-friendly slice.

With faux-solemnity, Taylor recited Guillermo's traditional description of the ritual. "I know there's some metaphor to be made, but it doesn't really matter. Slapping the cheese is fun because it doesn't have to mean anything. Just take a slap—a *real* slap—and pass it right along."

Taylor held the slice up and gave it a whack. The familiar crackling rattled in the narrow hallway.

The group president giggled. "Ooh, soy has a nice texture."

Despite everything that had happened, Ben and the rest of the Chorderoys proceeded with the same tradition they had performed before every other gig: Administering goofy, awkward, oddly enjoyable slaps to an undeserving slice of cheese. As always, the audience was none the wiser to their ritual.

When they heard Marianne's voice over the sound system, Taylor replaced the cheese slice in his pocket. The Chorderoys readied themselves in line.

The music director smiled. "Just sing your heart out," said Sid simply, as if his technical advice had always been secondary.

Marianne called out for them in her loud, excited voice: "Ladies and Gentlemen, the Brighton University CHORDEROYS!"

Ben rushed onstage. Immediately, he could feel the air vibrating from clapping and the heat of the bright stage lights. As he adjusted the solo mic stand, he smiled out into the abyss of shadowed faces.

Behind him, Sid blew the pitch pipe.

Ben opened his mouth to sing "Use Somebody," and as he sang, he felt an inexplicable electricity physically connecting him to the rest of his group. He *felt* the support of the sopranos singing a counter in a high-above octave; he *felt* the altos punctuate his solo with short, quick syllables; he *felt* the tenors' harmonies floating over the melody; he *felt* the basses driving home his melody with bold determination.

He was a rock star unfettered by instruments.

When the applause came, Ben had to force himself to stay in position rather than fist pump. His skin tingled from all the claps and cheers. From the back of the balcony, a familiar voice yelled, "BIG BEN! TOUCHÉ THAT SOLO!"

Smiling, Ben returned to the block of singers for song number two.

This time, it was Joanna who blew the pitch and counted off the tempo. From the block, Ben and Taylor made eye contact as they sang the crescendo-decrescendo swells of their tenor introduction.

In front of the block, Sid's voice came smooth and soulful. He took an assertive step forward, building up to the intense chorus of "Chasing Pavements." Although the song had been arranged for a female soloist, Ben knew that he'd been right to suggest that Sid sing it tonight. The music director's voice was a perfect fit for the theme of singing through a difficult time.

Looking over, Ben saw Nicole looking thrilled for Sid as she lip-synched the alto part, a model performer even without her voice.

Just before the second verse began, Akash walked slowly to the front-left corner of the stage. The freshman baritone grabbed the secondary microphone. He came in right on cue:

• • *Boom dama, duhv- Kah- / Boom dama, duhv- Kah-* • •

Ben watched his classmate sway back and forth naturally as he added his rhythmic pulse to the melody of voices. The first-time vocal percussionist made it look so easy! Ben listened for the guiding words disguised in his friend's percussion line: *boots, skirts. boots, skirts.*

Erin and Renee stepped forward, flanking Sid on either side. They sang above and below his melody line in warm alto and crisp soprano, an aural halo encircling his voice.

Akash waved his hand in front of the mic, creating a rattling "snare."

Renee and Erin stepped back into the block, which grew quiet. For the final line, it was just Sid's clear, melodious voice ringing out for the eager audience to hear.

Sid humbly bowed his head as the audience broke into applause.

When it had quieted, the Chorderoys gathered in a small clump for their third and final song. Sid blew the pitch, and Taylor stepped slowly forward.

As they began Queen's "The Show Must Go On," Ben and his fellow Chorderoys swayed back and forth with their president's yearning melody.

The song started slowly. Ben felt it build around him: Gary's ominous low pedal "organ," the altos dancing in and out of the melody line, the sopranos' haunting treble descant.

Then, all at once, the Chorederoys dropped a bomb-shell of energetic acasynchronicity on their audience. The group stepped confidently into Guillermo's "TRIANGLE OF THE APOCALYPSE" formation; the block took on a new, pulsating rhythm; and Taylor belted the heart-wrenching refrain.

The sopranos were responsible for initiating the key change in the second verse, an upward shift that began with Violet and worked its way downward to Gary's grumbly bass. Meanwhile, alone on his part, Ben sang out a high tenor line, wailing his "electric guitar."

Clutching his white oxford, Taylor was holding nothing back in his voice, as if he were channeling Freddie Mercury's own life-and-death determination. He seemed to be having a very intense personal moment before the enormous crowd.

As the song neared its conclusion, Ben and Dylan came forward and hoisted Taylor on their shoulders for the move Guillermo had called the "TOWER OF EPIC TRIUMPH."

The rest of the singers gathered around the "tower," singing their parts in bold *fortissimo*. Above him, Ben heard Taylor's booming voice, still holding the mic, defiant till the very end.

For the final note, their fists shot up on cue as Taylor finished, "The Show Must Go On!"

When the applause came, Ben's natural impulse was to throw Taylor's heavy thigh off his shoulder. But he kept his position, his body conditioned to the task after weeks of rehearsing.

Finally, their group president dismounted, and the Chorderoys backed up into a wide arc. All together, they bowed, then ran offstage.

Back in the waiting room, Renee was the first person to squeal. "YESSS!"

After the mandatory group hug, Ben found himself hugging everyone again, this time individually: Taylor, who had lines of smeared "eyebrow" across his forehead; Akash, whose shy smile stretched from ear to ear; Nicole, who blubber-croaked some incomprehensible compliment; Sid, who was still in utter shock . . .

When there'd been an acceptable amount of acaffection, Sid exhaled and said simply, "I'm proud." The music director shook his head, as if he couldn't believe what had happened during those critical twelve minutes on stage.

At last, the Chorderoys crept down the hallway and upstairs, to the highest row in the balcony of Blair

Chapel. From there, they could watch the last performances of the competition.

La*chaim had just introduced their second song, which they'd based on Psalm 67, "Let the Nations Be Glad and Sing for Joy." The arrangement modulated between major and minor keys, and La*chaim alternately sang in English and Hebrew.

By contrast, the final song in La*chaim's set was a mash-up medley of popular Jewish-American songwriters. "I Feel the Earth Move" by Carole King became "I'll Never Fall In Love Again" by Burt Bacharach became "Straight Up" by Paula Abdul became "Whataya Want From Me?" by Adam Lambert.

As Ben admired the creativity of an arrangement that mixed together so many disparate musical genres, he thought back fondly to his first experience of college a cappella at the Recruitment Concert. He felt the same sense of delight this evening as he had back then: A cappella was still freedom; he was still happy to have joined the cause.

La*chaim took their bow, and Marianne introduced the final group.

The nerdy nice-guys of the Dinos ran onstage wearing green vests and all types of ties—skinny, clip-on, bolo, even comically large bow ties. The effect was quirky and classy all at once.

Their first song, "September," was an old funk hit by Earth, Wind & Fire. As they sang, the Dinos acted out their roles in the band: The tallest man was a string bass; their slightest member was held horizontally as the "bow"; the baritones stretched their lanky arms as trombones; the tenors went wild with air trumpets. Ben spotted Greg's effervescent touch all over the choreography.

Dinos song number two began with smooth, rolling arpeggios, lots of *nim*s and *doo*s, and a relaxed, schmaltzy bass line.

Renee tapped Akash's arm excitedly. Of course she recognized *this* song! It was Billy Joel's "Just the Way You Are." Since Nicole's mixed CD had proven that it wasn't much of a secret anyway, Renee had recently outed herself to them as a Billy Joel – Elton John – Phil Collins fanatic.

The rest of the Dinos began interweaving the melody of the Bruno Mars song by the same name. It was a creative musical innovation, but Ben found his attention disturbed by Taylor's fidgeting fingers. Was the group president becoming more nervous about the competition results?

Greg seemed to be peering straight up into the balcony as he finished the song in his warmest, gentlest falsetto.

The Dinos' third and final number quickly had the audience laughing. "It's Raining Men" by the Weather Girls showcased the all-men ensemble's cheeky diva side. By the end, all sixteen singers were sassily snapping and shaking their hips.

In the final pose of that year's WAC competition, Ben spotted the only actual "jazz hands" of the evening. The Dinos flared their fingers high into the air.

After all the cheering, the Dinos exited, and Marianne announced that there was to be a short break while the judges deliberated. When the lights came up in the chapel, Ben continued to stare at the stage. All of the singing that evening had been exceptional. He had no idea how the six groups could possibly be measured quantitatively.

"So . . . how does this work?" he asked, turning to the others.

"Four judges—all experts—" croaked Nicole, "judge on musicality, choreo—" Her explanation was cut short by a fit of raspy coughing.

Renee patted her sympathetically and took over. "...Musicality, choreography, appropriateness of movement, audience engagement..." Renee rattled the rest of the judges' criteria in rapid-fire succession. She also told them about the judges. The panel this year consisted of a local high school choir teacher, a Brighton professor of musicality, a professional choreographer, and the Vice President of MASA, the Modern A cappella Society of America. Mid-explanation, the short soprano noticed the other freshmen's surprised stares. She shrugged and said, "So I studied a little."

Akash smiled and added, "Since Brighton has six groups, this round is intramural. They'll only announce one winner, though, and that group moves on to the semi-finals."

"And besides the first place group, they have the 'Outstanding' awards," added Renee. "Outstanding Choreogaphy, Outstanding Soloists, things like that."

At this point, Taylor motioned for the rest of the Chorderoys to join him at the front of the balcony. When they'd gathered together, he dialed Olivia on speakerphone.

"Hello, *darlings*," answered the alto, completely herself even on her sickbed. "And how did we perform this evening?"

Dylan hogged the receiver as the group phoned Guillermo, but the call was cut short by the flickering of the chapel lights. Marianne returned to the front and invited all six of the competing groups to join her on stage.

As Ben trekked down the aisles of Blair Chapel and watched all the groups gathering on stage, he felt an eerie sense of déjà vu. Like at the Recruitment Concert, the six groups stood in their separate packs, divided by their group colors: the Dinos in their green and black; the polished, purple-clad Notabelles; La*chaim in amber-gold and black; the Harmoniums in classy black and red, standing in two formal lines; the Gobfellas, already shedding their mismatched sports coats and bubblegum-pink ties; and Ben's own group, the Chorderoys, an ensemble of friendly white and blue. Per Nicole's request, they were holding hands, even Renee.

Marianne addressed them in her carefully crafted, singer-spokeswoman voice. "First of all, this was perhaps the most stellar intra-university WAC competition I have ever had the pleasure of witnessing. Rarely have I heard such *inspired* singing at the college level. Seriously, what's gotten into you guys?"

On stage, the singers laughed nervously.

"The judges would like to emphasize that they had an extremely difficult time making their decisions. The performances tonight were all of an exceptionally high quality." Marianne clinched her teeth into a smile. "But, they've made their determinations, and it's time to recognize tonight's winners. We'll begin with the judges' awards of special distinction.

"For Outstanding Arranging . . ."

Ben sensed that Marianne grasped the essential musicality of good theater. Before each announcement, she held her pause, allowing the tension to build, and providing Ben with time to think about the main contenders.

The freshman tenor considered the possibilities. He thought Caroline's arrangement of "Use Somebody" had

258

been hauntingly beautiful. And hadn't Greg done quite a bit of arranging for the Dinos? Still, Ben hoped the winner would be Sid. The music director had arranged all three songs in the Chorderoys' competition set list.

"The award goes to . . . Rachel Stein of La*chaim for her Jewish Lovin' medley!"

Ben nodded. That arrangement had been outstanding, weaving together so many types of music. Then again, the source materials she had started with were pretty good, too.

"For Outstanding Male Soloist . . ."

Although Ben imagined himself stepping out to accept the award, he didn't really expect to win. He sincerely hoped one of the Chorderoys' upperclassmen would get it, either Sid for his solo debut, or Taylor, for those wild, liberated vocals.

"The award goes to . . . Greg Hollis of the Dinos!"

The Dinos' president's face went bright red. His curly brown hair bounced up and down as he marched up to receive his award.

"For Outstanding Female Soloist . . ."

Ben knew this was a particularly deep playing field. Notabelle Kara's "Holding Out For a Hero" had been a crowd favorite, but how much had that performance been helped by the acrobatic choreography? Personally, Ben thought Caroline had absolutely nailed "Use Somebody," but was he perhaps biased? The judges would no doubt remember Dani's powerful Beyoncé interpretation, her masterful gift for controlling the audience's attention. Looking over, Ben saw Dani digging her fingers into her musical director's arm, bracing for her big moment.

"The award goes to . . . Caroline Cooper of the Harmoniums!"

Ben was the first to cheer. Already standing, he jumped automatically into the air, as if Caroline deserved more than a standing ovation.

It was obvious that the slim soprano wasn't expecting to hear her name. She didn't move at all until her groupmates gave her a friendly push, and she stutter-stepped forward to receive her certificate.

"Now, for two awards presented to the groups as a whole," Marianne continued, clearly excited by the transition. "For Oustanding Choreography . . ."

Ben thought this was an easier pick. He saw the Dinos and Notabelles as the two primary contenders, with the decision resting on whether the judges preferred hilarious dancing or elegant, acrobatic formations.

"The award goes to . . . those lovely ladies in the Notabelles!"

This time, a high-pitched, feminine "woo!" could be heard over the standard cheers. Kara walked forward to accept the award on behalf of the ladies in purple.

Marianne continued grinning with both rows of teeth. "One last group distinction award. For Outstanding Musicality . . ."

That was a broad category, thought Ben. He quickly considered Caroline's nuanced arranging, Dani's epic solo, La*chaim's diverse song mix, Greg's heartfelt love song . . .

"The award goes to . . . the Chorderoys!"

Nicole squeezed Ben's hand super tight; all around him, his fellow group members shouted and cheered. Together with Dylan, Ben pushed Sid forward to the front of the stage. After a year's worth of constant coaching, there was no one more appropriate to accept such an award.

At last, Marianne cleared her throat. "Now, the moment you've all been waiting for. The highest-scoring group, the winner of tonight's six-group a cappella competition, who will continue on to the Midwestern Semi-Final of the World A cappella Championship . . ."

Ben's mind raced. Given the song duplication, the mono, the laryngitis, Taylor's absence, the solo swapping, the abysmal soundcheck . . . It was too much to hope, wasn't it?

Then again, hadn't the Chorderoys just won the award for Outstanding Musicality? What could be a more important factor for judging an a cappella singing competition than the overall quality of *sound*?

"Ladies and Gentlemen, your champions tonight . . ." Marianne held her breath. "The Notabelles!"

On his right side, Ben heard such blood-curdling shrieking from the all-female group that he thought his eardrums might burst. The women stepped forward to receive the trophy before collapsing back into a giant group hug. Even with his disappointment, Ben couldn't help feeling some happiness on behalf of the "sisters in song."

Ben followed the Chorderoys, and the four other groups as they reluctantly left the stage, clearing the way for the Notabelles to sing their victory encore.

Before singing, Kara grabbed the microphone and yelled out, "Check Facebook for details on the afterparty! Non-acas are invited, too!" (Somewhere in the audience, Ben knew Wilson had just gotten very excited.)

As the Notabelles began to sing, the Chorderoys exited the chapel and veered off into the hallway behind the stage, gathering into a huddle. "I've NEVER been prouder to be part of this group!" yelled Taylor, straining to be heard over the boisterous rendition of Aretha

Franklin's "Respect" being sung on the other side of the door.

"What we pulled off tonight was incredible!" yelled the music director, smiling from ear to ear.

There were fervent, happy nods all around. Ben looked into the faces of his close friends, registering the moment. Not for the first time, he felt grateful that life had thrust this a cappella world upon him. Really and truly, it was these friendships that gave singing its true value.

In comparison, Ben knew winning didn't matter at all.

Chapter 21

Persuasion

. . . Well, it mattered a little bit.

When the Chorderoys arrived at the Notabelles' afterparty, the victorious ladies were already on their fifth bottle of champagne. Each lady took turns toasting something she loved about the group. With each toast they cried, "Chicago!"—the location of the next exciting round of WAC.

Though the "sisters in song" had most cause to celebrate, the other groups nevertheless enjoyed the standard a cappella revelry. Kelly Clarkson was blasting over the speakers, with several sopranos automatically singing the high harmony above the melody line; all around, drinkers were poorly estimating their liquor-to-mixer ratios, sharing cups without regard for basic rules of hygiene; one Dino was already showing off his vocal percussion in the corner.

"Gotta love the acatypes!" said Wilson, with a cheeky grin. He clapped Ben on the shoulder and veered off to join the growing blob of dancing.

On the other side of the apartment, Ben spotted Dani mixing herself another martini. Per usual, she'd brought the three required ingredients with her. He watched as she poured precise proportions of vodka and vermouth, shook the mixture, and tossed in an olive.

He knew Dani must be *devastated*. She'd been working toward Outstanding Female Soloist for months. Caroline had beaten her out, soloing on an arrangement Dani had specifically intended for Ben to sing when he transferred into the Harmoniums. It had to be killing her inside.

263

And yet, besides the fact that she was drinking alone, Dani revealed no hint of sadness. She'd applied fresh lipstick, stood with her usual perfect posture, and shot a wide smile to anyone who happened to walk by. Ben couldn't help admiring her.

As casually as possible, the freshman tenor began searching the apartment for Caroline. He spotted her standing with a group of her fellow Harmoniums, having what seemed to be a rather somber conversation. Elliot was not accompanying her.

On cue, Greg walked up and placed his hand on Ben's shoulder. "She just broke up with him," he explained. "Apparently, Elliot's been dating the owner of the indie music magazine that's been publishing his work."

Ben's eyes widened. He'd been wondering how the hipster was getting so many professional articles published at all of eighteen years old!

"Anyway, Caroline found out about her. Elliot apologized profusely, but Caroline said she couldn't trust him anymore. So she broke it off."

The Dinos' president examined Ben's face closely. "Something told me you'd want to know."

Ben nodded and took a deep breath. When Greg left, Ben spent a few minutes formulating his plan. He decided he would walk up to Caroline, congratulate her on her solo, and continue their conversation from just before the competition.

He'd finally gathered his courage and was taking his first step forward when he felt a hand grab his shoulder

"Can I speak with you outside, please?"

"Erm—but—uh—can it *wait*?"

Taylor shook his head gravely. "It's important."

Ben looked over at Caroline, then back at Taylor. Unfortunately for Ben, it's difficult to refuse someone with a half-missing eyebrow.

He followed Taylor into the hallway outside the apartment. The Chorderoys' president closed the door behind him, sealing in some of the noise. Greg was already waiting for them, a perplexed expression on his face.

"I know this isn't the best of times," began the Chorderoys' president, "But I need to tell you both what's going on. There's a reason why I almost didn't show up to WAC tonight.

"Greg, I'm hoping you might know how to handle this without causing a major disruption in ACUAC." Taylor turned and looked down at the freshman. "And Ben, I'm hoping you can tailor our message to the audience, given your dating history."

"What is it, Taylor?" asked Greg.

The Chorderoys' president ran his fingers back through his still-sweaty black hair. "Based on the performances tonight, Student Government will have an even tougher time deciding which group to cut."

Ben nodded. Even with the Outstanding Musicality award, the Chorderoys weren't yet in the clear. With the exception of the Gobfellas, who weren't going to be eliminated anyway, every group had won something.

Taylor took a deep breath, looking up with wide, determined eyes. "But if we play our cards right, perhaps we can save all six of us."

♫

The following afternoon, Ben waited alone in Badger's Café, feeling very much like *bait*. His untouched cup of coffee grew cold on the small table.

After what felt like hours, Dani finally arrived. "Ben Jensen. I must say, your message this morning came as a surprise. It's been some time since you last texted me."

Dani wore a fancy, all-black business dress, an indigo scarf, and her favorite red pumps. "Whatever did you wish to discuss?" As she sat down, he caught a whiff of her familiar perfume.

"Well, I heard you might know some people on Student Government," said Ben tentatively. "People who decide things like the budget. And I thought maybe you could, you know, use that power to help the rest of us a cappella people out." He tried smiling his cutest smile.

Dani sighed. "I suspected this, of course, but I'd honestly hoped for better. Forgive me, Ben Jensen, but you're not the most inventive communicator. If you're going to parrot whatever request Taylor asked you to make, why don't you just invite *him* here so I can reject the both of you simultaneously?"

Ben felt his cheeks burning red. "Um . . . er . . . I was hoping this would just be the two of us."

Dani smiled threateningly. "Invite Taylor to join, or I'll be on my way."

Reluctantly, Ben pulled out his phone and texted his group president.

When he'd finished, Dani shook her head, laughing to herself. "I can't believe he sent a freshman to do his bidding. What a chicken!"

Ben clenched his teeth. "I think he was under the mistaken impression that, at some point, you might have actually liked me."

Dani eyed him closely. "Mistaken impression?"

"Oh, come on, Dani. You know you were only pretending to be interested so that you could recruit me for the Harmoniums. It was all an act!"

Dani opened her mouth to speak but was interrupted by the arrival of Greg and Taylor. They'd been waiting nearby the café in case their young protégé needed assistance. It seemed to Ben that their lack of confidence in his independent negotiation skills was not unfounded.

Without asking, Greg claimed the chair next to Dani's. "Well, this is cozy," he said, in his usual warm tenor.

Dani straightened uncomfortably in her seat. "Start talking, then. If I'm going to be ambushed, I might as well know why."

"Taylor told us how you offered the Chorderoys protection if he didn't participate in WAC," Greg explained. "He also shared how you've taken over the Treasury Council in just the past few months. As ACUAC chair, I'm appalled. But as a fellow president, I have to admit: It's impressive."

Dani shrugged.

"We've come to ask you to use that power to prevent SG from cutting any of the a cappella groups," said Greg. "Sure, we're technically competitors, but all six groups bring something different to the table. It'd be a shame to see any of us go."

Dani shook her head. "I think, for once, you might be overestimating my abilities. The University is in desperate financial straits. Who am I tell SG that they should slash everything else, but a cappella alone must remain un-touched?"

The Harmoniums' president took a small sip of chai before continuing. "Furthermore, I disagree with your conclusion. There are clear advantages to the consol-idation of talent." Dani gave Taylor her most pointed green-eyed glare. "I honestly believe Brighton would be a better place with only five singing groups."

In response, Taylor's fingers leapt automatically for his brow. What happened next, however, was strange: From across the table, Greg nodded in Taylor's direction, and his hand fell slowly to his side.

Greg returned his gaze to Dani. "We thought you might say that, so here's our deal: If you don't use your influence to protect all of a cappella, we're going to go public with how you threatened Taylor. Sure, ACUAC might not have the means to seriously punish the Harmoniums for next year—our power is mostly ceremonial. But when word gets out in the *Student Times* that you tried to bully the Chorderoys out of WAC, SG will be forced to shut you down."

Dani actually laughed. "You seriously believe that you can blackmail me with no repercussions? Taylor here is not a blameless party. Has he told you yet about the dirty trade he engineered during this year's auditions?"

"Trade?" cried Ben. "You mean trading people? Does that actually happen?"

"It's not supposed to," said Taylor quickly, "But this year, Dani persuaded me."

Dani smiled with self-satisfaction as she revealed the news to Ben. "Your favorite soprano actually ranked the Chorderoys first, and Nicole ranked your group second. But Taylor desperately wanted an alto soloist, so we made a deal: I gave him Nicole McLain; he gave me Caroline Cooper."

Ben leaned back in his chair, his mind reeling. So Caroline *hadn't* changed her mind after they'd made their pact about group rankings. All year, he'd doubted her unnecessarily. And Nicole wasn't supposed to be in his group at all! "Wow . . ." he muttered, taking it in.

Greg frowned at Taylor. "No, he hadn't mentioned your trade. But what does it have to do with anything?"

"I kept Nicole's preference card as proof that she actually ranked the Harmoniums first," explained Dani. "If there is any attempt to discredit my name or the Harmoniums', I will produce it as clear and convincing evidence that the Chorderoys have been stealing singers."

"It wasn't stealing!" protested Taylor. "You just said we were trading!"

Dani turned to the ACUAC chairman. Her voice was cold. "Tell me, did you retain Caroline's card in your files?"

Greg fidgeted sheepishly in his seat. "Um, I think—"

"I'll answer for you: No, because that particular card hasn't existed since our presidents' meeting before the Draft." Dani leaned back, and smugly crossed her arms across her chest. "Taylor, I mean this sincerely and with the least possible hubris: If this becomes a muckraking contest, you don't stand a chance."

Ben felt his body temperature rising. He couldn't take it anymore. "Human trade? Destroying evidence? You've got to be kidding me! What's *wrong* with you older singers?" The freshman turned to Dani, specifically. "And why exactly do you hate Taylor so much? Whatever happened during your petty falling out, I'm sure it doesn't justify such hatred."

"Petty falling out?" she cried. "Trust me, anyone who heard my side wouldn't think *I* was the petty one."

"Try me," snapped Ben.

For a moment, there was quiet at their table, punctuated only by the soft chatter of patrons socializing at other tables throughout the café.

Dani looked at each of the three men. She took a deep, singer's breath and began her story:

"As you all know, I didn't make any of the a cappella groups my freshman year. It's no exaggeration to say that

I was devastated at the time, but that experience honed my skills as a performer and future leader in this community more than any other.

"I also made a friend that year, and for a while, he was a great help to me. Taylor and I were in Choir class together. We had real mutual interests: cooking, design, music, theater. We clicked instantly."

Ben looked to Taylor to refute Dani's story, but the Chorderoys' president wasn't disagreeing. In fact, he seemed to be hanging on every word.

"As freshman year wore on, we grew closer and closer. We always talked about a cappella, and I went to all his shows, of course. He told me he'd pull for me when I re-auditioned for the Chorderoys the next fall.

"This continued all summer. We spent long nights on the phone, just talking. We talked about the things we loved, our common interests, our dreams." She gave Ben a knowing glance. "Ours was a long, mutually-sustained conversation.

"As sophomore year began, our lives were suddenly hectic. I spent all day preparing for my second attempt at a cappella auditions, and Taylor was busy planning for recruitment. Still, he found the time to send me little text messages, wishing me good luck, telling me how happy he was to be reunited at school."

She sighed. "He was the cutest of flirts, talking about how much fun we'd have singing together on stage. But I warned him repeatedly that I intended to rank the Harmoniums first. The group was specifically recruiting altos, and this go-around, I was thinking much more strategically about placement.

"The night before the Draft, Taylor came over to my apartment. For the first time, he stayed the night."

To underscore the distinction, Dani shot Ben a particularly pointed look. In the few weeks they'd been dating, she and Ben hadn't had sex. He wasn't sure why, really. At various points, the timing hadn't felt right to either or both of them.

The Harmoniums' president exhaled slowly. "The next morning, he was strange, leaving quickly, almost forgetting to wish me good luck. That night, I finally heard my fate—the Harmoniums came to my door and sang me into the group! After so much waiting, I'd finally made it!"

Dani's green eyes shimmered beneath the café lights. "I waited for Taylor's congratulatory call, waited to celebrate what we'd talked about for nearly a year. But Taylor never contacted me.

"After a week, I finally stormed over to Taylor's apartment. I tried to be patient, tried to give him a chance to explain his behavior. But he didn't even want to look at me, much less *talk* to me anymore. All he said was 'This relationship isn't possible.' And with that, he closed the door in my face, without so much as letting me cry for a minute on his shoulder."

Dani took another of her deep, singer's breaths. Her cheeks were now as red as her shoes. "So, *yes*, Ben Jensen, I harbor some resentment for your esteemed group president. One day, he told me he loved me. The next, he told me it was all over because I'd joined a rival a cappella group!"

Ben gulped, wishing very much that her tale had been the petty dispute he'd been expecting.

Finally, Taylor said, "There's more to that story, Dani."

"Oh really?" snapped the alto. "What crucial detail did I neglect?"

271

Taylor's eyes darted from Greg, to Ben, and back to Greg. He shifted uncomfortably in his seat, taking short, gasping breaths.

"I knew early on," said Taylor, "Really early, actually. But it's not as simple as some people make it out to be. I genuinely believed I could do something about it. With determination, I thought I could make it work, or at least pass."

Taylor ran his fingers through his spiky black hair. He pulled his tee-shirt away from his neck, as if it were asphyxiating him. This particular angst seemed beyond his standard eyebrow-pulling.

He took several more shallow breaths, clearing and re-clearing his throat, before finally announcing in a careful, controlled voice, "I'm gay."

Dani shook her head, disbelieving. "No."

Ben looked back and forth at the two rivals. He had wondered about the orientation of his group president. To an outside observer, it could go either way. Which is to say, Ben wasn't exactly shocked by Taylor's news.

On the other hand, Ben knew how much Dani trusted her gut feelings, which had convinced her Taylor was straight. Her intuition wasn't often wrong, and never *this* wrong. She'd been blinded by her track record of accuracy.

She said it again. "No."

Taylor nodded solemnly. "I guess I knew going into college, but I hadn't accepted it. And when we met, we just had so much in common. I thought our friendship could become more. I really did try—I wanted there to be an 'us.' But, like I said, it wasn't possible. For me, at least."

"What about *Olivia?*" Even now, Dani said her name with palpable disdain. "You two were always so touchy-feely with each other."

For the first time that day, Taylor actually smiled. "Any romance between 'Liv and me exists solely on stage. We're just good friends. Since you and I weren't speaking, she's the first girl I came out to."

Ben thought back to Olivia and Taylor's hugs, her encouraging words, her reassuring pats on the back. It was true: Olivia was different with Taylor, not her customary *femme fatale.*

Taylor leaned forward. "I'm so sorry, Dani. I should have told you last year, but I just didn't feel ready. If it's any consolation, I've been waiting to come out publicly, even to most of my friends. I knew I owed it to you to tell you first."

Dani's eyes widened. She looked back and forth at Greg and Taylor, back to relying on her intuition, which was, after all, still usually correct. "And you two . . . you're—"

"We've been dating, yes," confirmed Greg, in his warmest tenor. "It's been difficult at times, because he didn't want to be open about it. But I tried my hardest not to pressure him."

Ben thought back to Taylor's reaction to Greg singing "Just the Way You Are" on the night of the WAC competition. In retrospect, the moment had new meaning.

There was a long silence.

At last, Dani stood up. "I'm sorry, boys, but you can't just gay your way out of this!"

"Wait!" said Ben. "What does that even mean?"

"It means Taylor and I were friends, and then he ditched me!" said Dani. "I have no problem with being gay, I truly don't. But that really, really hurt." She grabbed her purse. "And apologizing two years after the fact doesn't make it better."

Ben looked at Greg and Taylor, but neither group president seemed prepared to further argue the point. So much for his rescue crew!

The freshman leapt up, knowing he must act. "Then don't accept his apology right now. Wait until you're ready to forgive him."

The Harmoniums' president tilted her head; she hadn't expected this suggestion. The moment of hesitation provided Ben his opening.

"And with the budget cuts, you're missing the key issue," said Ben. "If one group is shut down, there will be many fewer spots for singers at Brighton, even though more people are trying out each year."

He looked straight into her green eyes. "Dani, if you let this happen, significantly more people are going to experience the same pain you did as a freshman. Sure, things worked out for you, eventually. But should anyone with your abilities be denied the opportunity to sing?"

For several seconds, the Harmonums' president was speechless. Both Greg and Taylor looked up at Ben, wide-eyed and impressed.

When she spoke, her voice was low and strangely monotone. "SG isn't just blowing smoke. The need for cuts is serious. It doesn't work anymore to tell them how much we love singing. We need an actual idea."

Luckily, Ben had one.

"What's the one thing the Gobfellas have that the other groups don't?"

♫ |

Chapter 22

Archways

It was a sunny April Saturday, and the Chorderoys were gathering in the campus quadrangle for their final performance of the school year.

Guillermo greeted Nicole as she walked up. "Well hello there, Madame President."

"President-*elect*," emphasized Nicole. "He's still in charge for one more gig." She smiled in Taylor's direction.

Taylor was smiling himself, relieved to be handing over his responsibilities.

In retrospect, Taylor couldn't believe how smoothly it had gone. Greg had insisted that both Nicole and Caroline be informed of the secret trade by their respective presidents, and given the option to transfer into the ensemble each had originally ranked first.

But when Taylor told Nicole, she had been adamant about remaining in the Chorderoys. Her heart and loyalties now rested firmly with the group in white-and-blue. In a peculiar way, however, the opportunity boosted Nicole's already fiery interest in a cappella, as if the second chance reinforced her belief that her plans were meant to be. Taylor hadn't been surprised when she submitted her name for the Chorderoys' presidency. Before the vote, Nicole shared her ambitious goals for next year—recording an entire album, organizing a national tour—but the real strength of her candidacy was her extreme dedication to the group.

For his part, Taylor was more than ready to retire from the presidency. The dutiful tenor was looking forward to finally having more personal time next year. Instead of standing for re-election, he offered to help Nicole in a more supportive role as the experienced upperclassman.

Akash arrived, late but excited. "I just heard none of the a cappella groups are getting cut now! Is that true?"

Taylor nodded to Nicole, encouraging her to explain this development.

"Student Government finally realized that the Gob-fellas were receiving thousands of dollars each year in unreported alumni donations," she recounted theatrically. "The Treasury Council voted that groups receiving vast amounts of private funds should receive a smaller percentage of the community a cappella allotment. The Fellas weren't about to give up their booster cash, so SG can now afford to finance all of us."

"Wow, that actually seems like a rational solution," muttered Dylan. "Are you sure SG came up with it?"

Taylor shot Ben a knowing grin.

Sid gathered the group in a circle and, for his last time as musical director, led them through vocal warm-ups. Together, they stretched their high ranges on a warm, major arpeggio:

I am a cow, Moooooooooooo.

Joanna seemed to be watching Sid extra-closely; the tough-minded soprano would succeed him in the fall.

After warm-ups, Taylor motioned everyone close for a brief chat. "While we're all still together, I want to make an announcement." Though clearly anxious, he held his hand firmly at his side. "I wanted to announce, err, tell you, no . . . specify that . . ." He stopped and caught his breath. "I'm gay."

Taylor waited, but no one said anything. "I'm still the same person, though," he added, a nervous afterthought.

"Okay, ten dollars!" cried Guillermo, holding out his hand.

Reluctantly, Dylan pulled out his wallet and thumbed through the bills inside. "We had a bet going about how you'd come out to us," he explained. "I said heartfelt group e-mail, he said touching public speech. So Mo wins."

As Taylor watched the financial transaction take place, he was unsure whether to be relieved or mortified.

Violet's maternal instincts kicked in. "What they mean is, we're all really happy and proud of you." There was a round of hugs, and comfortingly casual congratulations.

After the exchange of hugs, it was time to walk across campus to their gig. Brighton was designed in the classical university fashion, with a wide rectangular quadrangle, tall turrets, and echoing archways connecting the old buildings of stone. Their destination for this performance was the most acoustically pleasing of these archways.

Perhaps their smallest gig of the year, the Chorderoys' Senior Arch Sing was primarily put on for the group's own benefit. The intention was to send-off the graduating seniors in style, recognizing them for their years of dedication, thanking them for having offered their voices.

When the group arrived at their favorite arch, they found an audience consisting mostly of fellow a cappella singers. Caroline sat at the edge of the steps, chin resting on her hand, looking thoughtful. Greg sat cross-legged on the stone floor, smiling up at Taylor. In the back, Dani leaned against a stone wall, arms crossed. Taylor also spotted Rachel from La*chaim, Cory from the Gobfellas, Kara from the Notabelles, Melanie from the Harmoniums—representatives from every group, out to pay their respects for the departing voices.

The Chorderoys began the show with "Chasing Pavements." Per Sid's instruction, Nicole was back on the solo. With plenty of hydrating and some much-needed rest, her voice had returned within a few days.

As Nicole sang, she made full use of the performance space, bouncing her big voice across the curved ceiling of the archway. When she finished, her last note echoed in every ear.

Next came "Your Song" and "Ain't No Mountain High Enough/She Will Be Loved," two of Sid's favorite arrangements. As Taylor soloed on the second of Sid's compositions, he felt its interlocking harmonies reverberating around him as he never had before.

Finally, they came to Taylor's favorite a cappella tradition: The moment when each outgoing senior sang the song he or she had used to *audition* for the group four years previously.

The Chorderoys' sultry alto stepped forward to reprise TLC's "Red Light Special," slowly swaying her hips as she sang. Taylor smirked, remembering Ben's complete shock upon discovering last week that Olivia was attending Harvard Business School next fall. With all of Olivia's other qualities, Ben had somehow failed to notice that the alto was also a veritable marketing genius.

Next came Violet's solo, which revealed some significant personal transition. Straight out of high school, the bubbly soprano had imagined herself a punk rocker, strutting into the Chorderoys' audition room and busting out Avril Lavigne's "Complicated." Today, she sang it in her natural voice, a bright soprano lilt, as if she'd accepted herself for the sweet, agreeable person that she was. After this summer, she would begin her Master of Education degree, focusing on early childhood development.

278

Finally, Sid stepped forward to sing the Eagles' classic "Desperado." His baritone was smooth and warm, a gentle blend of head and chest voices. The veteran music director had announced last week that he'd decided to defer starting his Ph.D. in Philosophy in order to spend two years working for Teach for America, teaching high school Civics in one of the poorest school districts in the country. Sid had decided that, before committing years to academia, he wanted to have an impact on the "real world." Once again, Taylor found himself exceedingly impressed by his co-leader.

As Sid's voice echoed throughout the chamber, Taylor looked over to Dani. His fellow junior would never willingly relinquish her power as president. Luckily for her, the group also recognized her as the most competent person for the job. She ran unopposed, and was reelected unanimously.

Dani stared at Sid as he sang, with more than the usual intensity in her gaze. Taylor wondered whether she was thinking about what it would be like for her at this time next year.

When the concert ended, Taylor searched for Dani in the slowly disbursing crowd. He'd been meaning to thank her for convincing SG to adopt the "rich alums" solution, and for helping Greg plan tomorrow night's big party.

But the confident alto was nowhere to be found. She'd disappeared, as if the last ovation had been her cue to leave.

♪ |

Chapter 23

Choices

As the five freshmen—Chorderoys, plus Wilson—rode in the taxicab to the final a cappella party of the year, the guys discussed their sophomore rooming arrangements.

"We're definitely calling it the AcaSuite," kidded Ben. He smiled over his shoulder at Akash, who sat squished between Nicole and Renee in the back seat.

"No we're not!" protested Wilson. "I don't care that I'm about to crash a party full of a cappella people; I'm not letting you name our apartment the AcaSuite."

"What happened to Ryan?" asked Nicole. Ryan was a friend from Akash's freshmen floor; until recently, they'd been planning on rooming together.

"Told me a few days ago that he's transferring to Penn," said Akash. "Isn't that strange? He made all these plans to switch to an Ivy, and he never mentioned it to anybody."

Nicole and Renee exchanged a knowing glance, which the boys were unable to interpret.

The shy baritone smiled. "Anyway, now I'm a proud member of the AcaSuite."

"That's not its name!" cried Wilson.

The cab came to a halt just outside a cast-iron gate. The name was printed on elegant gold plating: THE WASHINGTON OAKS COUNTRY CLUB.

Together, the quintet walked a tree-lined path towards the faint sounds of music in the distance. Turning the corner, Ben was greeted with an unexpected menagerie of lights: The flames of tiki torches lining the back lawn; the pool shining blue beneath the humid summer air; the coals glowing orange in the barbecue grill; the neon lighting above the marble mini-bar.

To decorate this peculiar Midwestern oasis, the landscaping staff had planted palm trees in the lawn and installed speakers in the high hidden branches. Dance music floated down from the treetops, nature and artifice intertwined.

All in all, it was a pretty fancy establishment for a college a cappella party.

"How did we get this place?" Ben wondered aloud.

Greg appeared, once again perfectly on cue. "Dani knew a guy," he said, as if that explained everything. He held up a tray full of drinks. "Mojito?"

Wilson grabbed a glass. "Touché!" he said gratefully. Ben rolled his eyes.

As the five of them walked across the lawn, Ben observed members of every a cappella group mingling openly. Violet and the Notabelles' Kara were discussing how quickly their respective newbies had grown up. Men from the Gobfellas and the Dinos jockeyed amiably for the role of grillmaster, while La*chaim and the Harmoniums played Marco Polo in the pool.

Ben watched Olivia and Guillermo chatting together, having mostly recovered from their respective bouts with mono. Mo grinned as the sultry alto unbuttoned his Hawaiian shirt to reveal more chest hair. Perhaps there was more truth to Dylan's theory of contagion than Ben had thought!

Akash pointed. "Look, they have a springboard *and* a high dive!"

"Well, 'high dive' is a relative term," teased Renee. The twosome headed for the pool.

282

Noah Levinson—who was, indeed, a member of La*chaim—invited Ben to join him in a game of sand volleyball. The teams consisted of temporary confederations of a cappella groups. For a while, it was something like the Chorderchaimoniums versus the Dinogobfebelles, but each side quickly absorbed more people, and any alliances were hopelessly mixed up once again.

Ben had just dived to save the ball, missing it entirely, when he spotted her from the corner of his eye: Caroline Cooper in a powder blue sundress, walking away along the tree-lined path. He feared the worst—was she leaving already? But she couldn't! Tonight he really needed to talk to her!

Ben subbed himself out of the game and, although he couldn't spot her in the distance, ventured in the direction he thought he'd seen her go.

As he walked, Ben passed the deep end of the pool, where Renee was currently giving Akash swimming lessons. She demonstrated the proper butterfly stroke, flying over the water in short, athletic bursts. When Akash "imitated" her technique, he thrashed about, splashing all over, making her laugh.

Although the Chorderoys' upperclassmen had repeatedly warned against the dangers of a cappella-cest, Ben actually thought they'd make a really cool couple.

Returning to his mission, Ben thought he spotted Caroline turning the corner behind the clubhouse. He had just passed the emerging mob of dancing by the bar, when he was intercepted—

"Nicole and I are going to Drama Prom together!" Wilson proudly announced. He wrapped his arms around his roommate in a giant, very drunken hug.

"That's great, man," Ben murmured, his eyes still focused on the clubhouse.

"Oh yeah. I heard she was looking for a date, so I hinted that I was an awesome dancer to plant the idea. I've been trying to get lots of face time, too. Gotta capitalize on that Ingroup Bias . . ."

After several more minutes of this, and many assurances that he'd catch up with him later, Ben finally managed to pull himself away from his excited roommate. As he continued walking, it occurred to him that maybe it wasn't actually Nicole who'd been using Psych lessons in her dating life. Perhaps Wilson had been projecting *his* strategizing tendencies onto Nicole.

When Ben finally made it around the clubhouse, he stepped into a wide grass clearing at the edge of a dark forest. But Caroline wasn't there. A different woman leaned against the post of an ornate wooden gazebo. She wore her most elegant black dress and pearl necklace, and held her favorite cocktail in her hand.

Ben admired the brightly-lit gazebo on which she stood. Golden-white strings of light snaked around the wooden posts, their reflections shimmering in her martini glass.

Sadness thickened her voice. "Gin, olives, vermouth. Always my contribution to the party."

"They weren't your only contributions," replied Ben. "Without your connections, none of this would have happened. It's great that you organized this for the entire community."

Ben took a deep breath. "And I know SG didn't just decide to save a cappella on its own accord. Using your influence for that was very . . ." He hesitated, unsure of how to word it. "Very good of you."

For some time, Dani said nothing. There was only a wet gleam in her bright green eyes.

Finally, she said, "You know, Ben Jensen, I was surprised to hear about young Nicole's election. Not that I'm not looking forward to working with her," she added, "I am, truly—but I'd predicted leadership in *your* future."

Ben wasn't sure how to respond.

The Harmoniums' president pointed back into the trees. "Caroline went that way. She's like me, in many ways. We both require our breaks."

Dani set her glass on the wooden ledge, and walked slowly down the gazebo steps, to join him on the field. Even when they stood at the same level, Ben felt the contrasts between them: Her in her high-heels and stylish clothes, older and smarter; him standing barefoot, with sweat in his hair, and little red scratches on his elbows. He wondered if they could ever see each other as equals.

Her green eyes locked onto his. "If there's one thing I've learned this year, it's this: Speak early. You regret most what you wait to resolve." She took a deep breath. "Ben, I pursued you, in part, because I wanted you in my singing group. For this, I apologize. In itself, I know that wasn't right."

Dani drew so close that Ben could feel her breathe. Her lips were the most vivid red.

"But I know, and I think *you* know, that this is not the only reason I wanted you. It wasn't even the main reason. If it were, I wouldn't have reacted like I did."

Like any good performer, Dani knew to hold her pause . . .

"I'm attracted to you, Ben Jensen. I'm drawn to your goodness, your honesty."

Very slowly, Ben shook his head. "Dani, I don't want—I mean—I just don't think we should—"

Her fingers touched his lips, quieting him.

"I'm not expecting anything in return. It's like you said, don't accept it right away. Just know, this doesn't have to be the end for us." Her green eyes glimmered. "In fact, I don't believe it is."

With that, Dani turned and walked abruptly back up the steps. She polished off the rest of her extra-dry martini at once, even the olive. She pursed her lips as she enjoyed the familiar flavor, and flipped back her strawberry blonde hair, refreshed. "I've kept you long enough. Go find your friend. You should know, however, that Elliot's transferring here next fall."

The tenor frowned, surprised and disappointed to hear that name again.

As she spoke, Dani peered deep into her empty martini glass. "I guess he wasn't willing to give up Caroline without a fight."

Ben nodded. He understood the impulse.

The freshman turned to leave, then hesitated. "You know, I think you'll get it," he said suddenly.

She raised a thin brow. "What do you mean?"

"Your singing career, or whatever else you decide you want to do with your life." Ben nodded seriously. "Anyone who works so hard will make it eventually."

As Ben walked away, Dani wore a faint smile on her face.

Ben walked through the trees, treading lightly without his shoes, his path now lit only by the outer periphery of tiki torches and the occasional flickering of a firefly. In the distance, he heard humming. Caroline was sitting in another clearing, lying in one of three string hammocks tied to the tree trunks.

She jumped when she heard him. "Oh! Hi, Ben."

"Sorry. Dani told me you went this way." He didn't mention how long he'd been searching for her.

"I snuck away for a few minutes," said the soprano. Caroline eyed him closely, as if she were unsure just how much he knew about her situation. "I've been thinking a lot the past few days."

"Have you been thinking, perhaps, about something that happened during auditions season?"

Caroline nodded, realizing Ben was already in the loop. "Want to join me?" She indicated a parallel hammock tied to two nearby trees.

Ben lay back, staring up into the cloudless sky, feeling nervous as he wondered what Caroline would decide. He didn't want to press the issue, but the prospect of her joining him in the Chorderoys next year was very exciting. They would have so much more time together!

Tentatively, he asked, "Do you have a leaning yet?"

"I've already decided." Her soprano voice had never sounded clearer. "I'm staying with the Harmoniums."

Ben's leg twitched involuntarily in his hammock. The rope squeaked as it pulled against the tree trunk with his shifting weight.

"You're surprised?"

Ben forced himself to speak slowly, choosing his words carefully. "I mean . . . doesn't it bother you that you originally ranked the groups the other way? That everything would be different if she hadn't switched things on you?"

"Well, what Dani and Taylor did together was shady," said Caroline, placing particular emphasis on the mutuality. "But in Dani's defense, almost everything she does is because she loves her group so much. And it's strange. When Dani first admitted that she'd traded for me, I was really upset. But even then I felt *loyal* to her. At the

287

beginning of the year, Dani reached out to me when I was an overwhelmed freshman. I can't tell you how many times I've called her for school advice, or she's taken me out for frozen yogurt, or we've cooked dinner at her place when I've needed cheering up."

Caroline peered over from her hammock. "Dani's a good friend, Ben. She's got a real gift for empathy. And I think she uses it for good, most of the time."

Ben rocked his hammock back and forth. He wanted to tell Caroline that she had never seen the real Dani, but he knew it wouldn't be right. Still, the tenor wasn't ready to concede. "It's just that, my class in the Chorderoys is awesome, and I would love to see you join us. It's gonna be a great three more years."

Caroline leaned over the edge of her hammock, a smile on her face. "Isn't it amazing how quickly you bond?" Then, for the first time, really, Ben heard about Caroline's freshmen class in the Harmoniums: Max, the tenor dance major, who was hilariously blunt in his choreography critiques; Amber, who'd grown up in a small Missouri town and was always down for exploring the city; Phil, whose tough-guy-from-New-Jersey exterior hid his genuinely sweet nature.

As Ben listened to Caroline talk about how much she loved her newbie class, he felt the strongest draw to her. The way she cared for her friends made her seem very much *desirable*, even in the Olivia sense of the word.

"It's like a family," finished Caroline.

Ben thought it was one of the kindest—and hottest—things he'd ever heard. All he could say was, "Yeah, it's pretty awesome."

After a few seconds, Ben leapt up from his hammock, feeling newly inspired. He held his hand out to her. "Caroline, may I have this dance?"

Caroline took his hand, pushed herself out of the hammock, and together they danced alone to the far-off sounds of music. For a brief minute, Ben thought everything would be perfect.

He began, "You know, ever since freshmen orientation, I've felt—"

But then, she crushed him. "Ben, I think we should just be friends," Caroline blurted.

Ben stepped back, accidentally stomping on an acorn. "Ow . . . man! I mean, why?" he stammered, wincing through the pain. "Greg told me you broke up with Elliot. Are you still . . ." His voice trailed off, unable to finish such a depressing thought.

"No, no, that's not it. Elliot and I are over."

"But he's transferring, right?" Ben asked, still worried.

The soprano shook her head with disapproval. "I told him not to do it for me. I can't trust him after this past year."

Ben frowned. "But, if not Elliot, then—" He hesitated. He had wanted to ask how Caroline felt towards him, but was now too afraid to hear her answer.

Caroline sighed. "It's Dani," she explained. "Like I said, we're close. She sees me as her little sister. You two dated first, and she told me she still has feelings for you."

Ben smacked his forehead with frustration. The Harmoniums' soprano was holding back out of *loyalty* to Dani? He sensed his feelings souring towards the virtue.

"Trust me, part of me wants this," she whispered, peering into his eyes. "But I don't want to hurt anybody. I'd rather just be safe." She drew close, and laid her arms around his shoulders. "Is being friends okay?"

Ben lied. "Um . . . sure."

For a while, they rocked back and forth to the distant tuneless rhythm of the bass.

♫

Final exams came and went quickly. For Ben, they felt like five successive punches in the gut. And then it was all over. His mom had arrived to help him move back home to Chicago for the summer.

As Ben walked down the hall of his freshman dorm, he looked at the now-bare walls, the crinkled posters on the floor, the bags upon bags of trash, the oversized suitcases waiting by the doors . . . It was all ending so fast. His freshman year, his memories, were being packed up and cleared out, making room for next year's class.

Ben stepped over a deflated soccer ball lying in his path. He was supposed to grab the last load and bring it downstairs while his mother pulled around the car. In the disorder that was Freshmen Move-Out Day, Ben had been unable to say goodbye to most of his floormates. All afternoon, he'd received depressing texts to the effect of SRY. HAD TO RUN. SEE YOU IN THE FALL!

For some reason, Ben was preoccupied thinking about what he and his high school friends would discuss when he returned home. All year, he'd been so passionate about his new a cappella world, but would they care at all about this niche subculture?

What if they asked him about his dating life? His brief experience with an "older woman" had reminded him just how little he knew about actual romance. Now, he'd finally thrown his heart out to the one girl he'd loved since orientation—only to have her immediately flatten his dream of a real relationship.

It was all, decidedly, un-cool.

When Ben opened his door, he saw Wilson's stripped-down mattress. His roommate had moved out early this morning, still exhausted from his latest date with Nicole.

Turning into his room, Ben noticed something else: Two black instrument cases lying on his bed.

Caroline greeted him in the doorway. "I asked your mom if we could have a few minutes." She smiled softly as she held up a paper tray with two plastic cups. "I told her we've had a longstanding coffee engagement."

Closing the door behind her, she sat the coffee on his desk. She pushed herself up onto his raised twin bed and sat beside her Spanish guitar. "Maybe a coffee date/jam session combo?"

Ben felt his cheeks burn red, not wanting to get his hopes up. "Listen, Caroline, if you're worried about the two of us causing drama, I don't want you to . . ."

But this was Caroline's solo. Her eyes locked onto his, and he grew quiet.

"I talked to Dani last night," said the soprano. "Not to ask for her permission. I just want to start this honestly." She smiled, and patted the spot next to her on the mattress. "It's too good not to."

They each picked up their guitars. As they played, Ben could scarcely believe what was happening. Here she was, the coolest girl he'd ever met, choosing to spend her last moments of freshman year with him.

On cue, they laid down their instruments. Ben inched towards her on the bed. His voice was soft and earnest as he asked, "May I kiss you?"

♬ ♩ ‖

Acknowledgments

A very special thank you to my parents for believing in me. Thank you especially to my sister, Jessica, for reading the first draft of every chapter and for talking for hours on end about the characters. Next trip to Sonic is on me.

Thank you to my primary editor, Risa Edelman, for her painstaking efforts and constant warmth. Thank you to early readers Michelle Lindblom, Daniel Barber, and Greg Allen, and all of the enthusiastic fans on "Team AcaPolitics." Thank you to the graphic designer, Sarah Quatrano, for insisting on primary colors. Thank you to my writing teachers, especially Melissa Gurley Bancks, Marjorie Stelmach, and Steven Lund. Thank you to my longtime piano teacher, Barbara Taeger, for teaching me the language of music. Thank you to my alma mater, Washington University in St. Louis, and the Howard Nemerov Writing Scholarship Program.

Thank you to all my college a cappella friends, especially my friends in After Dark Co-Ed A Cappella Group. I was incredibly lucky to sing with you.

Thank you to the Contemporary A Cappella Society of America (CASA), the SoJam A Cappella Festival, Varsity Vocals, and the MouthOff weekly podcast, for introducing so many new readers to my work.

Thank you to A. Chandan Khandai for being perhaps the first person to use the word "acapolitics" in the Washington U. a cappella community.

Finally, thank you to my non-aca college roommates, who teased me frequently, but still showed up for all my concerts.

Stephen Harrison is a graduate of After Dark Co-Ed A Cappella Group and Washington University in St. Louis, where he was a Howard Nemerov Writing Scholar.

Made in the USA
Lexington, KY
29 April 2013